THE CITY WIFE

THE ISLE OF BURTONSHIRE SAGA

BOOK ONE

R. M. CARPUS

CARPUS

Miniver cursed the commonplace
And eyed a khaki suit with loathing;
He missed the mediaeval grace
Of iron clothing.

- Edwin Arlington Robinson

CARPUS

Copyright © 2022 R. M. Carpus
ISBN: 979-8-9865679-0-7

This is a work of fiction. Names, characters, places and incidents either are products of the author's imagination or are used fictitiously and any resemblance to actual events or locales or persons, living or dead, businesses, companies, events, or locales is entirely coincidental.

Edited by Arlene W. Robinson and Word Witch Copy Consulting LLC

Cover design by RL Design
www.gobookcoverdesign.com

For my mom, who left this world too soon.
You'll always be my favorite heroine.

ONE

"Jo, can you get that? Helen went home sick." Florence had called out from across the room, scribbling on a notepad. If she moved from the piano bench now the muse would float away, and it would take a miracle to revive. But I was too knee-deep in waffle batter and sticky syrup to come to her rescue.

The timid yet intrusive knock persisted.

"Hey, Jo? Can you please get the door?" Her pencil snapped against the paper. The hot griddle had my attention, but I didn't have to glance over to know that by now, her nostrils were flaring and she was pinning the broken pencil into her messy honey-brown bun. Or that this time of the morning she was covered in paint from her before-dawn session, which always preceded her composition work. The fainting couch was also smeared with the same color palette, whichever one she'd used to butcher the canvas. My mother made art the same way she kickboxed—with grit, blood, and savagery. She'd turned to kickboxing and archery during her turbulent youth, hungry for ways to practice self-defense. Dad and I never could figure out where all the aggression came from, though it was, without question, the reason my father was mad about her. She operated entirely from a paradoxical sphere, one that no one could ever find their way out of once they fell in.

Composed and fierce in a single breadth, Florence shaped a canvas into submission at six AM, shredded her Steinway to pieces by eight, and made it to the archery range for practice by ten. She did this with enough time to spare to chat with blind Sister Catherine from the convent on the corner of Third and Birch. Nearly every morning, without fail, Florence helped her cross the street, then moved to the bench in front of St. Rita's, where they'd sit and talk, sometimes for hours. Florence always made time for people, especially those most invisible to the rest of the world. Her voice was gentle, her hands soft, her posture as meek as the Blessed Virgin statue in front of St. Rita's.

Dad wasn't the only one mad about her. My mother owned every inch of my bleeding heart.

"Never mind." Florence's warmth radiated from the piano, carrying through the house to meet me. Wherever it was, it always had a way of finding me. The waffle batter splashed my apron as I watched her approach the entry, her baby blue silk robe billowing around her ankles. She inhaled deeply and pulled open one of the doors. "Yes? This really isn't a good time, I'm afraid—"

The silence punctured her poise.

"Hello?" Her shoulders slumped and she stepped forward, poking her head past the French doors. Peering left to right, she scanned the foyer. "Excuse me? Hello?"

"Who is it, Mom?" I set the spatula down and joined her.

"No one here. What do we pay this ghastly amount of rent for anyway? Isn't some of it supposed to go toward the building's posh security system, or something?"

"According to Dad? Yes." I chuckled, wiping my hands on

the apron. Florence grinned like a lovesick teenager. That was the effect my dad, Asher, had on her. Nothing, absolutely nothing, could soothe the innate irritability that flared whenever something distracted her from the bench like the thought of Asher Kowalski. Oxford graduate, *New York Times*-bestselling author, award-winning philanthropist, and devoted father, Asher was a Philadelphia native and an institution across his hometown. The man beamed brilliance, but he couldn't fry an egg, much less pick a building in Rittenhouse Square with a decent doorman. Unfortunately for us, Florence was equally unversed in domestic life, even though she'd been living one for over two decades now.

Which was why we employed Helen, our cherished maid, personal assistant, and all-around superhero, part time for the last fifteen years. Now *that* woman could fry a mean egg, and she had no problem handling visitors. Naturally, her waffles also put mine to shame.

Florence shook her head. "Your father and his lavish taste. He's lucky we love him."

"We're lucky he's lucky."

With a wry smile, Florence stepped back inside, a silent directive for me to finish cooking breakfast so she could return to her next great piece. It had taken my entire twenty-two years of existence—and counting—to figure out how to speak Florence, but I'd become almost fluent in the language. Today was one of her dark days. Whatever she was working on this morning agitated her as much as the sonata she wrote after my grandma's funeral. She was more pensive then, only lashing out when a block hit, but the tension was the same: constantly bubbling, just beneath the surface, on the verge of boiling over.

I suspected today's episode was about last week's newspaper article, which now had seven whole days to simmer in her mind, giving her plenty of time to dwell. The one by the snarky columnist who announced that Mom was being replaced on the orchestra's board of trustees by a younger, equally esteemed up-and-coming prodigy who happened to look like a modern-day Marilyn Monroe. This new celebrity could apparently offer a greater time commitment than Mom, and the board felt she could also serve as a fresh new voice for negotiating the committee's future agendas. Marilyn 2.0 might have had more hours to offer the board, but the fresh voice? Come on. It was about the face.

It was always about the face.

The columnist subtly mentioned Mom's looming birth date, and was kind enough to hint at the idea that perhaps the time was approaching for her to retire from the classical music scene altogether. The writer was so gracious, she even referred to a recent photograph of Mom on stage, commenting on the "dark, tired circles under her eyes," as if she'd been commissioned for an adult diaper commercial or was in need of a seniors cruise to catch up on her rest. Good, old-fashioned biased journalism at its best. The article was not up for discussion. There was no need for dialogue anyway. She strolled toward me from the entry, abandoning her notepad and piano bench to flick off the stove and drag me to the studio, where she always made her feelings perfectly clear.

"Wait," I objected weakly, tugging my apron off. "What about breakfast? And your composition?"

"It can wait." Once she had me in front of the easel, she wasted no time. "Well?"

I stood there, staring dumbly at the vibrant piece she'd unveiled. "Well, I . . . uh . . ."

Her brows lifted.

"I mean, it's so very . . ."

"Yes, go on. Say what you mean." She circled the painting, studying it, fingers tapping her lips.

"Well, it's kinda . . . Munch's *Scream* had a lovechild with Tim Burton's *Corpse Bride*."

"Does the woman you see have Helena Bonham Carter's voice?"

My forehead broke into a sweat. The macabre 1950s starlet stared back at me from the canvas, warning me to tread carefully. "That matters . . . how?"

"Helena's voice is *everything*. The woman in the painting either has it, or she doesn't. Does she have everything or nothing, Joanna?"

"Okay." I gestured a farewell salute and beelined it for the exit. "And on that note, I'm gonna head to the theater. I'm working on some new designs. Enjoy your breakfast."

"Jo."

"Mom." I halted at the door. "I don't know what to say, I'm sorry."

"Don't analyze. Just react. Tell me your vision. Come on."

"Can we talk about it tonight, when I get home? Give me some time to think about it."

"You don't have time, Jo, that's the point. Time mocks us the moment we're born."

My body slumped against the doorframe. Ladies and Gentleman, *je te présente* my mother, about to slide straight into nuclear mode. Close proximity to my exit tempted me to make my escape now, before she roped me into the detonation zone, but my feet instinctively rooted my legs to the floor. Her abrupt silence ensnared me, and just like that, I was clay in her hands, ready for the mold. A spark flared in the center of my chest, warming my whole body as she careened around the utility table to commence the show.

She lifted a can of paint with a dainty twist of her wrist and carried it over to the canvas. "Immunity is the most ancient of lies, and yet we're all too happy to believe it." She clicked open the lid and splashed the paint onto her starlet bride. The rich garnet cascaded down the image. She waited for the *drip* to hit the floor, waited for the bride to suffer, then pressed her bare palms against the canvas. She spread the paint around, her deft fingers swirling wildly in every direction. She stilled when the slice of her fingernails shredded the canvas cloth. "The deception flooded the sidewalk as I was cruising down Third the other day. It reached out through the crisp autumn air and saturated the entire street, as if it had been summoned. Everyone was right there, in the center of the great lie. The sun assaulted our backs, frying our butter-soft leather coats like overdone eggs on a rusty skillet. Women with blond highlights checked their reflections in windows as they passed by, mistaking the silver glint of their gray manes for sun-kissed streaks. The fast-paced click of our heels on the Monday morning pavement masked the sound of our weakened arteries. And yet we all kept moving, *click, click, click,* as fast as we could toward those office cubicles, swathed like babies in history's greatest hoax." Her scorching gaze raked over the mangled bride, sizing up the damages.

Sailing back over to the table, she retrieved two paintbrushes. With a sleek press of a button on the stereo, she cranked up the volume. Florence and the Machine's "Bird Song" filled the space, lifting off and rising up to the ceiling, offering smoke plumes to heaven. She coyly strolled in my direction and extended one of the brushes with a maroon-slathered hand.

"Now," she said, leveling me with mystifying green irises, "show the cubicle-worshiping slaves your vision, Joanna."

I couldn't control my smile as I accepted the brush. The song's drumming pulsed against my veins, pounding an anthem into my bones. My shoulders lapsed into a little hop and my body soon followed, rolling into the song's rhythm, surrendering to every beat. Mom padded backward, head bobbing, watching me. She pumped the air with a raised fist and broke into a spin, tossing off her robe to reveal her tiered maxi dress, thrashing the skirt around as she swayed back and forth. I skipped and bounced over to the table, popping off one paint lid after another, dipping my brush into each color. I ran the brush along my throat and cheeks, then flew back to the table and dipped my hands into a deep, luscious purple, flicking the vibrant color at the canvas bride.

Mom's claps fell into step with the music. She shook and shimmied in circles, threw her head back, and belted out the words, howling in tandem with the tune's intensity. The bridge's crescendo brought us higher and higher, then plunged us into a euphoric dance fit. Our paintbrushes morphed into drumsticks. Mom's skirt became a curtain, then a harp. Paint lids transformed into tambourines. Latching onto each other's forearms, we whirled around the room, slipping and sliding on shades of fuchsia, royal blue, and sunburst orange, the paint matting our hair, crusting over our elbows. We wrapped up the performance with a mock wedding ceremony. Mom hopped up onto the center table. Every single art supply took flight to the floor, along with leftover Vietnamese takeout containers and piles of theater props, making way for her barefoot waltz. I offered up a canister of paintbrushes to serve as her makeshift bouquet, and a Victorian-inspired steampunk hat I'd made for one of my last shows. Gloriously wrecked and straight-faced, she stalked regally down the table.

The song finished and I met her at the very end of the table with a reverent bow, presenting her with a gilded birdcage from the pile of show props. "Do you, Florence Josephine Kowalski, take this bird, Liberty, as your lawfully wedded creed, till death do you part?"

She curtsied and knighted me with the paintbrush flowers, then bent down to open the birdcage door. "In sickness and in health," she replied, releasing the make-believe bird. We lifted our eyes to an imagined sky, bidding the invisible creature a farewell in its departure for another world. Mom jumped down from the table and we both collapsed to the floor in hysterical laughter, onto a cool rumpled sheet that lined the space for events just like this one, a heap of oily, multicolored, tangled limbs.

"Mom?" I panted.

"Yes, my darling?"

"You have Helena Bonham Carter's voice."

Her greasy, ruby-stained fingers found my grape-stained forearm, and the room slid back into silence. It wasn't long before the landline's shrill ring echoed through the house, attempting to disrupt our peaceful bubble, but it couldn't touch us. In moments like this, a cell phone on silent mode or even an old-fashioned answering machine would be nice, but Florence didn't believe in such things. She yielded to modernity's brute force to a necessary degree, but stamped out any weak link, claiming what small victories she could.

An aroma of cinnamon waffles swam around us. The phone continued its assault and Mom started to hum an old lullaby she sang to me when I was a little girl. I hummed, too, until the noisy intrusion drifted where it belonged, back out into the city's concrete labyrinth.

Two

"What do you think of Ireland in the spring? I spoke to Kirstie the other day about meeting with the Dublin Asylum Network. She'll make the arrangements." Mom nursed her espresso as she scanned the paper. After our studio dance party, we'd cleaned up and finally made it to the breakfast table. "The recent attacks are appalling. So brazen."

"The Poles again?"

"Yes. More pub brawls. The reports call it an 'undercurrent of prejudice,' but *undercurrent* implies subtly, don't you think? There's nothing subtle about aggressive insults and blatant violence." She set the paper down, drumming her fingers on the table's edge. "I love Ireland, just as much as I love Poland. This tears me in half, Jo."

"I know." I reached over my waffles and cupped my hand over her fidgety knuckles. "I would love to go with you in the spring. I just have to sort out my schedule at the theater."

She observed my evasive gaze as quickly as I sensed her penetrating stare, burning into the clock above my head. Both Florence and I were immensely talented when it came to the art of poker faces, but the skill was only useful on strangers, or vague acquaintances. No matter how well I maintained cool indifference, Florence's x-ray vision lanced straight through me. The uncanny part was she didn't need to study my face to use her gift. Nothing flew under Florence's radar, especially where my future was concerned. Still, dodging eye contact made the exchange easier on me. The moment those compelling viridescent pools ensnared me, there was no hope of sneaking anything past her.

"No Yale?" Her focus remained on the clock.

I cut into my waffles. "No Yale."

"You have to tell him."

"He'll find out soon enough when Kirstie books our trip to Dublin. I've been stalling for a while now, Mom. If the gap years after highschool and the last deferral didn't tip him off by now, I don't know what to tell you."

"You know Yale's deferral policy after admittance. You can't stall this any longer, honey. He thinks you're leaving after the holidays and starting classes in January. He thinks you've had a change of heart this time."

"Well, he thinks wrong."

"Your father wants you to be happy."

"I *am* happy. I'm happy working in theater. I'm happy helping you with the refugee work. I'm happy just being your daughter."

"So tell him that. He'll respect your decision. He'll understand."

"Florence."

"Joanna." Her chin dropped, and there they were—those verdant irises, slicing into me.

"Dad will not understand, and he definitely will not respect my decision."

"I never attended an Ivy League school. Your father understands."

"You went to Julliard." My fork clinked as I dropped it onto my plate. "You're naturally brilliant, Mom. Of course he understands. You and I are different, and don't pretend you aren't aware of that fact. I'm normal. Privileged, yes. Special? No."

"*Special*?" Florence's chair screeched across the floor as she stood fluidly. "Special has an expiration date, Joanna, just like everything else in this life. Special fades. It's shiny for about ten minutes. And then the next shiny, special thing comes along. People are fickle, Jo. Fickle, vain, and easily discontented. They're always looking for the next best thing, so stop worrying about being so damned special. You're smart, driven, and compassionate. Is that really your perception? You have nothing special to offer the world? Have you really allowed this position, as your so-called brilliant mother's daughter, to alter your perspective so greatly? Have you truly given your power away that easily? If so, you're lost, Joanna. Your views are severely distorted. You are special because no one else on this planet has your fingerprint. You can be normal too. That's fine. There's nothing wrong with being plain. Don't let the shiny people shame you for it. You've got money? You've got privilege? Great. Okay, then. Use them. Be a voice. Speak up for those who can't. Don't hide behind me, and don't give me all the credit. Harness it—your normalcy, your unique spirit, what you are, what you aren't, all of it. Just make sure you hold the reins. Don't dull or deny your light because of someone's expectations—not even your father's." A wave of lavender and honey, Mom's signature scent, rolled over my shoulders as she breezed past me toward the kitchen sink. "I'm wearing your dress tonight," she said, voice softening. "The black deco one, with my favorite amber brooch. Help me with my hair?"

"Of course." I pivoted in her direction, but she didn't turn to meet me. She ran the water, scrubbing furiously at a lipstick stain on her espresso cup. For a moment, I considered reminding her that Helen would be here any minute to take over the kitchen work, but opted for surrender. Leaning against the back of the ladder chair, I glanced up at the clock. "I'll tell Dad tonight. After the gala. He flies home tonight, right?"

"Yes. He'll miss the reception, but he'll be there for the performance. We'll drive home together."

"Mom?"

"*Hhhmm*?"

"Are you excited? About tonight's show?"

She buffed the sponge against the cup's rim, knuckles whitening with the flex of her grip. "Always, darling."

"I'll be by your side during the entire reception. I promise."

"I know you will." She dropped the sponge into the sink and sighed, finally turning to face me fully. "You know what?"

"What?"

"We're overdue for a trip to Aunt Marie's. I want to fit in a visit before Christmas madness begins. We need to get out of here and clear our heads."

My heart instinctively lurched in my chest. "Oh, yeah. I couldn't agree more. When do you want to go?"

"Maybe next week. I'll call her in the morning. Sound good?"

"Sounds perfect."

Florence sighed again, but this time she brimmed with relief. The energy resonated with me completely. Our road trips to Aunt Marie's place in the country had been a sort of life raft ritual for years. Any time we needed to escape the pressures of the city, Aunt Marie's offered us a rustic, picturesque oasis, where we could roam barefoot on the farm, hang out with the horses and sheep, and help make strawberry jam. My aunt's jam was legendary, and her pies were even more epic. So much so, her local farmer's market monopolized her baked goods each season, requesting nearly all her inventory before she had the chance to sell it anywhere else. Marie didn't mind one bit; she made a comfortable living for herself, and the work kept her busy after my uncle Bob lost a battle with pancreatic cancer.

After the media's latest swipe at Mom and finally facing the reality that I'd rather design costumes and devise scripts than join the Ivy elite, a road trip to Aunt Marie's was exactly what we needed.

"I have to get the rest of this paint off me and get ready." I carried my dishes to the sink, reaching up on my tiptoes to plant a kiss on her cheek. "See you at four?"

"Don't be late."

"Me? Late?"

"Joanna . . ."

"I'll be ready."

As Florence whipped a dish towel at my hip the landline rang, inspiring a collective cringe. "Jo?"

"Nope!"

"Traitor!" she whined, but too late. I dashed for the stairway, bounding up the steps in giant leaps and strides. One of these days, Florence would have to give in and get over her aversion to answering machines. In the meantime, her struggle to submit to the telephone's ring served as great amusement. A feral growl emanated from the kitchen, followed by the crumpling of paper—Mom stubbornly snatching up her handwritten phone message pad—and an irritated, "Yes? Hello?"

I waited at the top of the stairwell, biting back a laugh, just so I could imagine the poor soul on the other end of the line receiving her wrath. I loved feisty Florence just as much as I loved wise, maternal, collected Florence.

Disappointing silence spiraled up the stairwell.

"Mom?" I called down to her.

"They hung up again." She released an exasperated groan, slamming down the receiver. "Listed as private on the Caller ID. I'm done answering this demon contraption, Jo. I mean it. From now on, you and your dad can handle it."

"Dad and I have cell phones. You're the one who wanted the landline in the first place!" I snorted, shaking my head. "You know, you can put the ringer on silent."

"Then what's the point of having a phone in the first place?"

"My point exactly." My voice carried a smile with it, soaring down the hall to meet the baffling woman who brought me into this world. "Just unplug it and quit stressing yourself out."

She grumbled something unintelligible.

"I'm going to get ready now. Promise not to break anything while I'm at work today?"

"I only make promises I intend to keep." The playful, affectionate echo of her voice, traveling up to reach me, charged the air with something I could bottle up and patent. In another universe, the ingredients would sell out due to overwhelming demand.

I let her have the last word—she loved that—and continued upstairs, bracing myself for the day.

———

"Oh, my darling, you simply can't imagine my horror when I saw the column." Calista van de Berg, wrapped in an obnoxious orange taffeta frock, rested a condescending hand on my mother's forearm. A heavy stone, I anchored myself at Florence's side, her free arm linked with mine. "I told Ted you'd be positively wrecked. Yet, here you are, absolutely stunning as usual. I'm quite amazed. And your style . . . so demure, so understated. That gown is simply divine."

Florence delivered a measured, polite smile. "Why thank you, Calista. This is one of Joanna's designs. Divine, indeed. I'd wear it every day if I could."

"Oh, how marvelous. That's just lovely, Joanna. How sweet and thoughtful of you, looking out for your mother. This media circus is atrocious, isn't it?" Calista leaned in toward me, as if sharing a smug secret with a trusted confidante. "The nerve of these people, running your mother through the mud. Honestly, who do they think they are?"

"Calista, how is Bethany these days?" Smooth as always, Mom swooped in. "She's a junior now, isn't she?"

Calista's thick lash extensions fluttered. "Ah, yes. She's doing splendidly, thank you, dear. The poor girl loves Harvard, though. She's already devastated at the thought of graduating. I can't say I blame her. Harvard was the most gratifying experience of my life." Winking in my direction, Calista eyed me up and down before diving into yet another mindnumbing topic. "Speaking of university life, Joanna, you must be thrilled to finally be attending Yale. Why, after all these years, we were beginning to worry ourselves sick about you, sweetheart. Delaying college is a bold move, even for you. You're lucky they let you in at all after that wild stunt of yours." A boisterous laugh, as loud and tacky as Calista's dress, burst from her lips. "Running off to Mexico with that boy? When that tabloid photographer caught you at the airport . . . Oh, Joanna, what on earth possessed you to get involved with—"

"With what?" My body advanced, closing the space between us, but my brain struck it into whiplash, pulling me back. "Someone so *brown*?"

"I beg your pardon?" Calista stuttered, her eyes darting around the room. "How dare you put words in my mouth."

Florence's dignified elbow jab was impressive; it only half punctured my lung.

The projectile words bypassed my filter. "Oh, but they *are* your words, are they not? You made no effort whatsoever to conceal your opinion last summer, at my birthday party. A party, need I remind you, that my mother was kind enough to invite you to out of courtesy, despite the fact that you've done nothing but trash our family privately and publicly for as long as we've known you."

"Joanna Grace Kowalski," Florence whispered beneath her breath, "not tonight."

"Calista, you might want to powder your nose," I spat through clenched teeth. "You have a little something right there. It's simply grotesque." I discreetly tapped my nose and gestured toward the ladies room with one last hard glare. Unsheathing my arm from Florence's, I turned for the exit. "Excuse me. I need some air." Pushing past swarms of the Northeast's most prominent socialites, I fought my way through the clinking glasses of champagne and trays of hors d'oeuvres, all being passed around like my mother's dignity, ripe and ready for consumption. I tugged at my ruffled silver tie, windpipe protesting the restraint. I dashed outside into the nightfall to inhale the sharp fall air. My sleek wide-legged pantsuit's material was no match for the temperature, but I sailed around the corner and squeezed down the side alley anyway.

Flush with the building's frigid wall, my body caved, head falling back as my lungs demanded oxygen, aghast at what I'd just done. The one person on the entire planet who understood the true depth of the crater in my chest was inside right now, swaying in a sea of phony flatterers. My untamable temper won out, and I'd broken my promise. I'd left Mom alone. All it took was one mere mention of my relationship with Miguel, and I'd lost all ability to function and reason. Florence understood the triggers. Not once did she judge me for still being gutted nearly a year after the split. She grasped the irreplaceable nature of young, passionate love, lost to the limelight and pressures of the world.

To the average adult, our engagement was sweet, yet hopeless. Romantic, but fragile at best. Our friends and family didn't even give Miguel and me a year; they bet their money we'd crash and burn in six months. We defied the odds and lasted the senior year of high school, then all the way up to last summer. There we were, celebrating his birthday, and the inevitable unfolded like a slow-motion nightmare. Me, returning the engagement ring after months of arguing about our differences. Somewhere amidst the clash in goals and dreams, opposing values, and the vast valley of needs not being met, no amount of love could save all we'd built. I wouldn't keep him from returning to Mexico to take care of his sick mother, and he wouldn't keep me from the Ivy League track fate had set me on. The odds were against us, and the longer we tried to hold on, the greater our knees buckled. It was exactly the kind of classic, tragic tale the press—and Mom's false cheerleaders—wanted.

The others didn't understand, and they didn't need to, because Mom did. She alone knew my desire to marry Miguel was more than young, blind, ambitious love. It was rooted in the recognition of something raw and real and one-of-a-kind, something bright and beautiful in a dim, harsh world. Mostly, though, it was victory. With Miguel I was a warrior, just like Florence. I kicked, screamed, fought, and bled as she did, carving her heart right onto the canvas. With him, I was awake, and I was brave. Wasn't that what love was supposed to do, make you strong? Yet here I crumbled, a wounded warrior in the theater's alleyway, hyperventilating a year after the loss, a neurotic artist's daughter incapable of dominating my sharp tongue and unruly emotions.

Everyone's *I told you so* could claw its way down my throat all it wanted, but it couldn't keep me from my mother. Not tonight. Not ever.

Adjusting my tie and blazer, I pushed away from the wall and wiped at my mascara-stained cheeks, stalking back inside the theater in search of the woman with enough strength for both of us.

THREE

B ack in the theater's main lobby, I hurried toward Mom, rolling to a stop when I saw the crowd formed around her, caging her in. I marveled at her sophisticated timbre, and the chic drape of the faux-fur shawl over her delicate shoulders, a deliberate fashion choice doubling as an ethical statement. Ambling mindlessly over to one of the emergency exits, I found myself huddled against the wall, enveloping myself in the shield of a large ficus. From afar, I joined the enraptured admirers, listening as she dazzled us with an amusing reenactment of our trip to Moscow the year I graduated from high school. Though the trip was for her to harvest research for her latest humanitarian project, Florence was thrilled when I decided to go with her following my monumental breakup with Miguel. Neither of us spoke Russian, and our interpreter's flight was delayed, so we braved the winter weather by ourselves and headed for the hotel. Our taxi wound up crashing, the driver passed out from a concussion, and we were stranded in a blizzard at night on a strange highway, attempting to call for help with no interpreter to rescue us.

Mom's amber brooch sparkled beneath the grand chande-
liers. She spoke animatedly with her hands, her teeth flashing
with a tender laugh as bright as the glistening stones against
her dress's sweetheart neckline. "Still to this day," she entertained the crowd in a sing-song voice, "Asher is awestruck by
the miraculous improvement of our charades skills on family
game nights. I just keep telling him, 'My dear man, Joanna and
I took lessons in Moscow, and I can't recommend it highly
enough.' Speaking of my husband, he'll be fashionably late
again this evening, but fret not, everyone. I have every intention of berating him with the charades expertise I picked up
on that dreadful winter night. I assure you, it will be quite the
show. You're all very welcome to attend after the recital—two
shows this evening for the price of one." More pleased
laughter surfed around the captivated flock, followed by a new
round of toasts, some in honor of my parents and their work
abroad, others in honor of tonight's anticipated performance.

Florence caught sight of me over her shoulder, hiding
behind the plant like a timid five-year-old. She gave me a
discreet wink, and her fans immediately pulled her back into
their bubble, vying for her attention, bombarding their
sovereign with endless requests and accolades. The ficus
concealed the adoration that must have been etched across my
face. There, blended among the mass of false flatterers, existed
loyal supporters with genuine regard for my mother. Pride
seeped into my heart, and I absorbed it quietly in my not-so-
secret hideaway.

Two female figures came into my peripheral vision, stirring
me from my trance. Just a few feet away, their whispers, laced
with contempt and intermittent snickering, pierced me the
moment I registered their words.

"Honestly, I'll never understand what they all see in her."

"She's in her mid-forties now, isn't she? Poor thing, trying
to pull off that dress. So pathetic. I mean, she's classically

pretty, I guess. In that boring, outdated way. The sooner she realizes her prime is behind her, the sooner she can stop making a fool out of herself."

"*Ugh*. I couldn't agree more. I'm sure her family is sick and tired of her being in the limelight. How embarrassing for them."

"You know they only laugh because they feel obligated. I hear the committee's been trying to replace her for the last few years, they just didn't have the guts to get rid of her."

"Yes, I heard the same. So she's talented, who cares? *Yawn*. She's had her twenty seconds of fame. Nothing more pathetic than a washed-up, middle-aged housewife still trying to play dress-up. It must take her hours to cover up those crow's-feet."

More snickering elicited a hot rush of rage along my spine.

"Which charity is this event benefiting again?"

"Something for orphans, I think. I don't know. Tom dragged me here. Why are you here?"

"Same. Charles wanted to make an appearance. I tried getting out of it, but he's such a petulant child when he doesn't get his way. At least Asher will be here soon. *Yum*. That's a perk."

"Oh, yes. I could watch that man walk around in a tux all day. Shame he's tethered to yesterday's news. She better enjoy tonight while it lasts. A few weeks from now, none of these people will even remember her name."

"Oh, we're so bad."

"I know. Isn't it *fabulous*?"

The women's salacious giggling made my stomach roll. My limbs, rigid and trembling, moved on their own accord. I stepped out from behind the ficus, ready to pounce. Until my eyes darted to my mom. Something about the slight, almost imperceptible tilt of her head made me freeze in place. The gathering around her was dissipating, her fans breaking up into smaller, more intimate pairs to chat over brandy, bubbly, and brie. She glanced over her shoulder, gaze drawn down as if she were studying the design patterns in the carpet. Even, steady fingers lifted the champagne glass to her mouth. She brought the rim to her lips, took a measured sip.

Olivia, a regular with the theater's catering crew, breezed by, balancing a large tray of hors d'oeuvres on her left and drinks on her right. My possessed body resumed movement, thrusting the toe of my shoe into forward motion, directly in her path. As she tripped and started to go down, I clumsily intercepted the fall, flipping and launching the trays toward the vicious women. Precision and aim were on my side; one tray splattered them neck down with hors d'oeuvres, while the other drenched them with martinis. The trays crashed at their feet and the collision knocked Olivia to the ground. Startled, her cheeks flamed as she hurried to rebound.

"Oh, so sorry Olivia." I feigned surprise and leaned down, offering a hand, too pumped with adrenaline to feel the sting of my sin. "I'll get someone to help clean up . . ." Faking an accident wasn't enough. The boiling fury rose and demanded greater satisfaction. I swiped a fresh martini from the stunned Tony, another member of the waitstaff, and waltzed up to the phony scandalmongers. A flick of my wrist splashed the glass's contents in their faces. Their shrieks drew every pair of eyes in the lobby. Heads turned, whispers commenced, and the vengeful, victorious beast bellowed from within me.

"For the record?" I tossed the last droplets of martini at them. "You're not my father's type, she's ten times the woman you'll ever be, and all the Botox in the world can't fix your poisonous, cold, barren souls. There are more reporters outside." I pointed to the entrance door. "Your twenty seconds of fame await. That's what you want, right? You want everything my mother has. So, go ahead. *Get out.*" Searing them with one final pulverizing scowl, I stormed past them and peeled a hard left toward the onsite restaurant. The anger, still raw and rallying, carried me all the way into the kitchen, where I could grab some towels to help clean up, and hopefully collect myself before returning to face the woman I knew I'd disappointed. More than anyone who'd just witnessed the spectacle—peers, mentors, professional acquaintances, members of the press—Florence alone was the only one who mattered. A thousand scenarios did cartwheels in my head, pantomiming versions of her possible reactions. There was no escaping the damage done; Mom's people would be talking about this for days, and it would undoubtedly make it into the papers by Monday.

Tony appeared behind me, racing on my heels into the kitchen. "Joanna Kowalski, you are my hero." His hand touched my back as he doubled over in laughter. He smoothed back his thick, black, wavy hair, shaking his head. "Oh, that was so, so good. Too good. You totally made my night."

Palm to my forehead, I took a deep breath and steadied myself against the wall. "They had it coming."

"Hell yes, they did. I've had to deal with them before. They've been to a few of your mom's benefits, and I swear, they're more and more vile each time they come back."

I moved to a shelf by the utility sink and started rifling through the linens. My flustered fingers latched onto a heap of towels and yanked them from the shelf. "Damn it. I mortified Olivia, though."

"Liv? She's tough as nails. She can take it."

"Not so sure about that. She looked pretty humiliated. I have to find her. Trash bags?" I spun around in search of the storage closet.

"Here." Tony veered around me and walked us to the closet. "Don't sweat it, Jo. You did us all a favor. She'll recover. I was in earshot of that entire conversation, and once I tell Olivia what went down, she'll understand. Trust me."

"I'm going to make it up to her." Scanning the supply

shelf in the closet, I yielded to tunnel vision as it directed my every move. I spotted the trash bags, grabbed a few and stuck them under my arm, then frantically rummaged around for a broom and dustpan next. "Buy her dinner. Or a puppy. Pay her rent. Something, I don't know—"

"Hey," Tony's voice turned soothing and earnest, and his hand found the small of my back. "Chill, Jo. Take a breath. You meant well. Shit happens. I'll smooth things over with Liv, I promise."

I stilled at his sincere, affectionate touch. He meant well too. But I wasn't ready. I wasn't sure I'd ever be ready. As drastic as the thought might be for a young twenty-something, it was reality. Miguel changed me. The relationship changed me, and though I knew it was over, something in my aching chest continued to light hope's candle. The cavernous pit his absence left remained dimly lit, feeding me with dreams that maybe someday, we'd find our way back to one another.

Tony and everyone else in my circle called it denial.

I'm sure it was. But I was also certain that getting involved with anyone else wasn't possible. Not now. Maybe ever. For now, I adjusted to the updated version of myself. My work with the playwright group was thriving, and the theater company that employed me offered to extend my contract. The last few months proved some of my most inspired, productive months to date, and Mom's calendar was filling up at rapid speed with commitments to various refugee asylum networks. Florence trailblazed, and I plucked up the debris in her wake, studying each speck of stone and dirt and ash until the breadcrumbs molded a new vision, one much clearer and sharper than my own. Sternly anchored by my compass, I'd never drift astray. Submerged in my designs, my mother's convictions, our art and our purpose—that was enough for me.

"Tony." I reached for his hand, intertwining our fingers.

"Oh, I've heard that tone before." His tall frame inched closer, and he smiled softly, squeezing his eyes shut. "Please, Jo, just let me down easy. You're such a heartbreaker, ya know."

"Yeah. Part of my charm." I cleared my throat, waiting for his eyes to open. "I want to say this, and I need you to hear me. In another universe, one where my life wasn't governed by my past experiences and choices and a brilliant, complicated mother, or our world of all-consuming, continuous creativity . . . I'd say yes in a heartbeat."

"I didn't ask you anything yet."

"I know what you want, and I'm sorry, but I just can't give it to you."

"Dinner at my place this weekend? It's sort of a house-warming party. My roommate and I just moved into a new apartment a few months ago. You can invite your friends from the playhouse if you want. And some of the catering crew will be there. Just a low-key dinner. That's it."

"We both know it isn't. The pieces of me that you're after? They aren't available. I can't even reach them myself."

"You're not ready."

"It's more than that."

"Meaning?"

"I'm taking time to put myself back together. This is hard—maybe impossible—for a lot of people to understand, but I won't ever love again the way I loved him." I shrugged. "We can always find someone new, but that's not the point. We're all unique, completely irreplaceable. It takes time to let go of something one-of-a-kind. Choosing someone new is like moving to a new town, thinking that changing the scenery will help you forget whatever painful thing you left behind. It doesn't work that way. The pain follows wherever you go. You can't go over, under, or around a storm, you have to go straight through it."

He gave me a playful smirk. "Airplanes ascend above storm clouds until they're out of the storm's range."

"Passing over a storm doesn't make it disappear. It's still out there, wherever you left it."

He skimmed his thumb over mine. "Well, I believe we can choose to leave the storm alone. We don't have to be tornado chasers, Jo. Happiness comes down to choice."

"You're absolutely right. I agree, believe me. And I choose to hold onto my heart and protect it, for however long it takes. And I'm a firm believer we can't force something as fragile as love."

"Well, I can wait. I admit I can't relate. I haven't been where you are. But I *do* understand where you're coming from." Gently cupping the back of my skull, he guided my forehead to his lips. "You'll love again. When you're done chasing those tornadoes, let me know." Releasing me, he reached over and plucked a broom and dustpan from the nearby wall rack, then handed them to me. "I gotta get back out there. I'll let Olivia know you're looking for her."

"Thanks." I reached up and squeezed his shoulder, gripping the broom in my other hand, steeling myself for a reappearance in the lobby. My pantsuit swished as I followed him out of the storage closet, the sound intruding on a silent prayer that the reception portion of the evening would be over soon. A glance at my wristwatch filled me with relief; Mom would be due backstage for the performance any minute.

Hushed murmurs flit quietly around the lobby when Tony and I returned. We didn't have to search far for Olivia; she was hunched over, linen napkin in hand, still wiping at bits of crumbled pâté and globs of cream on the carpet. I swooped in to rake up the broken glass, showering her with apologies, then went to one knee and started scrubbing the carpet with one of the towels. Tony pulled the trash bag from under my arm and gave her a hand, shooting me a glance.

Olivia didn't speak. Her head down, she worked diligently, careful to avoid eye contact. The sight of her stripped me of all thought about Florence's whereabouts.

"Meet me in the kitchen," Tony whispered to her. "We can talk. She didn't mean to throw you under the bus." She rose to stand as I did, and the three of us surveyed the lobby over one another's shoulders.

"Are you that dense?" she shot back, still refusing to look in my direction. "Her people never *intend* to do anything. They just make messes and expect us to clean them up."

"Please let me explain," I interjected, lifting a hand to silence Tony's attempt to defend me. "I have no excuse, Olivia. Except those women were tearing my mother up and . . . it was a knee-jerk reaction. I snapped, and you were there, and it was terrible, and I'm really, really sorry."

"For crying out loud—just stop. As if you have any idea what it's like to be on the receiving end of your *knee-jerk reaction*. You're sorry? I don't feel sorry for any of you. Your whole *oh-my-life-is-so-hard* thing? It's overplayed and insulting to every single person in this room *not* padded by a trust fund or some prodigy parent paying their way into Ivy League. Stop pretending as if we even live or breathe in the same realm, because we don't. Anyway, you aren't sorry. You're just sorry that putting me in the middle made you look bad. Get over yourself." Olivia tossed the food-filled napkin into Tony's open trash bag and slipped away, weaving through the surrounding clusters of nosy onlookers.

"She'll calm down," Tony said beneath his breath. "She didn't mean all that. Here, give me the broom and pan. You shouldn't be doing this in that outfit." He gently pried the broom from my numb grip.

I shifted on shaky legs, brushing specks of broken crackers from my knees. "She meant it."

Tony opened his mouth to speak. His focus veered left,

roaming somewhere across the room, then up to the ceiling, homing in on the lobby's central chandelier. "You feel that?"

"Feel what?"

The chandelier's crystals jingled then, and a tremor reverberated in the bones of my feet. A subtle flicker prompted a collective pause in the crowd, then shouts of surprise as the lights went out. Stronger, more pronounced rumbles rolled beneath the carpet, the sensations pummeling against my shoe soles like bowling balls hurtling down their lanes toward their targets. Seconds stretched in the darkness, peppered with startled gasps and panicked cries. The absurd notion of an earthquake in Philadelphia rattled around in my brain, but the odds were smothered by a dire imperative: I must find my mother, and as quickly as possible.

FOUR

"The show must go on, darling," Florence said matter-of-factly, dabbing a romantic rosy hue onto her lips. Serene and stately, she sat in the backstage dressing room at the vanity table, awaiting her cue. Normally, this scene wasn't surprising; Mom was never more tranquil than the moments before she took the stage. Somehow, the preparation for transition from reality to performance art's alternative universe lulled and centered her, transforming her into the unearthly entity that so regularly beguiled mere mortals. Given the scene I'd made during the reception, plus the brief power outage and potential earthquake, her regal equilibrium unnerved me.

"Mom."

"Joanna."

"You're still going to play?"

"Of course I am. Why wouldn't I?"

"You're not at all freaked out by what just went down."

She powdered her nose in the mirror. "If you're referring to the assaulting of benefit guests and humiliating the waitstaff, no, I am not. If it's the shaking ground you're talking about, yes, I must admit that is a little concerning."

A barrage of images pelted my mind: memories of pushing and shoving through the flustered crowds, of then racing through a flickering theater hallway to track Mom down, over-hearing alarmed talk that their cell phones weren't working. When the chaos settled, some moved on to the theater, while others contemplated leaving. An array of assumptions made their rounds, ranging from terrorist attacks to results of global warming. "Oh, I'm sure the news will fill us in later," a dismissive voice had said as I'd scrambled to the dressing room. Whatever it was, it seemed to have instantly turned my lobby outburst into old news, but I wasn't so sure Mom agreed.

"You're not angry." Warily, I stepped forward.

She sighed, pivoting on the stool to face me. "I'm appalled."

My cheeks flamed. "If I said I'm sorry, I'd be lying. Those women were talking about our family and I lost it. I'm sorry for involving Olivia, but I'm not—"

Slender fingers waved in the air. "Don't."

"Don't what?"

"Bother explaining yourself. You were impulsive. And while I'm shocked you chose tonight, of all nights, to lash out, I'm not surprised whatsoever." She tilted her chin and dead-panned me. "Impulsiveness is genetic in this family. It's hardly a revelation."

Either I was imagining things, or a spark of humor flared in her eyes. My lungs expelled a quiet, relieved breath.

"I heard the women."

"You did?"

"Yes. Though I didn't need to hear them to know what's being said about me because it's splashed all over the papers." She swished a wrist in the direction of a newspaper that rested on the edge of the vanity table. "The venom that's circulating is entirely out of our control, and it's not your job to defend me or fight my battles."

I crossed my arms and bit my lip. How could she, of all people, not see the flaw in her thinking? The woman who knew me better than I knew myself, who'd possessed the reins of the invisible cord linking us, should know more than anyone. Of course it was my job to defend her. It would always be.

"Anyway," she continued, "there are more important things happening right now."

"Understatement of the evening," I mumbled.

"Starting with this tremor that has everyone so riled up. Cell service is still spotty. Without our precious technology, we humans resort straight to meltdown mode, don't we?" A playful wiggle of her eyebrows relieved me further. "We need to make sure bodies are in those theater seats. Some already filed in, but there are at least dozens still out there in the lobby, thinking about leaving because no one knows what caused it. As for your lobby tirade, all I have to say right now is that there's a time and a place to speak up, and only you can discern when to act. Sometimes silence serves a purpose, sometimes it's more effective than the most thunderous roar. Own your decision. I love you, my darling."

"You forgive me?"

"Already forgotten." Her tall, languid form deserted the vanity stool and moved toward me. "Now, I know exactly what we need to help calm the audience down."

"Xanax goody bags?"

She winked. "Oh, *très drôle*." Bringing tender hands to my cheeks, she smashed them together. "You. Singing for them."

I suppressed an inner groan, swallowing down the protest. If Florence was willing to let tonight's episode in the lobby roll off her shoulder, then the least I could do was present some sort of peace offering, show her a little gratitude. Besides, I knew what this performance meant to her, and I'd be damned if I'd let her down again this evening.

"Well?" Her dimples appeared, accenting a hopeful grin. "What do you say?"

"Singing would distract me too. And if it'll help turn this night around, I'm in. If that's what you want, I'll do it."

"Tomorrow's game night—extra ice cream, whatever flavor you wish, and I'll let you win charades."

My mother, the negotiator. She knew I loved beating my father at charades almost as much as I loved ice cream. *Almost.*

"Do we have a deal?" Florence's hands landed on her hips.

"I already agreed, Mom. Deal."

"Perfect."

"What should I sing?"

"'If You Were the Only Girl in the World.'"

"Yes." Envisioning the song's effect, my heart fluttered with approval. A classic choice—one I loved to sing, and one that would surely lift spirits. "Love it."

"Figured you'd be pleased. Okay, sweetheart. Let's do this." She wrapped me in an embrace, bringing me home. I watched our hug through the vanity mirror over her shoulder. She sighed against my head, slipping into recitation. "This royal throne of kings, this sceptered isle, / This earth of majesty, this seat of Mars, / This other Eden, demi-paradise . . ." She waited, squeezing me tighter.

Skipping ahead in our favorite *Richard II* scene, I continued, "This land of such dear souls, this dear, dear land, / Dear for her reputation through the world, / Is now leased out—I die pronouncing it."

Pulling back, my mother smiled softly, brushing my bangs across my forehead. "This place will take everything from you if you let it, Jo. Beauty fades and talents wane, but inside us exists an eternal, consuming fire. Focus on what you can give, not on what's taken from you. Tonight, give the world a song.

Tomorrow, you can put this evening behind you and start anew."

A tangled knot lodged itself in the back of my throat. I only wished starting fresh was that easy for me. My mother knew how to tear out a page, how to write a new chapter. She knew how to exist on her own and also as someone's partner. Nothing she had today had been handed to her. The diamonds dangling from her lobes, her name in glittering lights, the cushy bank account—none of it was a result of prestigious family breeding or a life of privilege prior to my father's financial padding.

Abandoned at three years old and separated from her sister, Marie, Mom bounced from foster home to foster home. The sisters lost touch and Mom wound up out west, hitchhiked through California and all along Route 66, until at last, at sixteen, she found a way to reunite with Marie on the east coast. She'd survived on funds from odd jobs, jazz club gigs, and private piano lessons. After settling in with Marie she applied to and wowed Julliard. The scholarships rolled in, she went to New York, and fame soon followed. A feral yet refined dichotomy, she'd been acquainted with the world in a way foreign to me. She'd sunk her jaws into life as a mere child, and I'd barely taken my first bite. I'd come close, with Miguel. Life with him should have been—could have been—a one-way ticket to an unsheltered existence, untainted by the glitz, glam, and illusions of my father's realm. He loved me for who I am, beyond the flash of the limelight. The moment he disappeared, it seemed my opportunity to be fully immersed in life vanished with him.

Dad would be home this evening, and it was time to tell him about Yale. I could only conceal myself in my mother's womb for so long. I wasn't going to college—not now, not ever—and it was time to grow up, to be real.

"Mom?"

"Yes?"

"I'm not patient, strong, or brave like you. I'm starting to think . . . I don't have what it takes to make it. In Dad's world, I mean. It's time for me to figure out how to make it on my own, ya know?"

"Oh? Where is this coming from?"

I shook my head and took a step back. "Forget it. I don't know what I'm saying."

Florence closed the gap between us, pinching my chin firmly in her grasp. "You know exactly what you're saying, Joanna. Go on."

"Me snapping on those women tonight. That, and something Tony said to me afterward."

"Tony, your waiter friend?"

"Yeah. He said something about how I'm chasing storms, instead of veering around them."

"Do you think you're chasing storms?"

"No. I think there's a difference between chasing them and choosing to go through them, to prove yourself resilient, or to learn something. I told him I wasn't looking to give my heart away to anyone new until I rode this storm out. I feel like I need to self-preserve right now, retreat and recover. So, that's what I've been doing, by focusing on my work—our work."

"Well, I think that's wise."

"I do, too, but I also don't want that to be an excuse to close myself off to other things."

"Like?"

"Not being honest about the life I'd like to live. Like not telling Dad about school, and . . . maybe moving out."

"*Ah*. I see." Her brows furrowed as she offered a comforting elbow rub. "Darling, you are plenty strong, and plenty brave, or you wouldn't have confronted those women, and you wouldn't be standing here telling me this. Patience . . . well, patience is yet another one of those endearing qualities elusive for the Kowalski women." Her eyes rolled and we both laughed. "I don't know the context of this conversation you had with Tony, but I'm assuming it had something to do with your great love. I understand he stole your heart, inspired you, and helped paint this picture in your mind that you'd both ride off into the sunset with one another. He loved you deeply, Joanna. Passionately. And you loved him equally."

"Still do," I stuttered, choking on a hot swell of pain, rising in my chest.

"I know. Everything you feel was as real then as it is right now. I believe what he really did was wake you up, and I think you woke him up too. I think that was the very reason you crossed paths. When you're ready, with time, it will be up to you to set your brush to the canvas and restore the painting. No one, not me, not Tony, not your father, can tell you how to make that happen."

"You're right." I swiped a rogue tear from my cheek.

"Of course I am," she teased, adjusting the edges of my suit blazer. "You don't have to figure it all out tonight, Jo. You'll get there in due time, you'll see."

"Promise me something? If I leave the city, you'll visit me as often as you can."

"You're thinking of leaving the city?" If there was an ounce of disappointment or sadness behind the question, no hint materialized on her face.

"Not until after I finish my contract at the theater, but yeah, I am."

"Have you given any thought to where you'd like to go?"

I hadn't, not really, but now that my decision was formed and verbalized, I had to say something. "Maybe west. Maybe abroad. Definitely a country life, like Aunt Marie. Away from this concrete circus—Mom, stop dodging. Do you promise?"

"Jo, you could move to the moon and I'd find you

there. Wherever you decide to go, as long as this aging, feeble body allows, you can rest assured I will visit. Often." She gave a teasing smile. "You can count on me harassing you, in fact. You can forget about a husband, kids, or pets. You can basically kiss any semblance of a life goodbye the second you leave. You won't have any physical or mental space for anyone other than your hopelessly devoted mother, who has an uncanny knack for smothering her only child. You're stuck with me for eternity, darling."

"Okay, good." I grinned. "That's exactly what I want. No space."

"Living in the country is definitely going to give you space . . ." A shadow passed over her irises, like a curtain dropping over her thoughts. "And with it, great perspective. Perhaps for both of us."

I rushed forward, determined to meet her before she delved too far into the possible horrors of empty-nest syndrome. "Hey, Mom. Let's not talk about this tonight, okay? We'll sort everything out later. Let's handle Dad first, right?"

She blinked, returning from wherever she floated off to. She folded me into a hug, cheering me on with an upbeat tone. "My battles to fight, remember? Not your job to rescue me."

"Speaking of Dad, I hope he makes it on time. I'm sure he's flipping out, not being able to get hold of us. Did you hear from him before the power outage? He should've landed over an hour ago."

"No, no word from him all evening. He'll get here when he gets here. Everything will be fine."

A knock on the dressing room door, announcing it was showtime, stirred us from our private universe.

"Ready?" She released me and straightened her posture,

then removed her formal evening gloves. "You lead, and I'll jump in."

"Whoa. Wait, what? No way." Any time I've ever performed with Mom, I was the one who jumped in. Florence always led; it was the natural order of things.

"Start a cappella."

"You can't be serious."

"Do you trust me?"

"Yes, but . . ."

"Okay, then. Move it." She ushered me toward the open door, where an antsy stage director paced while mumbling into her headset. Mom filled the nervous woman in on the change of performance plans, and then a mic was shoved into my hands, and I was rushed out onto the stage, positioned in front of the orchestra musicians. The orchestra feverishly shuffled pages of music as they were briefed on the changes, laughing and wiping sweat from their brows.

Just another day's work with the unpredictable, usually infuriating, always magical Florence Kowalski.

I clasped one hand behind my back, cutting off the circulation in my fingers, waiting for the velvet, deep mahogany curtain to rise. In seconds it lifted and the houselights flooded the space, jolting me with a heavy dose of adrenaline.

Adjusting to the brightness, my eyes scanned the front row in search of my dad. Both of our reserved seats remained empty. My heart flip-flopped, but I didn't have time to dwell on his absence. I began to register the audience's massive turnout despite the earlier drama in the lobby. Silence swam all around, faces chiseled with anticipation, staring up at center stage. My shaky hand moved to my stomach, and I closed my eyes, calling on the power of my diaphragm to deliver the first note. The words embarked from my lips and flew out over the audience, sprinkling them with the wistful, lighthearted melody. Theatergoers exchanged curious looks, eyeing the empty piano and the still, mysterious orchestra in the shadows.

I didn't have to see my mother take her first step onto the stage. The audience's cheeks grew rosier, their smiles stretched wider, and their eyes twinkled with childlike wonder. The Florence effect. Continuing to sing, I waltzed over to join her at the Steinway, my beating heart less nervous, less burdened, simply because she was near. A living, breathing, celestial creature, her elegant frame floated over to the bench, where she perched and began to play. She swayed from left to right, encouraging me with each determined keystroke, carrying me to the final verse. The audience joined in the chorus with me, infusing the theater with undiluted joy, transporting us all back to a simpler place and time. I pushed off the piano's edge and prepared to take a bow as the song rolled to a close, but Mom's gaze latched on to mine. She gestured for me to join her on the bench, continuing to play, then nodded in the orchestra's direction, cuing them.

So naturally we almost missed it when Florence slid from one melody right into the next, her demeanor shifting with the music. The veins in her neck strained and her shoulders tensed as she rocked forward, then back, striking each key like the sharp tug of a wrangler taming a wild animal. The orchestra complemented the rhythm, vigor building as if ascending a mountain. As transfixed as those observing from their seats, I rested beside her, watching her fingers fly over the keys, bending each note to her will. Wisps of hair fell loose from her braided updo, the strands meeting the thin sheen of perspiration spreading over her temples and cheeks. Her jaw flexed as each keystroke drew more blood, and with it, a steady stream of tears down her face and throat. The intense vibrations of bass and explosive violin harmonies built up and crashed over me like a tsunami. This was it—her latest piece, the one I'd only heard bits and pieces of during the composition phase. She'd refused to let me hear the final product until the show.

Applause erupted across the theater when she concluded the performance, sweeping over the aisles like voracious flames, devouring each seat in a succession of waves. She took a moment before moving to rise, acknowledging the recognition with a slight bow. My heart lifted as the applause turned into a standing ovation. Florence's ethereal, statuesque presence continued to absorb the praise, lowering her head further, as if genuflecting before a royal court. I gawked at the display of quiet strength. Tonight she fought the media's attacks with her very own ammunition, an infectious resilience, a battle cry that reverberated throughout the theater. *You want to annihilate me, but you can't have me,* it said. *The love in this room is stronger than your hate,* it roared. *You can tear at my withering flesh and revel in its ailments, but you can never take my soul.*

In that moment, watching her in the epicenter of her element, a primal truth surged within me. Someday, I wanted to be exactly like her. For now, I'd happily be her infinite *protégé.* I stood and moved to her side, slipping my arm around her waist. Her teeth flashed in a blinding smile as she returned the gesture, pulling me closer. Together we basked in the uproarious energy.

A shimmer rippled in the distance, mingling with the glare of the lights, calling my attention upward, to the mezzanine balcony. I squinted against the harsh flicker and saw a raven-haired woman in a chic scarlet gown. Stance motionless, her hands rested on the railing before her. Her face, devoid of emotion, drew a sharp ache from my core. How could someone witnessing this dazzling event remain so unaffected, so numb to its enchantment?

We locked gazes and her form blurred, became a ruptured mirage fracturing in the distance. I blinked, and she was gone.

FIVE

Keys jingled, and the front door clicked, sending Mom bounding around the corner.

"What do I have to do to get a kiss around this place?" my father shouted from the entrance, tripping on a laugh as she tackled him, squealing and smothering him in a deluge of kisses. I wiped brownie batter-covered fingers on a dishrag and rushed over to meet my parents. After a late night stranded at the airport, he'd given in and stayed at a hotel, then resumed the journey home today.

"Too much?" Mom grinned up at Dad's face, her long arms wrapped around his torso in a vise grip.

His cheeks glowed as he peered down at her with a smile that should have cut his face right in half. "No such thing, babe. Never, ever."

I rolled my eyes and pretended to gag. "Speak for yourself." Launching myself forward, I body slammed them both, and all three of us tumbled sideways against the door. Dad's briefcase flopped to the floor and his suitcase and jacket followed, everything piling into a heap. We stood there, entangled and immobile in a group hug, with our eyes closed.

"I just want to smell you," Mom said, inhaling deeply against Dad's *U2* band t-shirt-clad chest.

"You're such a creeper," I said, and laughed, poking her side.

"Joanna Grace Kowalski, where are your father's welcome-home brownies?"

"Not ready yet."

"You deign to greet this Adonis without the sacred brownies?"

"Excuse me, I'm baking like five things at once. Pardon me for being unable to multitask as well as you, your majesty." I bumped her hip and separated from the group hug, then started back for the kitchen. "Welcome home, Dad. We missed you kinda-sorta."

Dad's brows lifted and he gave me a lopsided grin. "Ah, my clever, articulate daughter. You've been working on your vocabulary since I've been gone, I see."

I dismissed him with a smirk and a wave of my wrist, resuming the baker's position in the kitchen, leaving my parents time for their makeout session. The scene grew increasingly sickening each time Dad returned from one of his business trips. His research trips were always the longest, so that meant an equally long smooching marathon upon his homecoming. There were moments, like right now, when I couldn't help but peek over my shoulder and smile at the nauseating sight. Dad's strong, protective hands gripped my mother as if she were a paragon of virtue dangerously close to sinking through a dissolving, clouded throne, a fragile creature in need of cradling. His crisp blue eyes latched onto her in the same vigilant manner; they regarded her carefully, as if trying to decode and preserve the inner workings of her intellect. The scruffy five o'clock shadow that never seemed to leave his cheeks and chin remained in place for the mere fact that my mother preferred it to a clean-shaven face. The sprawl of ink tracing the length of his left forearm—a medieval illustration of ferocious lions resting leisurely beside a flock of gentle sheep—served as yet another ode to his queen, etched onto his skin during the time he spent in Estonia writing his very first novel. My mom loved lions and lambs in equal measure, yearning for the day when humans coexist in a place as harmonious as the lions and lambs of her dreams. My father's body was a work of devotional art, a temple of adoration for the woman we couldn't live without.

I looked away, resuming the stir of brownie batter as their embrace deepened, and the intimate whispers commenced.

"Well?" Mom asked, clearing her throat. "Dare I ask how the trip home was?" They parted reluctantly and she took his hand, towing him into the kitchen.

"Utter nightmare. A five-hour layover, two delayed flights, and then another delay this morning. Once we finally boarded, we still sat on the tarmac for an hour, waiting for take-off clearance. Then, there was a storm just below Toronto."

"Of course there was." I giggled while pouring the batter into a greased pan.

"So, the pilot had to take us up and over that. Mind you, all of this was in the midst of last night's aftermath. The airports, the restaurants, the planes—everyone, everywhere, completely caught up in the commotion of the great Philly mystery."

"No longer just the Philly mystery," Mom said, taking a seat on a barstool. She reached across the island and swiped up the day's paper, handing it to him. "Manhattan and Boston, too. Shaking after midnight, just in time for the press to catch the update before going to print."

"Yeah, I heard." He shook his head to decline the paper, rubbing at the darkened circles beneath his eyes. "It's all anyone could talk about this morning. I'm sorry I didn't call earlier in the day, but our service wasn't restored until sometime after my last flight took off, and then I realized I'd been so out of it, I left my charger at the airport. By the time I landed, I was so knackered, I couldn't care less." I chuckled at the sound of Oxford's influence, always sneaking into his American speech. "I just wanted to get in the car and get home to my girls as quickly as possible."

Mom thumbed through the paper, and I moved to the oven, pulling the lasagna out before popping the brownies in. We'd been working hard all afternoon, cooking Dad's favorite comfort foods. Tonight also called for an overboard feast, in honor of our customary family game night.

"Wise man," Mom said, chucking the paper to return full attention to her other half. She pushed up on her elbows and leaned across the counter to give him another kiss. "You must be exhausted, sweetheart. Joanna's been watching the news all day, driving me mad with updates. The general consensus seems to be some sort of terrorist attack, but they still don't know for sure. An oil line went down in the Southeast just before Philly shook, and they're saying it's linked to the cell tower disruption . . . who knows. What amazes me is everyone seems so stunned, as if this is all somehow a shocker."

"Here we go." I exchanged glances with Dad.

"Invincibility is an illusion." Florence threw her hands up. "Our fragile infrastructure is no secret; it's our society's Achilles' heel, and yet the media runs around, fear-mongering and sensationalizing every sordid detail of these events, as if it's all breaking news. All they truly want is control. They already have it. They have us right where they want us."

"Watch out," I mimed in Dad's direction. "She's one step away from becoming a prepper."

"Way ahead of you." Florence pitched us a salty glare. "I've been prepping for months now. Catch up, kids."

"You have not." Dumbstruck, I slid halfway onto the empty stool beside her. "Mom. Please tell me you're joking."

"Your mother is many things," Dad warned, reaching for a packet of hot chocolate from the cupboard. "A comedian is not one of them."

"I resent that." Mom pouted. "I can be very funny."

I coughed as I lifted my tea to my lips, spilling it on the island countertop. "Now that's funny."

"Joanna Kowalski, whose side are you on, anyway?"

"Dad's, obviously." I snatched up some napkins to wipe the spill and blew her an air kiss.

A dramatic sigh puffed from her lips.

"Seriously, though." I attempted round two of tea sipping. "You're not prepping, are you?"

"Maybe, maybe not."

"Mother . . ."

"Florence," Dad chided, matching my tone.

"There may, or may not be some supplies in the spare bedroom. I refuse to say anything further until my attorney is present."

"Mom!"

"In the spare bedroom?" Dad chucked the hot chocolate packet onto the counter. "Where, in the closet?"

With a smug shrug, Mom puckered her lips. "I'm not saying there's anything stored in the walk-in-closet, but if there was, it may or may not be stored on the first three shelves on the left."

"Florence." Dad pinched the bridge of his nose with a laugh. "I can't leave you alone for ten minutes, babe."

I jumped off the stool. "Ten minutes? Look at what happens when you leave for days, Dad. Do you see what I have to deal with here?"

"So, you knew about this?" He wrapped his hand around my ponytail, tossing it loosely over my shoulder.

"No, this is news to me too." I turned an accusatory glare on Mom. "You little sneak. You've been slipping supplies away behind my back this whole time? What, do you wait until I leave for work?"

"Who do you think you are?" Mom dipped a cracker into a bowl of hummus and flicked some at us. "The prepper police? I store goods however and whenever I choose, thank you very much."

I planted my hands on my hips. "Oh, this I have to see."

"Shall we?" Dad gestured for me to lead the way.

I stalked past Mom out of the kitchen and across the great room, toward the last bedroom at the end of the hall, Dad fast on my heels. With an imaginary monocle raised to his eye, he scrutinized the room as he stepped inside, releasing exaggerated gasps as he examined each piece of furniture.

"No, no, nothing here." He inspected the dresser drawers, then beneath the bed. "Nor here. Nothing here, I say!"

Swinging the closet door open, I flicked on the light and peeked at the shelves. My eyes bulged. There, on the first three shelves to the left, an assortment of materials lit up the ivory wall—enough food and supplies to provide for a small army. Of course, my mother neglected to mention that the first three shelves were the *only* three shelves on the entire wall—she'd installed an entirely new shelving system since I'd last stepped foot in there—and each one was stocked to maximum capacity, from the top of the ceiling to the fluffy carpeted floor. The rest of the walk-in was bare, ready and waiting for whatever my mother had in mind next.

Dad surveyed the closet, giving a jaunty bow before stepping inside and joining me down the rabbit hole. "Ah-ha! By Jove, I don't believe it!" He wiped the invisible monocle and stuffed it back inside his nonexistent coat pocket. "She's indeed lost her marbles, my dear Joanna."

"Indeed, she has."

Mom traipsed into the room, watching us from the doorway. "I suppose it was only a matter of time before I'd be found out."

I smacked my palm to my forehead. "Mom, this is out of control."

"This?" She rolled a flippant shoulder. "This is nothing, darling."

Dad and I stood in the middle of the walk-in, mouths agape as we stared at Florence's work in progress.

"Jo, your mother says this is nothing."

"Mom."

"Joanna." She crossed her arms, fingers tapping her elbows.

"It's *The Walking Dead* in here."

"Well, when the zombies finally arrive—and they most certainly will—you'll both be thanking me, now, won't you?"

Dad's lips turned white as they pressed together, squashing the bout of laughter I knew was raging inside him, begging to be let out. Dad was never one to resist any opportunity to tease my mother. He'd bat at the mouse as long as Mom let him, and right now, she was more than willing to play along.

"Tell me, babe. What exactly do you plan to do to the zombies when they arrive? Serve them olives and fancy jam preserves?" He moved to the shelves, plucking one olive jar and one strawberry jam jar from the dozens on display. He held one in each hand, eyeing them curiously. "Or are these delightful delicacies for us humans to snack on *before* the zombies snack on us?"

Unable to help myself, I jumped in. "Yes, Mommy dearest, do tell." I snatched up the first items I set eyes on—canned pineapple juice and a bulk box of mending kits—and adopted my very best game show host persona, showcasing the pineapple juice first. "If the zombies win, let's see what prizes they'll take home. Behind Door Number One, these mouthwatering beverages will transport them to the tropical island getaway of their dreams. Oh!" I presented the mending kits next. "And should they find themselves a little worse for wear, behind Door Number Two, they'll enjoy these handy-dandy sewing kits, so they can stitch themselves right up."

Dad rested the olive jar melodramatically over his heart. "Babe, I feel so very honored to have such a considerate, meticulous doomsday prepper in the family. Joanna?" Glancing my way, he shot me a mischievous grin. "I think it's time we show your mother our true appreciation for her contribution to our lovely family." He drew me immediately on board, though I didn't know where he was taking me just yet. As inherently different as my mother and father proved to be over the years, one quality they undoubtedly had in common was their insatiable desire to surprise one another.

Mom took an instinctive step backward. "Oh, that isn't necessary. Jo, your brownies are in the oven. You wouldn't want them to burn, right darling?"

I inched toward her. "They won't be ready for twenty more minutes at least."

"Asher." Mom's crafty eyes narrowed. "Your lasagna is going to get cold. Let's eat dinner, so we can start charades."

"It's too late, babe." Dad darted through the closet doorway and seized her, scooping her up and off the floor as he growled and howled like a crazed monster. "The zombies have overtaken the kitchen. Can't you hear them?"

"Asher!" My mother kicked and wailed over his shoulders. Dad spun her around and carried her into the closet, and I quickly shut the door behind him, shutting us all in. "Put me down, you wild man!"

"No can do, sweetheart. I'm afraid we'll have to settle for a feast right here."

She wriggled and shimmied and flopped back and forth

like a ragdoll, but Dad didn't set her down until I fully block-aded the exit, splaying my arms and legs across the doorway.

Dad winked at me, dropped Florence onto her feet, then started popping open anything and everything he could get his hands on. She shrieked as he rubbed jam and peanut butter across her cheeks and neck, immediately grappling with him to get hold of the boxed juices lodged beneath his underarms, the next piece of artillery in his arsenal.

"Asher, don't you dare!" She fumbled desperately with his hands, working to pry the items from his grasp. "Joanna, if you don't help me put a stop to this, I'll disown you!"

Reaching up with a pleased grin, I snatched a bag of marshmallows from the shelf just above her head. Tearing it open, I fired them at the back of her head, one after another, extracting another exasperated squeal. Dad chucked a juice box over her shoulder, and I caught it, ripping open the plastic wrapper. I jammed the little straw into it to force a hole, then aimed and squeezed, spraying her with fruit punch. Dad poured more on top of her head, saturating her hair, and she finally managed to wedge past the scuffle and retaliate, yanking boxed milk and a jar of honey from the middle shelf.

"Oh, no you don't!" I cringed when I saw the honey, imagining the horrific clean up ahead of us. Then I grabbed a jar of my own, because, why not?

Frustration and hysterical laughter ripped between the three of us as we launched into a full-on, ruthless food fight. A sticky, gooey bundle of entangled arms and legs, we sparred and screamed inside yet another personal time capsule. We'd invented so many over the years, including the guest bedroom, where my parents had barricaded the doors, rolled me up like a burrito in the down comforter, then proceeded to have a feather pillow fight. I was their captive, wiggling and wrestling around on the floor in an attempt to fight back while an explo-sion of feathers rained down all around me. I'd finally managed to peel myself out of the burrito comforter, but they'd had me beat, ten to none.

My bathtub, another memory capsule, temporarily served as Mom's alternative private spa during renovations on my parents' bathroom. She didn't want Helen to have to clean an extra guest tub just because she wanted to keep taking baths, so she used mine. One night, Dad and I sneak attacked and spoiled her bubble bath time with an MC Hammer "Can't Touch This" performance, followed by an ice cream sundae assault. We doused her with must-have toppings: cherries, whipped cream, chopped peanuts, chocolate syrup—the works. For the first few seconds, she moaned and wailed about *unsanitary* this, and *how-dare-we* that, until, in true Florence fashion, she nabbed some of the toppings from me and Dad and surrendered, making a sundae for herself. I sat there cross-legged on the chocolate-syrup floor, eating my *unsanitary* sundae, while Dad ate his on the bathtub ledge, dotting Mom's nose with cherry juice.

As it had that day, our laughter roared, the echoes ricocheting off the closet walls, until the muffled sound of the landline ringing broke through our rambunctious fit.

"Asher, about that telephone," Mom said, still winded. "It has to go."

Dad looked at her with a patient, knowing smile and wiped peanut butter from his cheek. "This again, babe? You need a phone. If you still refuse to have a cell phone, then I insist we at least keep the landline. It's a matter of safety."

The annoying ring made me cringe. I opened the closet door. "Anyone gonna answer that?"

"Safety?" Mom's voice jumped an octave. "That contraption was ringing off the damned hook the entire time you were gone. It's a threat to my sanity, Asher. *Safety*."

"Well maybe if you answered it once a while, it would shut up, dear." Dad pinched her peanut butter-covered cheek.

"Guess not," I mumbled, moving out into the bedroom to answer the phone. "Hello?"

Silence.

"Hello?" I glanced at the Caller ID. *Private number.* Again. A breath rustled on the line. "Listen, whoever you are, speak up or stop calling. This game is getting old, and we won't have this phone much longer, so you're going to be seriously disappointed when—"

Click.

I chucked the phone onto the bedside table, biting my lip. The presence was there, and then it wasn't, melting away as quickly as the scarlet-clad presence on the balcony had the night of Mom's big show. "You guys?" I paused, then shuffled over to my parents, leaving sticky honey footprints in my wake. They continued to ramble on about answering machines and the evils of cell phones. "You guys!"

They both glanced at me.

"How about we eat dinner now?"

"Who was it?" Mom asked, wiping jam from her lips.

"Unknown number. Another prank. I heard them breathe this time, at least."

Confusion stirred Dad's features. "You've been getting prank calls? That's still a thing?"

"When you still use phones made for the 1960s, yes," I chuckled, gesturing to my stubborn mother.

Dad smirked at Mom. "I agree with our daughter, sweetheart. Time for real grub. But we're not finished with this conversation. You're either going to agree to use a voicemail service for the house phone, or I'm setting up a cell for you before I leave for Seattle the day after tomorrow—"

"You have to leave again?" I wasn't able to hold back a pout. "Already?"

"I know. This is just a quick one, though. Three nights max. Meeting with the new publisher to discuss plans for translation rights. They're antiquated, like your mother. They want to do everything in person."

Linking her arm through his, Mom rested her head on his shoulder, and they both headed toward the bedroom door. "That's okay," she released a forlorn moan, "Jo and I have been talking about a trip out to Marie's. If Jo can take a few days off from the theater, maybe we'll do that while you're in Seattle."

Dad murmured against my mother's ear as they exited the bedroom, and I trailed behind, already aching at the thought of my dad going away again. The yearning quickly dissipated, though. Any minute now, I'd be dropping the I'm-Not-Going-to-College bomb. Worse yet, it wasn't just any college. It was *the* college. The only one Dad had his heart set on seeing me attend. My stomach twisted as my family migrated back to the kitchen, reminding me the timing of the Seattle trip wasn't entirely a bad thing. A little space might be necessary after tonight.

It might even be heaven sent.

SIX

"You're telling me someone's been making it past building security, sneaking onto the elevator without a key card, and knocking on our door, completely undetected?" My father's disapproving stare traveled across the dinner table. Sticky and disheveled, we lounged back in our mismatched provincial dining chairs, chowing down on lasagna. "That's impossible. And unacceptable. I'll speak to Todd in the morning and find out what's going on. One look at the security video footage and we'll get to the bottom of it."

"Poor Todd," Mom said with a chuckle, giving Helen space to pour her another splash of lemonade. Nothing topped Helen's homemade lemonade. She made it year-round, and we drank it year-round, with nearly every family meal. Helen circled the table, admonishing us in Croatian with a shake of her head as she observed our food-stained clothing. She'd stopped by to drop off my father's dry-cleaning, which she'd forgotten to deliver that morning, and ended up walking into a post-food fight warzone. The minute she saw us sitting down to eat, she insisted on cleaning up the kitchen, and after discovering our shenanigans, the closet too. Doing the dishes quickly turned into dinner service because workaholic Helen couldn't help herself. She didn't always serve our family dinners but usually demanded to whenever we celebrated one of Dad's homecomings. She bustled around the table like a flustered mother hen, scrubbing at my cheeks with a wet cloth napkin and picking pieces of marshmallow out of Dad's hair while she hurried to clear our salad plates.

"Poor Todd nothing," Dad grumbled, stabbing a radish from his bed of leafy greens before Helen whisked his plate away. "It's you two I'm worried about. I explicitly discussed our security needs with him when we first moved into the building, and as property manager, he assured me he'd go above and beyond to ensure our privacy and safety. The press is more vicious than ever since . . . well, you know. The orchestra board matter. They're unhinged, Florence. All it takes is one erratic photographer, one disturbed reporter to break in this apartment and do God knows what."

"No need to get carried away," my mother lovingly shushed him. She gave Helen's hand a gentle pat as she replenished the lemonade carafe. "Though you're terribly cute when you get all worked up over our safety."

"Really, Dad? Deranged paparazzi? God help anyone brave enough to mess with me or Mom. People in this building are scared of *us*, not the other way around. You should've seen the look on Mrs. Rodriguez's face the other day when I left for work. Think she heard Mom yelling at the phone when I ran into her out in the hall."

"Don't forget sweet Mr. Merkle," Mom gasped, eyes dancing with humor. "He called the cops that one time, remember?"

I almost spit out my lemonade. "How could I forget? Pudding balloon day. He heard us slipping and sliding and hitting walls . . . thought you were trying to kill me."

Amusement momentarily melted Dad's austere mood.

"You two are trying to kill *me*, aren't you? I can't leave you alone for two minutes."

"You miss all the fun, Dad."

"Not always." He winked.

Florence took another bite of lasagna. "We haven't even told your father about the episode before last night's performance, have we, Jo?"

"Mom," I hissed, setting my glass down.

With a teasing, patient smile, Florence dove straight into the other unpleasant news. "Joanna made quite the scene during the reception."

"Mother."

Dad slid me a leery glance. "Oh? What kind of scene?"

"Don't worry," Florence intercepted. "I'm sure the papers will fill you in soon enough. That is, if there's any room for the subject on top of all the earthquake news. I was certain there would be mention of it today, but it seems to have gotten lost among all the power outage commotion. I suppose the timing of it all might actually allow Joanna to escape this scandal unscathed."

I squirmed in my seat, dodging eye contact.

"Well, then." Dad pushed his lasagna plate away. "The details can wait. I'm going to need a shower and a full night's sleep to face whatever it is you two are talking about."

"Oh, no." Mom stood and walked over to rub his shoulders. "We've worn you out. You've had such a long day. Ready to turn in? We can do game night tomorrow."

"You haven't had your brownies yet," I blurted. An overwhelming feeling that my time with him was slipping further away snuck up and suffocated me. His travel obligations had been intense the last six months, and the announcement that I was passing on Yale and moving out might drive the wedge deeper between us. Waiting to tell him right before he left for

Seattle might diffuse the tension a little, but it still wouldn't make the task easier.

"Shocking, I know, but I'll have to skip the brownies too." He yawned. "I'm sorry, Jo. I'm starting to feel the jetlag. And I'm pretty sure I have honey in my ear because I can barely hear you on my left side. The brownies smell delicious, as always. How about breakfast tomorrow, just me and you, while your mom's working?"

"Yeah, that sounds good." I swallowed hard.

"Great, sweetie. It's a date." He groaned. "All right. Time to hit the shower. I'll see you girls in the morn—"

"Hey, Dad?"

"Jo?"

"I'm not going to Yale." The words tumbled off my tongue and landed in a splat on his place setting. Mom froze.

He sat up straight. "What did you say?"

"I'm not . . . going to college. My design contract at the theater's been extended, so I'm going to finish out the contract, and then I'll be moving away. I'm sorry to bring it up right now, but . . . I didn't know you were going away again so soon, and I just . . . needed you to know."

"Either the honey is really lodged in my ear, or you just said you're not going to Yale."

"Um. Both, I think."

My mother slipped quietly back into her chair. Helen approached the table with mints and chocolates, immediately backpedaling into the kitchen, eyes wide.

"Joanna, help me to understand." Dad's jaw flexed. "You already took time off and already deferred—possible only because of the strings we were able to pull—and you're telling me a month and a half before classes start that you're backing out."

"Yes, Asher," Mom chimed in. "I believe that's what she's trying to say."

"I didn't make this decision lightly, Dad. I've been thinking about my options for a few years now and I realized that—"

"Excuse me, your options?"

"Yes, options."

"There is no alternative to Yale, Joanna. The institution is incomparable. You don't replace it with another *option*. Is this about a boy? Is Miguel back in your life? Because if he is, he damn well better support your decision to attend, instead of distracting you again from your goals—"

"Of course he would support me." My voice cracked, dangling on a ledge with the painful realization that my statement was hypothetical. He wasn't coming back. He was gone. "Miguel is in Mexico, Dad, remember? It's over. This has nothing to do with him. Can you please, for once, just consider the possibility that I'm choosing this because I want to? For me? Not for anyone else?"

"Each time you've delayed starting college, you did so because you were fighting with and crying over that boy. He drained every ounce of your energy, Joanna. You allowed him to derail your academic career. So, yes, forgive me if I jump to the conclusion."

"Asher," Mom's leveled voice cut in, "this isn't helpful. There's no need to remind her of the toll the relationship took on her. She's well aware of its effects; she's still grieving. If I recall, our whirlwind romance interfered greatly with your work when we first met."

"Damn it, Joanna." Dad's fist slammed the table. "It's time to prioritize. Yes, your mother distracted me in those early years, and I paid for it, believe me. I lost my very first agent and delayed my progress by five-plus years because I fell in love with your mother."

My eyes roamed to Florence. She didn't flinch, didn't

blink, but a stinging shadow—the same kind I'd seen pass over her gaze the night before—rolled across her green irises.

"Love is grand," Dad's stern voice blasted across the table, " but you fail to see the difference, here. Your mother lifted me up, encouraged me, fueled me toward my goals. However unintentional, Miguel weighed you down, added to your burdens, can't you see that? I didn't dislike him, Joanna. He was a great guy. I understand that you loved him. But your involvement with him was far too consuming. He's still taking, right now, as you sit here a year later, telling me you're pulling out of the most important decision you could ever make, one that alters the rest of your life. It's asinine—"

"Asher, you're not listening," Mom said. "Let her speak."

Rubbing a rough hand over his scruffy chin, Dad inhaled and waited.

"I don't expect you to understand, Dad. You're right. You and Mom have something very different. Maybe you're right about all of it. The relationship changed me, I'll admit that. But this decision . . . it's mine. You don't have to remind me he's gone. I've accepted what I've lost. And I don't belong at Yale. I don't belong in this house anymore. I can't hide beneath Mom's wing, or yours. I was hoping that maybe you'd be able to see that, but I think I was kidding myself. You're not here to see it. You're never home. Just because I'm having trouble letting go of what happened with Miguel, just because I still love him, doesn't mean I'm not moving forward with my life. Sounds like you're the one living in the past, not me." I pushed my chair back and rose to my feet but stood in place, staring down at the remainder of my meal. "I was wrong to think that you might know what it feels like to be assigned a role you were never born to play. You were made for this existence. It's in your DNA. I might share your blood, but we have different dreams."

"Joanna," Mom said. "Your father needs a hot shower and

some sleep. I suggest you both resume this conversation in the morning."

"No." Dad ripped the napkin from his lap and flung it on the table. "There is nothing more to discuss because this decision isn't up for debate. Joanna, you're attending Yale in January as scheduled, and that's final."

"Last time I checked, I was a grown adult."

"Then act like it."

"Asher." Mom stood. "It's taken every ounce of courage she could muster to tell you these things. Please, go get some sleep and revisit the subject in the morning."

"Forget it, Mom. His mind's made up."

"Florence. Tell our daughter how foolish she's being. Tell her not to waste her energy on pining over a boy. Tell her not to throw away the greatest opportunity of her life."

Helen cautiously reappeared from the kitchen with the candy dish, stiffening when she caught sight of my mother's pallid complexion. Once again, she slunk back into the shadows, disappearing around the corner. We all held our ground, head-to-head in a hopeless standoff. The Kowalski family was a brewing hurricane that couldn't be stopped once it made landfall.

"Asher," Mom's voice, hollow now, broke the momentary silence. "The greatest opportunity of Joanna's life might be staring her right in the face." The words whipped around the dining room. "It's foolish of us to demand she give it up."

Dad faltered but rebounded in a flash. "Theater costume design. That's the great alternative? Moving out and living with your vagabond friends and doing what, exactly, Joanna? Making props for the rest of your life? Then what, join the circus and go on tour?"

"Are you blind?" I shot back, anger rushing hot and fast in my veins.

Taking the very words from my mouth, Florence gritted

her teeth. "Asher, you belong to a family of nomads. You *are* a drifter. You're being entirely unfair, here. You're not seeing things clearly right now."

"You know what?" Resigned, Dad raised his hands. "You're right, Flo. I thought I had a partner in this, someone who'd fight right alongside me to protect and support our daughter's future. I haven't been home much, I take responsibility for that, but this isn't a matter of me not seeing things clearly. I'm going to bed. When you two decide to see some sense, you know where to find me."

The second Dad's presence evaporated, I walked to the front door.

"Jo." Florence moved to follow me.

"Please don't." I lifted my purse from the wall rack and put on my coat. "I'll be back in a few hours. I love you, Mom. Thanks for trying to help. Please thank Helen for taking care of dinner for us."

"Where are you going to go, covered head to toe in peanut butter?"

"To another dinner party," I said with a glum laugh, running my fingers through my wet, gooey hair. "I'll fit right in."

"He didn't mean it, darling. All will be well when the sun rises again."

"Yes." I opened the door, one foot out of the apartment. "He did." Strolling hurriedly down the hallway, I fished my cell phone from my coat pocket. Walking into the elevator, I eyed the lift's ceiling. The camera's glossy orb shone from above, discreetly nestled in the right corner, and I pondered the millions of secrets, the countless snapshots, the inconceivable amount of intel the device had collected and captured over the years. Like characters on a stage, aware the audience was always watching, we invited the technological gods into our most intimate moments, the vulnerable spaces we called reality.

I lowered my eyes to the phone. Scrolling to Tony's contact, I sent him a text. *Change of plans. Coming to your party tonight. On my way now. Just have to make a stop at the store. See you soon.*

SEVEN

Our family game night died a gruesome death, but determination propelled me toward the idea that something could still be salvaged by the end of the evening. Like resurrecting any semblance of a social life, particularly one that didn't involve the friends from my usual theater circles. Nothing against them—they were great people, and I couldn't imagine life without them—but the confrontation with Dad served as a stark reminder that some circles created barriers, and barriers had no place in life. Not for Florence Kowalski's daughter. I'd had a chance to venture out during my time with Miguel, but the road was cut short before I'd been able to crash fully through those barricades. Demolishing walls was more than just a priority for my mom, it was a lifelong pledge, and her example was my mission.

Before the cab rolled to a stop outside the drugstore on Walnut Street, I'd made up my mind: the past was a dress rehearsal, and this was opening night.

"Thanks," I said to the driver, leaning over the seat to pass him some bills. "You can keep the meter running. Be back in ten."

Tacky, upbeat elevator music met me as I rushed into the store. Customers, annoyed that I'd come to a full stop in front of the seasonal aisle, veered around me to get to the register line. A lanky, trench coat-clad man with a sardonic grin eyed my tangled ponytail as he bumped into me. I cocked a brow at him. "Yes? Can I help you with something?" He scurried away, merging with the throng of people around the front counter. Thanksgiving was just days away, and the stores were already packed with hurried, grumpy bodies in a race to snatch up cheap bottles of wine and overpriced greeting cards.

My attention landed on a shelf of gaudy turkey figurines, each one boasting some sort of defect: chips, cracks, half-painted wings. A preschool ceramic class could probably produce a higher quality product than the knickknacks on sale here, but time was short and it was the thought that counted. I selected one of the sad turkeys, hesitating at the overwhelming array of color choices. What kind of turkey would Tony want sitting in his new apartment? One with a bright orange and black pilgrim hat? Or one with a festive garland wrapped around its neck? Why were the turkeys smiling? What kind of sickos came up with these decorations? My inner Wednesday from *The Addams Family Values* groaned in protest. I should've just made a gift myself. Oh, well. Showing up for a party on the fly required improvising.

I glanced down at my watch, then made my way through the rest of the aisle, randomly grabbing anything that looked homey: a fuzzy throw blanket, a cookie-cutter pumpkin spice candle that oozed American consumerism. A raccoon door mat, dotted with fall leaves and a welcome message woven across the top in frayed, flimsy thread, because raccoons were cute, cuddly little sweethearts, when they weren't trying to claw your eyes out. Finally, a box of mystery chocolates, wrapped with a taupe faux satin bow, because . . . who didn't like chocolate? A frustrated sigh whooshed from my lungs.

Again, my homemade brownies would've been nice. Better than any of this junk, but it was too late to turn back.

Keeping watch out the store window to make sure the cab driver didn't split, I endured more curious looks and awkward side steps until I reached the register. Unceremoniously dumping the hodgepodge of items onto the counter, I chewed my lip and watched the cashier ring everything up. The plump, rosy-cheeked lady carefully scanned one item at a time, the pace so painstakingly slow I almost dozed off. She cleared her throat, and I swiped my credit card, grabbed the bag, then dashed out of the store.

The cab driver eyed me over his shoulder as I plopped into the back seat. "If you don't mind me saying so, miss, you might wanna . . ." He rumpled his hair, signaling me to adjust the mess. "You know, in case the paparazzi man catches you."

I pulled a compact mirror and brush from my purse. "Thanks for looking out," I said with a laugh, forcing the brush through my mangled mane. "Don't ask."

"Sergio doesn't ask questions. Sergio drives."

"Can you take me to this address, please, Sergio?" I offered him a peek at my phone screen. Tony's reply included his address and a flood of excited emojis.

"Yup, I got you."

"So . . . the paparazzi, huh?" Our gazes met in the rearview mirror.

"Yeah, I know you. I keep up with what's happenin' in my city. You're that writer's daughter, yeah? Your mom's pretty big stuff too."

"Musician."

Sergio nodded, messing with the radio volume as he drove. "Ya know, they say all the crazy stuff happens up in NYC, but I always tell 'em, *nu-uh, you haven't seen nothin' yet. Not until you spend time in Philly.* You kiddin'?" His head shook with a dark laugh. "All those bodies in the Delaware River. Gangs, shootin's, lootin's, one thing after another. Rittenhouse Square is so shiny, isn't it? Hides all the crazy. Now these earthquakes and cell tower outages? Philly's no joke. Wild place. One day, I'm gonna get as far away from this city as the good Lord'll let me."

"I feel ya, Sergio. More than you know."

A radio host's voice crackled through the cab's speakers as we drove toward Tony's building, filling the car with more news of gun violence and the ever-growing mystery surrounding our city's latest earthquake event. A soft hum emanated from my throat, drowning out the noise. An inner melody pushed it out the windows and into the city streets, far from the recesses of my mind.

———

The Pixies's "Where is My Mind?" blared from inside Tony's apartment when he greeted me at the door.

"A low-key dinner?" I smirked, peeking over his shoulder for a glimpse of the scene.

"Yeah . . . about that." Chuckling, he held the door open to invite me in. "It was low key until about an hour ago. My friend Brandon told his coworkers, and the next thing you know, the whole building decided to show up. Please, don't let it scare you off, though. I'm so happy you're here." He stepped back with open arms. "Come on in. Can I take your coat?"

Packed with warm bodies and a lit fireplace, the apartment was stifling. I began to slip eagerly out of my wool trench but came to a halt, shrugging it back up over my shoulders. "Actually, I think I'll keep it on."

"Oh?" Tony's hands hesitated at my side, studying the peanut butter smeared denim overalls beneath my coat. I wore them over a gray, long-sleeve Henley t-shirt, also stained, with traces of brownie batter splattered along the forearms for good measure. "Okay, then. As long as you're comfortable, that's all that matters. You look great, by the way. Nice outfit."

"Flatterer."

"You gonna tell me why you have pieces of marshmallow in your hair?"

"Food fight."

"Another one? Man, you really have a thing for food slinging, don't you?"

I mimicked a fake kick to his shin.

Tony's amused grin revealed a dimple I'd never noticed before.

"What's that look?" I wrung my hands together, twisting the handles of the plastic drug store bag that dangled from my wrist.

"You smell like a bakery."

"I brought you stuff," I deflected, drawing his attention to the bag. "Happy housewarming. This was the best I could do on such short notice."

"Oh, wow, Jo. Thanks. You didn't have to bring anything. Just you is enough."

Warmth spread over my cheeks.

"That was cheesy, I know. I should've learned by now that my lame lines don't work on you."

"Give yourself some credit." The words spilled out so fluidly, with such natural ease, I didn't recognize my own voice. "I'm here, aren't I?"

Speechless, he blinked.

"So, there was a big blow-up at my family dinner. That's why I'm here. I mean, I'm here because I want to be. I mean—"

"Are you trying to say you're done chasing storms?"

"No. Not exactly. But I'd like to be friends, if that's cool with you." I transferred the plastic bag to him and he accepted, stepping back to invite me farther inside.

"I thought we were already friends."

I exhaled. This was harder than I thought it would be. "I'm open to spending more time together."

"Hey, I'm just messin' with you. I get it." He shut the door behind me and led me forward into the living room. Inquisitive glances followed us as we navigated the crowd. Whether everyone was staring because I was a disheveled mess or because Tony and I were talking, I wasn't sure. Squeezing into the kitchen, Tony set the bag down and pulled open the fridge door. "Take your pick. We've got a pale ale, your run-of-the-mill soft drink selection, plenty of H2O, or—"

I leaned forward and snatched up the chocolate milk.

"Or that." He laughed.

"This is a great place," I said, seeing the wall-to-wall built-in bookshelves and collections of classic movie knickknacks, scattered across nearly every visible surface in the apartment. "I didn't know you were such a big movie buff."

"You don't know the half of it." He shut the fridge, swiped a spring roll from a tray on the counter, and offered me one. "My roommate is borderline fanatical. He's more into the foreign film scene. I'm all about classic Hitchcock stuff. It's a good arrangement. We're both certified nerds."

I took a bite of the spring roll and washed it down with a swig of chocolate milk. "Do you know everyone here?"

"Not quite." Scanning the room, he pointed out people in his immediate circle, moving in closer to talk over the noise. A surge of laughter billowed from across the room as the front door opened and more people piled in. "That's my roommate," he said, gesturing to the short, bearded guy welcoming the steady stream of new visitors. "I'll introduce you to him at some point. Don't be surprised if reporters start showing up. I'm sure people will start alerting the media that you're here any second now. I think they're a little starstruck."

"They recognize me?"

"You're joking, right?"

"I'm nobody. Crowds don't usually notice me unless I'm in the same vicinity as my mom. Same with my dad. He's lucky he's a writer, he gets to live out his fame in private. The media doesn't usually harass either of us, unless we're out with her."

"Well, I think this has something to do with the scene from the other night."

"Oh. Olivia." Realization sailed over me as I surveyed the group of onlookers gathered around the sofa. "Of course, how could I forget?"

"Don't worry about it. I think they're more stunned that you're here to see me."

"What? Why? Why wouldn't I be here to see you?"

"Isn't it obvious?" he laughed. "You're way out of my league, Jo."

"Please don't say that."

"I say it because it's true."

I squirmed, rubbing a thumb over a glob of peanut butter, smattered across my wrist.

"Sorry it's so loud. This is definitely not what I pictured for our first . . . our first time hanging out."

I slipped around him and returned the milk to the fridge. My brain scrambled to construct some kind of strategy. I wanted to open up, meet new people, put forth some effort. Getting to know Tony better seemed like a good place to start. The catering company he worked for served all the major theaters in town, so we'd bumped into each other regularly over the last few years. We'd been friendly acquaintances, but nothing more. Being here meant leading him on, though, I just realized. The moment I crossed the apartment's threshold,

I stepped into something I couldn't get myself out of without hurting him. And maybe myself.

"You're a thousand miles away," he said, breaking through my thoughts. "What's going on in that beautiful mind of yours?"

More laughter sounded from the left, and a new track boomed from the speakers. It wasn't the time or place for this conversation, but I took a stab. "I'm aware the friend thing can get complicated fast. If it's not enough for you, I'll understand."

"Jo, I hate to break it to you, but it was complicated long before you texted me tonight."

"I don't know how to do this."

"No pressure, all right? I'm not expecting anything from you."

"We're already in deep trouble if you actually believe that." We both smiled. Something unfurled in my chest, a dormant sensation that traveled through my veins and filled me with relief.

"Do you always have to be this difficult?" He reached up and brushed my cheek.

"Always."

"In that case, let's start with something simple tonight, okay? Like rummaging through this gift bag." He retrieved the drugstore bag from the counter and began picking through the items one by one, a little kid digging for buried treasure.

"This is my first housewarming party," I confessed, watching him display each thing on the counter for all to see.

"Really? I thought your entire life was fancy parties."

"Key word *fancy*. I've only been to maybe two normal parties in my whole life, and they weren't housewarming parties." My brain tried to convince my fidgety limbs to calm down. I didn't like where this conversation was going. Those other normal get-togethers were Miguel's birthday parties, and the mere thought of them twisted my heart, cutting off its circulation.

"*Ah*, I see. Well, welcome to the real world, my friend." Entertaining himself with the deformed little turkey figurine, he made it dance across the counter. "You're welcome to stay as long as you like."

"Thanks. That means a lot."

"I love every single one of these gifts. I've always wanted my very own racoon door mat."

"Oh, yeah? Did Santa miss it on your wish list last year?"

"Santa's a cruel, cruel man."

"Please, don't hold back your Christmas cheer."

"This year I might change my tune. My biggest wish of the year already came true, the second you told me you were on your way tonight." He chanced a sappy, playful grin in my direction.

Heat flamed the tips of my ears. He wasn't going to make this friend thing easy on me. "Tony, what are you doing to that poor turkey?" I averted his gaze, but couldn't conceal a ghost of a smile. He continued making the turkey tap dance, and we both lapsed into a simple exchange, some banter and some laughter, light and untouched by the crowd around us. The easygoing vibe relaxed my muscles and lowered my heart rate, but the enjoyment was short lived.

Tony's posture straightened, and his carefree laugh disintegrated. "Great," he mumbled, glancing behind me. "Incoming."

I turned around. Homing in on us from across the living room, Olivia approached, working her way through the sea of prying eyes.

"Hey, Joanna," she spoke at me but not to me, her eyes fixed on Tony. "I'm surprised to see you here."

I adjusted my coat. "Hey, Olivia. I'm surprised to see me here too."

She turned an indifferent stare my way, appraising my outfit. "A little hot in here to be wearing a coat, don't you think?"

"Liv—" Tony walked around the counter, ready to jump in the ring.

"I was just leaving," I said. "I came to drop off a few things and say congrats on the new place, that's all."

"What? No, Jo. You just got here." Tony touched my hip. "Please, stay. Olivia, we were in the middle of something."

"I can see that." She eyed the medley of gifts on the counter with a smug grin. "How cute. Gifts from the drugstore. Was that your first time in one, Joanna? Saks Fifth Avenue is more your scene, isn't it? How considerate of you, though, lowering yourself to Tony's level to bring him something more suited for his kind."

I worked my fingers over my coat buttons. That was my cue to bounce. "Wow. That's not . . . accurate. Or fair, but okay."

"Really, Olivia?" Tony snapped. "What's wrong with you?"

She ignored him and lifted her cup in my direction. "Hey, I come in peace. Sorry, Joanna. Does that make everything better? Are we cool now? Saying sorry fixes everything, right?"

Tony wedged himself between us, cutting her off. "Damn, will you let it go already? That's enough."

The music continued to flow from the speakers, but the apartment's lively chatter thinned out as more eyes landed on us.

Fully buttoned up and ready to go, my fingers twitched at my sides, conflicted, like my emotions. Embarrassed, I wanted to dart, wanted to flee from the apartment and never look back. Enraged, I wanted to pounce. "You've made your point," I said, moving to make my exit before I released anything I'd regret. "I hear you loud and clear. Don't worry, I'm on my way out."

"No." Tony was fast on my heel. "You don't have to go anywhere, Jo. I invited you here. You're my guest. Come on, let's go up to the roof where it's quieter."

Olivia mirrored my steps, fencing me in. "Should I spell it out for you? Because someone needs to. It doesn't matter that he invited you here. Just because he invited you doesn't mean you belong."

My fists balled at my sides. The music's volume lowered. Whispers sprung up all around us. "Is that what this is all about? You're hung up on the money?" I asked calmly. "I can promise you, more money doesn't equal more freedom, it means a more spacious gilded cage, with more chains, more spectators, all waiting, watching for that one misstep. It's not a charge card at Saks, it's a prison. You want it? Here, please take it. Have it all." I stuffed a hand into my pocket and pulled out my wallet. Popping it open, I retrieved a thick, folded wad of hundreds and shoved it against her chest. "By all means, take it. I'm sorry I'm rich. I'm sorry I humiliated you at the gala. I'm sorry I wanted to try to be friends. I'm sorry, I'm sorry. Yes, sorry should be enough when it's a sincere apology. I don't know what else you want from me."

"I'm one thing you can't buy, Joanna." Fuming, she chucked the cash in my face. The bills broke apart and fluttered to the ground. "You can't buy my friendship, and you can't buy his, either." She jutted her chin at Tony. "Someday your whole world will come crashing down. I don't know where or when or how, or what it's going to look like, but I do know this: you'll finally know how it feels—what it's like to slum it with the rest of us."

Tony flew forward, reaching for her elbow. "Liv, back off. That's not fair."

"Don't touch me." She yanked her arm away, then shoved

him back. He stumbled, knocking against the edge of the kitchen counter. Someone killed the music. "What were you thinking, bringing her here? Let me guess," she laughed scathingly, "you think she's just gonna meld right into your world, right? What, you'll visit her at Yale on the weekends, dine with her preppy friends and then she'll come kick it with you on weekdays in your apartment off Lincoln? With leftovers you bring home from your gig the night before? That shit happens in the movies, but you know what? That's one thing you both actually have in common: you both live in la-la land, while the rest of us live in servitude to the reality of the daily grind."

"Okay, that's it." Tony's voice was harder, harsher. "I said back off. We're done here."

"Oh, you're right about that. I'm done, for sure." Olivia's eyes suddenly welled with tears as she glanced down. Her lashes swept back up at Tony, then her bitter stare returned to me, and that's when I knew.

Tony really was a fool for inviting me here, and I was downright delusional.

"Olivia." My gaze dropped. "I didn't know." I wanted to douse her in I'm sorrys—but I knew better now. More than anyone on the planet, I knew what it meant to love someone you couldn't reach, couldn't keep, couldn't ever truly have, not the way you wanted and needed to have them. The pain of her tears resonated with the agony buried in the marrow of my bones, linking us in a way she'd never know.

"Jo, don't," Tony whispered, leaning into me, pleading with those determined dark eyes.

"She's right." I held up a hand. "I shouldn't be here. Thank you for the invitation, but I have to get going." Pushing my way past them both, I was relieved to find I didn't have to fight my way to the door. A clear path had formed, leading the way for my escape.

When I reached the door, my balance faltered, knocking my hand from the knob. Bodies collided and tripped over one another as the lights went out, dropping a dark blanket over the apartment. Vibrations spread from the ground up, rattling my teeth. Behind me I heard books jumping from their shelves, and crashing glass evoked a string of screams across the pitch-black space. The earth roared below my feet. A layer of terror spiraled into oblivion, and this time, I couldn't get to my true anchor, my true north. Without Florence, I was panic's prey.

EIGHT

Ten *flights.* I only had to make it ten more flights down the stairs. The building's hallway lights flickered on, then off. An electric buzz hummed along the walls as emergency exit signs came to life. Pushing and shouting swallowed the narrow space, almost drowning out the wailing of ambulance sirens, drifting up from the city streets into Tony's building. Images of Sigourney Weaver in the first *Alien* movie, racing desperately for escape with her caged cat in hand, flashed sharply in the back of my brain. I guessed this was what it felt like, to be forced to fight for your life in a claustrophobic space with strobe-light effects. Only, unlike Ripley, I wasn't alone, trying to make it out of this place alive. Elbows punched my ribs as people shoved me aside. My cheeks smashed against the grimy walls as they flattened me like a pancake to make way for their families, scrambling to remain linked to one another, bobbing and weaving through the chaos.

Hyperventilation kicked in. I cursed the out-of-order elevators as I drew closer to the stairwell exit, then felt a mass of dread plunge straight down to my stomach when I passed by their doors. Heavy pounds and screams emanated from inside, driving against the metal, the whimpers of the poor people trapped inside yanking on my heartstrings. Had I disengaged from the blow-up with Olivia and fled Tony's apartment just a few minutes sooner, it could have been me, stuck inside one of the lifts. As bad as my situation was, it could no doubt be worse. I faltered, wishing I had the super-human strength to pry the doors open and release them from their prison. The ongoing stampede knocked me back into motion, ushering me away from the elevators and toward the emergency exit at the end of the hall. Hope sprung against my chest when I flew through the stairwell doorway.

Ten flights. Just ten more flights.

People moved at a rapid pace here, bodies flowing like a surging, downward waterfall, giving the hope in my chest a turbo-rush. Shadows danced against the stairwell's reddish neon light, making me dizzy, but I kept up with the herd, counting the flights as I descended. The limited ventilation and musty smell of old cigarettes assailed my lungs, triggering a wave of nausea. I willed the sensation away, dropping two more flights. Somehow, in the blurry span of immeasurable minutes, I arrived on the first floor, sweaty and winded. Fresh air bursting forth from the exit, the cold stung my nose and cheeks, so fresh and alive it brought moisture to my eyelids, and silent tears trickling down to my chin. My heels clacked on the bustling sidewalk as I put as much distance as possible between me and the building's exit, tucking myself into an alleyway on the left.

Dragging my phone from my pocket, I blinked spastically, swiping and tapping at the screen, chancing a text to my dad. A string of texts and missed calls from him were already wait-ing, sent to me just minutes ago. I nearly dropped to my knees in relief when my typo-riddled response processed instantly. I sent it again, this time managing to correctly spell out Tony's address, then did a quick scroll through my news feeds for updates, in case I lost service. Word that large chunks of Philadelphia were out of commission rolled over my phone screen, followed by other seismic activity highlights from around the globe: tsunami warnings near the Oregon coast. Just yesterday, Haiti—hundreds lost, residents desperately pulling their loved ones from piles of rubble. Crumbled buildings, living tombs. Though we'd been spared that level of destruction here, the abnormal, sudden tremors were no less concerning, as our city streets made clear.

Fed up with the internet, I buried my phone in my coat, instead tuning into talk that littered the nearby sidewalk to fill in the odd gaps of scattered news bits I'd discovered on my own. I tried to make sense of whatever was happening, head rolling back as I searched high, far, and wide for the sky's sanctuary. A blanket of onyx rained down on me. This place, this city, was electrifying and exhilarating, but it also had no problem shoving its people in front of the first moving bus to make way for the next promising prototypes, those willing and desperate enough to be amenable to its mold. My mother managed to excel in its hostile environment, but beneath its weight, I withered.

My head dropped back down, leveling my gaze with the alley's dim path. My mind was made up. The second my theater contract was up, I was leaving this concrete wilderness and never looking back.

The glimmer of a limping silhouette flared in my peripheral vision, an auburn-haired girl in a familiar oatmeal-colored sweater dress. Hunched over and gripping her side, she stumbled into my alley. Her head lifted, revealing a swollen, bloody cheek. My brain stalled out then sputtered back to life when I registered her face.

"Olivia?" I rushed over to her, slipping my arm around her back to hold her steady.

"No," she moaned when she saw me, squirming away. "This night just keeps getting better and better."

"Lean on me, come on."

"Get away from me."

"I promise to leave you alone as soon as I call 911. What happened, did you get trampled?"

"*Gee*, I don't know, what does it look like?" Her eyes rolled as she released another groan, wincing with the shifting of her weight.

"Wait, hold up." I gently guided her along the cobblestone passageway, concealing us deeper in the alley's fold. Maneuvering her against the wall, I adjusted her shoulders and gently tapped her kneecaps, signaling for her to bend and rest back. Calling 911, I gave them our whereabouts, fingers shaking when I ended the call. "Do you need to call someone? I still have service. Who knows how long it will last."

"No. There's no one."

"Not even a friend? Someone you work with?"

Our eyes met.

I looked away, but chanced the question. "Is he okay? Do you know if he made it out safely?"

"I got out before he did. I don't know."

"You sure there's no one you want to try and call?"

She grit her teeth, the skin around her swollen eye spasming. "I already told you. No, all right? I live alone. Family's dead. I'll figure it out, just back off."

Moving to give her some breathing room, I stuffed my phone away. A cell phone with full battery and service was a hot commodity right now. The thought of offering it to others on the street who also needed to call for help pricked my conscience, but I knew the moment I offered it up, there was a chance someone would snatch it away and I'd lose my only lifeline. My gaze gravitated up to the dark sky again as I worked to catch my breath. Somewhere up there, amidst the line of skyscrapers, beyond the city's light pollution, existed a million stars, dusting the universe with their magic, and a moon so bright, it made my chest ache. How I yearned to be there, rather than here, in the aftermath of another wave of east coast tremors.

"Okay," Olivia winced, shoving at my shoulder. "You said you'd go away after you called for help, now go."

"I'm not leaving you here. Not until the ambulance shows up."

"Look around." She jerked a hand toward the city street. "It might take them hours to get to me, and I don't want you here. Now leave me the hell alone!"

The acidic edge in her voice made me flinch. My hands shot to my sides, and I stepped away.

"Fine." She pushed off from the wall, face contorting in pain. "I'll go, then."

"No. Olivia, please. Stay and rest. They'll come for you and everything will be okay."

"Right," she laughed. "Easy for you to say."

"I'll leave as soon as they get here and then you'll never have to see me again, I promise." I glanced nervously toward the street, knowing it was a half lie. If Mom and Dad got to me before the ambulance arrived, I wasn't leaving her here. She was coming with us and we'd get her help, even if it meant holding her hostage against her will.

"Will you get it through your thick skull? I don't want your help." With one strong heave of her limbs, she launched forward, hobbling out of the alley toward the street. I hurried after her, attempting to snag her elbow, but she yanked her arm away and turned to give me a hard, uneven push, then disappeared around the corner. For a moment, I didn't move. Just stared at the space she'd vanished from, as if I'd hallucinated her presence. My shoulders felt heavy as I lingered near the alley's edge to peek out at the commotion, taking it all in.

Some of Tony's party guests flew past, cell phones in hand, mouths moving, eyes wide. No sign of Tony or his roommate, though. Shaking myself from the daze, I fumbled around for my phone once more. My fingers flew over the screen as I sent him a frantic string of messages, praying he'd receive them, that he'd made it outside in one piece.

My toe tapped the sidewalk as I waited. No response.

Risking a few steps farther out onto the sidewalk, I slipped around the corner, dodging the rush of the crowd, and made a move for the same apartment stairwell I'd exited from. I scanned the faces as they poured from the doorway, casting intermittent glances over at the street, watching for signs of Mom and Dad. If I let my mind linger on where Oivia had run off to, I'd lose focus on what was right in front of me. I backed up flush against the building's wall, continuing to watch for Tony. Car horns blasted in the street, mixed with shouts and expletives. Whipping toward the commotion, I hesitated.

"Jo!" Florence's voice boomed from a distance. "Joanna!"

I searched for the direction of her voice. The moment I spotted the car, I bolted. She rolled the window back up when I reached her, and I jumped in the passenger seat. The locks clicked. I buckled my seatbelt. Not that I'd be needing it. Lincoln Avenue was barely moving.

"Where's Dad?" I asked, bracing the armrest.

"He thought it would be safer if one of us stayed home, and one of us came to get you."

"And it had to be you? He sent *you* out in this?"

"I insisted."

"Well, I agree. Someone should be at the house. Where's Helen? Is she okay? What about Aunt Marie?"

"Helen's still at the house. She can't get hold of her family. She's a mess. I told her to stay the night. Aunt Marie is safe. The tremors weren't as strong out her way. Cell and landline are in service. She's more worried about us. Your grandparents called from LA. They want us to fly there and stay with them. Your father declined. They're offended, as usual. Of all the nights you decide to make a dramatic exit, Joanna."

I snuggled into the warm seat. "Tell me about it."

"How are Tony and his friends? Was anyone hurt?"

"Olivia was hurt during the evacuation."

"Waitress Olivia? Oh, no. How bad is it?"

"No idea. She looked pretty rough. I wanted to stay with her but she took off. We had a fight at the party. It was a mess. I couldn't find Tony and he's not responding to my texts. It was all a blur. I was leaving when the tremors hit; I was one of the first ones out of the apartment. I think his place is wrecked. What about the house? Your studio? Did we lose power?"

"Some broken frames and dishes, some knickknacks ruined. Studio's in okay shape. Power's on. This side of town was hit worse. Your father's calm. I've never seen him this calm. Ever."

"Get out."

"Deadly serious."

My father calm under pressure? Unheard of. Mom and I knew better than to be within a mile radius of him whenever a book deadline approached. With each calendar day that passed, bringing him closer to doomsday, he defaulted to Kowalski crisis mode—a hilarious, though nerve-racking spectacle.

"I can't look at any more news." I sighed.

"You don't need much. You've seen one report, you've seen them all. I've seen enough since I got your call to know this will pass, just like the last episode did."

"Mom, this is insane."

"Unusual and alarming, yes. What you're seeing is what happens when control is put into perspective, darling. We have very little of it. All we can control is the way we think and how we react. Don't let it scare you. We're going to be okay."

My fingers fumbled with the seatbelt strap. "I wish I had a fraction of your confidence."

"Oh, it's in there." Mom's hand left the steering wheel to pat my knee. "We just have to reach in there and shake it up a bit. We're frail humans, but we're mighty."

Keeping my focus fixed on Mom to avoid the street's mayhem, I caught a glimpse of dark moisture smeared beneath her eyes. "Mom?" I leaned over and rubbed her cheek. "Have you been crying? Are you okay?"

Indomitable exterior still intact, she smiled softly and lifted a hand to wipe the runny mascara away. "This? This is nothing. Yes, I'm fine, sweetheart. Like I said, don't let this worry you. Everything's going to be all right."

"You can tell me if you're scared, you know. You don't always have to have it together for me. Please don't lie to me. Not ever."

"I assure you Joanna, I'm not lying to you. I'm fine, just overwhelmed." She gestured to her face. "This isn't really about the earthquake."

"Oh? Then what's going on? Talk to me."

"Your father and I had a fight before I came to get you. It's infuriating when he refuses to listen."

"Oh, no. About Yale? That's my mess, I'll straighten it out."

"No. About his trip to Seattle this week."

"What about it?"

"He says he's still going."

"He is absolutely not going."

"That's what I said. I mistakenly assumed that tonight's events would naturally mean postponing the trip. He flipped out, we exchanged unkind words, and there you have it. When it comes to his work, he has selective hearing. One moment, he's as affectionate as the first month we started dating, and the next, he's pushing me out, building walls to keep me on the other side. I hate the distance he creates. It feels as if I'm pinned down underwater, clawing to the surface for breath, witnessing his abduction. His attacker drags him farther and farther away, and I can't reach him. No one can hear my screams. I'm still down there, thrashing about, unseen and unheard."

The distance my mother spoke of became a tangible mass of raw energy, passed to her from my father. No matter what she said, the withdrawn longing swirling in her green eyes gave her away. "Please don't cry, Mom. We'll sort it out." I rested my hand on her forearm as she drove, inching us closer to the next intersection. "I'll talk sense into him. I don't want him clear across the country right now, and we can't sit at home worrying about him getting on a plane while all this is going on."

"He refuses to stay. You can plead your case, but you won't get very far, I'm afraid."

"Well, I'll make him listen. He's not going to push me aside. I won't let him get away with it."

"He loves us. He's blinded by ambition, which is one of the reasons I fell in love with him. But it's a double-edged sword. You either choose to take control of that drive, or it drives you."

"You're right, he does love us, but love is so much more than emotion, more than feeling. Love is also action. It means showing up for people, being considerate of their feelings."

"Your father is his own man, Jo. He isn't your average soccer dad, in case you haven't noticed."

"Yeah, I'm aware of that, but I still think we make too many excuses for him sometimes. You're an artist, too, you also travel for your work, but you still show up for your family. You don't just run your own ship and expect us all to get on board at your beck and call. He's being selfish, and it pisses me off."

"Couples fight. This is family. While I love you for coming to my defense, try to remember that your father is human, too, Jo. This is his personality, these are his eccentricities. It's all a part of the Asher package. Give the guy some credit, kid. Your mother isn't the easiest person to deal with either, you know." She turned her head, feeding me a small grin, and its effect was contagious. The tension in my shoulders melted, and I couldn't help but smile back.

"Well, you have me there," I mumbled. She gave my knee a playful squeeze, then we suddenly rocketed forward as she slammed the brakes.

A heavy thud hit the car hood, a sweaty, suit-clad professional in his mid to late thirties, flinging himself across the vehicle. He pounded the windshield, cursing at my mother, demanding she give him the car keys. "Give them to me, now. Let me in!" Enraged, bulging irises seared us through the glass. "Now! Get out of the car, lady." Mom revved the engine and hit the gas, attempting to knock him off the hood. The bumper-to-bumper traffic hedged us in, blocking any chance of escape. The move only provoked him further. He tore at the windshield wipers, ripping at and struggling to snap them like toothpicks.

"Mom!" My body sunk back into the seat, wincing with each of the man's erratic movements. "What do we do?"

"Don't make eye contact," she replied, unbudging. Her hands remained stationed on the steering wheel, gaze trained straight ahead.

"He's going to break the windshield."

"Let him."

"Mother! Hello? We need to do something!"

"Get in the backseat. Do as I say."

"And then what?"

"Joanna. Now."

Unclicking my seatbelt, I pushed myself up and wedged between the arm rest, clumsily tumbling into the backseat. The man was screaming now, his speech slurred and unintelligible. Cars darted around us and cut us off as the traffic jam inched forward with a new greenlight. Tires peeled on the asphalt, leaving us to fend for ourselves. *Tough luck, baby*, said the mocking, cutthroat squeal of the rubber. *Sucks to be you.* The bright city lights illuminated the backseat, casting a dim glow on a long piece of metal near my feet.

"Slide me the bat," Florence commanded through the rearview mirror. "Quickly."

My eyes popped wide. "Forget it! No way are you getting out of this car. What if he has a gun?"

The belligerent man lifted one fist high in the air, then brought it down like a heavy hammer. The loud smash made me jump.

"He would've used it by now. Give me the damn bat."

A tiny fracture from his bludgeoning fist gave way to the first sign of a spiderweb ripple on the windshield. Blood trickled along the glass. He wiggled down the car hood and landed on his feet. Limping, he felt his way along the hood of the car to hold himself upright as he wobbled toward Florence's door. I plucked up the baseball bat and slid it toward her. Her stealth maneuver happened so quickly, I blinked and almost missed it. Within a fraction of a second, the driver door opened and she was on her feet, stalking around to meet him head on. A gust of wind blew her long, ivory, A-line coat back as she raised the bat and brought it down on his knuckles.

My eyelids snapped shut at the sound of a sickening crack against the car hood.

The man's scream permeated the air, overpowering the surrounding street traffic. Opening my eyes too soon, my gut twisted as I watched Florence deliver another strike—this time to his knee. The second blood-curdling scream seemed to offer her some assurance. Gliding smoothly back to the driver door, she slipped inside the car, slammed a foot on the brake, then threw the gear into drive. She wrenched the wheel to the left, veered around the wounded man, and cut off an SUV approaching from behind. Hitting the gas, we lurched forward and sped through the light, putting just enough distance between us and the now crippled, hunched-over man. Florence stared head-on as she fought to turn a hard right at the next intersection, bobbing and weaving through lane after lane of densely packed vehicles.

Jaw clenched and chest heaving, she tightly gripped the wheel. "Buckle up back there, please."

Words grating against my windpipes, I immediately obeyed.

"Your father isn't getting on that plane. We'll stuff and lock him in the trunk if we have to. He's going to Aunt Marie's with us. We'll spend the week there, stay through Thanksgiving. We'll hunker down and return when things settle down. Agreed?"

"Uh, sure. Yeah, sure." My lashes fluttered. Crushing drowsiness pressed down on my lids, sweeping me away like driftwood. Florence's voice echoed from some vacant, hollow hall until finally, it disappeared.

———

The slow crawl on Lincoln eventually led us home. Mom heaved me up and out of the car and then upstairs to our apartment. I leaned weakly into her, vision still blurry.

"Asher?" she called out, lowering me onto the edge of the sofa.

Helen raced over to us from the kitchen with a glass of

water, lifting it to my lips. "Please drink, Miss Joanna. You're too pale."

"She fainted." Mom's voice was strained.

"How long was she unconscious?" Helen asked, watching me carefully as I took a sip.

"Long enough. She's had a shock, but she's coming around."

Helen pointed to the hallway. "Mr. Kowalski is in your studio. Since you left. I tried to convince him to come out and drink some tea to calm his nerves, but he refuses to move. He's staring out the window."

Mom and I exchanged looks.

"Oh, boy. I better get in there," Florence said, rubbing Helen's shoulder. "Thank you for taking care of us, Helen. I only wish we could return the favor. I'm so sorry you're cut off from your family. I'll drive you to wherever they are as soon as I'm able, I promise. Any luck reaching them by phone?"

"No. Nothing. Thank you." The pronounced wrinkles on her forehead brought out the faint, stray gray hairs near her temples. "I doubt I'll sleep one bit tonight."

"I doubt any of us will. It's getting late, though, and heaven knows we need it."

I returned the glass to Helen. "I'm going with you, Mom."

"Don't you dare move, Joanna. You're staying right there until you've had some time to catch your breath. I'll get you settled in bed once I've checked on your father."

"Oh!" Helen caught my mother's wrist. "You're bleeding, Florence. What happened to you? Come into the kitchen at once. We'll clean you up."

As if she'd wandered into a spacey fog, Mom vaguely studied the smattering of blood on her hand. "Oh, no need to worry. It isn't my blood. You're right, though. I do need to wash up."

"Not your blood? What on Earth are you saying?"

"Mom almost killed a man tonight," I replied, pulling myself to the edge of the couch. I refused to sit there like a lump while my mother looked after everyone. It was kind of Helen to play nurse, but she hadn't witnessed what I'd witnessed tonight. And she didn't speak Florence.

"Joanna, please," Mom hushed me.

With a horrified gasp, Helen made a sign of the cross. "You almost killed someone? Is this true? Why? How?"

"Joanna's exaggerating, Helen. It's true, I did have a run-in with a disturbed man on the street. He threatened us and I needed to send him a message. He's wounded, but he's far from dead."

Helen clutched her chest. "I can't believe what I'm hearing."

"I'm not exaggerating." I said. "She could've killed him. And he could've killed her. She needs rest just as much as I do. So, if she insists on taking care of Dad right now, I'm going with her, and she can't stop me."

Mom exhaled, lifting her hands in surrender. "You are *so* my daughter."

I stood and gestured for Helen to lead Mom into the kitchen. "I'll be waiting in the studio with Dad."

Helen and Mom hurried into the kitchen. The running faucet offered a comforting sound, something ordinary and mundane. The evening's events, including my confrontation with Olivia at Tony's party, swamped my overloaded brain. Keeping one hand on the hallway wall as I started for the studio, I denied my body's attempt to knock me down with another wave of dizziness. I wouldn't faint again. I wouldn't give into the need for sleep. Not until I knew Florence was okay too. When she'd surely recovered and felt well enough to call it a night, then—and only then—would my head hit the pillow.

NINE

I found Dad sitting quietly in Mom's studio, propped leisurely on a wooden stool, gazing at one of Mom's oldest works, a portrait of Poor Joanna from Jewett's *The Country of the Pointed Firs*. Poor Joanna huddled beneath a little shack on Shell-heap Island, her self-imposed exile, adorned with gifts from Dunnet Landing's mainland: a warm blanket draping her shoulders, a little bottle of thyme and sage tied loosely around her neck, and a mysterious sack clenched in her fist, overflowing with flower petals.

"You can smell Mrs. Todd's sweetbrier, mint, and molasses, can't you? I can almost taste it when I look into Joanna's eyes," Dad said, observing the image with the same awe and wonder that seized his features time and time again. The deliberate yet effortless intricacy of the brush strokes, the deep, vivid hues that pulled you right into the scene—so rich you nearly drowned in them—fully entranced my father, rooting him to the stool on which he sat. "The way your mother painted her, it makes you wonder why one of Mrs. Todd's herbal remedies couldn't save her. I suppose none of them were strong enough to persuade her to leave the island."

"She made up her mind to be there. I don't think any remedy in the world could have been a match for Poor Joanna's will."

"How dreadfully bleak."

"I disagree." Our eyes met. I rested on the desk's edge beside him. "I think exile brought her comfort. She knew she wasn't really alone. Everyone was there on the mainland, ready to welcome her back with open arms if she chose to return someday. Even after all that time, the people of Dunnet Landing never let her memory die."

"That's the difference between you and me. Perspective."

"I love you, Dad, but you messed up."

The haze holding Dad hostage dispelled as he blinked. Silence's chasm opened up and we both fell into its ravine. An eternity passed before he spoke again. "You'll never have my blessing to withdraw from Yale, Jo. But I accept your decision, and that's going to have to be enough. I'm sorry for how I reacted. I think the only answer with this one is to agree to disagree."

My teeth burrowed into my bottom lip, nearly drawing blood. "I wasn't asking for your blessing. And I'm not talking about Yale. I'm talking about you sending Mom out to pick me up. She was attacked."

"What?" Dad rose and strode toward me, eliminating any traces of the daze. "I told her to stay here. I wanted to get you. Where is she?" His firm hands pressed into my shoulders, fingers digging into my skin. "Are you all right?"

Florence's unwavering, tranquil presence emerged from behind us. "We're both fine. We had a bit of a scare, but we're here now and we're safe, and that's what matters, right, Joanna?"

The pressure lifted from my lip as I forced my teeth to relent. "If you count crippling some dude on the street with a baseball bat and me passing out fine, then sure. We're both fine. Just peachy."

It took less than a second for Dad to register the redness sprawled across my mom's knuckles. He flew forward, folding her fingers into his large, rough hands. He went to one knee to pay homage to his madonna, planting kisses on her palms. "Tell me what happened, babe. Talk to me. I'm so sorry I wasn't there. I'm an idiot. I'll never forgive myself. Tell me and don't leave anything out. We need to get you both to the doctor. Right now."

For a few moments, the twinge in my chest at the sight of Dad's adoration made his comments about Yale sting a little less.

"Asher. Get up, you sweet, silly man. I doubt we're going to be able to see a doctor tonight. It's a mess out there."

"The emergency room."

"There is no emergency. We need hot showers and rest. We'll reassess in the morning."

He clutched her tighter, bracing her forearms. "Who attacked you? How? When? Why?"

"A stranger on the street. Some frantic, unhinged man, desperate for a car. I handled it, but the incident shook us up a bit." With a glance, Florence delivered one of her classic, silent directives. As always, I wanted to obey the order. But Dad needed the truth, not some cushioned, sugar-coated version of the incident to shield him from whatever it was she was attempting to protect him from.

"Shook us up? That's an understatement," I spat. "The man threatened her and tried hijacking our car. Helen was just in the kitchen, cleaning his blood off Mom's hands. Our windshield is cracked, and we're lucky we made it to the freeway without some other deranged person running us off the road. I don't remember anything else because I was unconscious the rest of the ride home."

Florence's eyelids pressed shut.

Dad stood to his feet, both unable and unwilling to release her from his grip. "Is this true?"

"No, Dad, I'm making it all up, just to make sure you're paying attention."

He finally let go of Mom and stepped toward me. "Now, wait just a minute, Joanna—"

"Stop it," Florence hissed, sliding between us. "Both of you—"

"I don't like your tone, Joanna Kowalski." Dad veered around her, pointing a finger in my face. "I understand you have a grievance you'd like to express, due to the unfinished business we need to discuss, but I'm still your father, and as long as you're my daughter and you live under my roof, you're going to respect me, are we clear?"

"Wow." I pinched the bridge of my nose, pushing back a dizzy spell. "Forget it. I can't have this conversation right now."

Mom stumbled slightly, drawing Dad's attention back to his queen.

"Flo?" He swooped in, steadying her. "Let's go. We're leaving for the hospital."

I rushed forward to brace her from the other side. "Something Dad and I actually agree on," I said to her. "I think you should get checked out, Mom."

"No." She leaned against us, allowing us to lead her out of the studio. "I refuse to go back out into the city tonight. Please just take me to the bed so I can lie down." Her loose braid unraveled over her shoulder as we guided her down the hall and into the master bedroom.

"I'm going to bring some things from the kitchen," Dad said as soon as we lowered her onto the bed. "I'll be fast. Jo, don't let her out of your sight."

"Aye, aye, Captain."

Florence groaned as Dad flew from the bedroom. I climbed onto the mattress and carefully tucked the sheets and blankets around her feet and sides, then clasped her hand tightly in mine, snuggling up next to her.

"Let him take care of you, Mom," I said with a sigh, hugging her tight. "Stop trying to shield him. He never worries about shielding us from his stupid temper tantrums."

Suddenly kicking the blankets away, she threw her hands up behind her head and rifled around beneath the pillow, retrieving an unopened chocolate bar. "Oh, for heaven's sake, Joanna." She tore at the wrapper with her teeth. "I have no interest in shielding your father from anything. I simply wanted to keep him calm in preparation for the Seattle conversation because we needed any leverage we could get. We lost any hope of that, thanks to your smart mouth."

My jaw dropped as faint, feeble Florence vanished and vigorous, roiled-up Florence returned. I snatched the chocolate bar, broke a piece off, shoved it in my mouth, then handed it back. "You're so sneaky. I might have a smart mouth, but at least I'm not faking illness. You're gonna give Dad a stroke. You know that, right?"

"I'm not faking it. Just . . . embellishing."

"Always an actress." Did she ever turn it off? "Where were you during auditions for my last show?"

"Busy coddling your father, apparently."

"*Ugh.*" I leaned over and dropped a playful kiss on her forehead. "All I'm saying is Dad needs tough love sometimes. Being a melodramatic, self-absorbed artist doesn't give him a lifelong hall pass to act like a pubescent teenager."

"Doesn't it, though?" she snorted.

"Okay. So, where are our hall passes?"

"My darling girl, sometimes you have to think about Act 5 when you've barely made it through Act 1, Scene 1."

"Hurry and tell me, then. What's the plan?"

"Just follow my lead." She stuffed the half-mangled chocolate bar beneath the blanket. "*Ssshhh*. Here he comes."

Dad raced back into the bedroom with a tray full of treats: my brownies, tomato soup, crackers, water, and ginger ale. "Helen gave me this, too, for your knuckles." He gestured to the ice pack next to the ginger ale. "Your hand looks swollen."

Feigning a sharp wince as she shifted her weight on the bed, Mom accepted the tray, resting it on her lap. "Thank you, sweetheart. I hope you didn't keep Helen from going to bed. She needs sleep too. She's worried sick about her family."

"She helped heat up the soup, but she's gone to the guest room now. I assured her we'd help her with whatever she needs in the morning."

Remnants of chocolate dissolved on the back of my tongue as I watched my mother carefully. She might have fooled me when it came to physical weakness, but she couldn't fool me when it came to her mind. Florence opted for calculated deliberation, revealing only the wounds she believed I should see. She didn't account for the intuitive superpower daughters share with their mothers.

Dad brought a spoonful of soup to her lips. His tone and demeanor altered as the cogs turned in his brain. "Damn it, Flo, a baseball bat? Did you have to hit the guy? You could've killed him. He could've turned the bat on you. He could've had a knife or a gun. Why did you get out of the car? How could you be so reckless? Have you lost your mind?"

My shoulders tensed. "Whoa, Dad. Slow your roll . . ."

Florence knocked the spoon away. Tomato sauce dribbled onto the comforter. "Excuse me?" Agitation laced each syllable. "He was attacking us, Asher. He cracked our windshield and tried to steal our car. Did you want us stuck clear on the other side of the city during this? With no way home? I confronted him because I had no choice."

"What about a cab, for crying out loud? If someone

attacks, hand over the damn car. Give him what he wants. Don't risk your lives!"

"A cab?" Florence pressed her lips together until they turned white. "You expected me to abandon our car and hail a cab after an earthquake, with raging lunatics roaming the streets."

It was my turn to play referee. "Guys, stop. Please. I have a headache. We're all tired and overwhelmed. Mom's right, we need hot showers and sleep. Arguing isn't going to solve anything right now." I swallowed down a surge of hot anger. It did a little dance with my heartstrings, stirring up a whirlpool of emotions. I loved my father's concern for our wellbeing, but Dad's tendency to act as if everything always happened to him, and only him, wasn't new, and since he'd taken it upon himself to orchestrate my Ivy League future, that tendency multiplied tenfold.

Florence reached over and pulled the food tray closer, then snatched the spoon from Dad's hand to feed herself. "What's done is done," she snapped. "I don't feel well, Asher. We're all exhausted. We're home and we're safe, and that's enough."

Rubbing the stubble on his jaw, he dropped a defeated hand onto his knee. "I'm sorry, babe. You're right. That's all that matters. I just . . ." His shoulders slouched. "If anything ever happened to you or Joanna . . ."

"You can't protect us all the time, Dad." I scooted over and rested my head on his shoulder. He was an infuriating father, but he was my infuriating father.

"It's true," Florence agreed, lifting the glass of ginger ale to her lips. "There is something else you can do for us, though."

"Name it."

"Cancel your flight to Seattle."

"Florence."

"Asher."

"Dad." I pouted and closed my arms around his neck, snuggling closer, curling into him the same way I did when I was seven years old. "What kind of man denies a sick woman?"

He sighed and kissed my forehead. "A smart man, trying to keep his job so he can provide for the sick woman."

"The publisher will understand. Family comes first."

"They will, and yes, it does. Me showing up, attending this meeting, *is* putting family first. I cannot afford to lose momentum right now, Jo. Everything I do affects you and your mother too."

"Mom makes a mountain of money on her own. She doesn't need yours. And neither do I, as much as you disagree with that whole idea. This is about your career, not us. I wish you'd just admit it."

Gently pulling back from our embrace, he peered down at me. "And what kind of man would I be if I said it wasn't?"

I studied his face, fatigued and troubled, as if he'd ran a thousand laps around the track in his brain. "Even if you lost your deal with this publisher, you have enough clout to publish with anyone you want, Dad. You could go indie, have more control over your work."

"This isn't a book deal we're talking about. It's a long-standing business relationship that I've worked very hard to cultivate and maintain over the last ten years. It's my lifeblood and livelihood, but it's much more than that." His worn-out gaze swung to my mother's face. "It's who I am as a husband and father. The only thing I have some say over. Everything else is . . . chaos."

A wrinkle formed on my mother's forehead as she gazed back at the weary, stubborn man she shared a life with. She set the food tray aside and leaned forward, cupping his face. "It's not all of you. No matter how many times you hit the best-seller list, you'll always be our hero. And we support your career, you know that. But this is one time we're asking you to please make an exception. Say no. Don't get on that flight. Come with us to Marie's and we'll all come home after Thanksgiving, after things have calmed down around here. It'll give us a chance to recharge and regroup. Talk them into an online meeting, just this once. I know it's not their style, but make them work with you."

He instinctively leaned into her caress. Leading her hand to his lips, he kissed her knuckles. We all slumped forward, our weight caving in and drawing us together in a tangled hug. Dad's arms, still strong despite his weary mind, infused me with fortification. "Let me sleep on it," he pleaded. "Our internet and phone service aren't reliable right now. There's no guarantee I could make an online meeting happen, even if by some chance they agreed to one. How about we get you both to the doctor tomorrow, get Helen to her family, and get you packed for Marie's. Then see how we feel. We don't have to make this decision tonight."

Resuming her original position, Mom fell back against the pillow and tapped the food tray. Resting a hand against her forehead, she closed her eyes. "Thank you for feeding me, sweetheart. Will you take this back to the kitchen? I'm too tired to shower. I need to sleep."

"Of course," Dad replied, lifting the tray from the comforter. "Goodnight, babe. I love you."

A soft hum purred from Mom's throat and she rolled onto her side, hugging a pillow to her chest.

I tucked her hair behind her ear, said goodnight, then quietly rose and walked with Dad out into the hall. I stopped and took the tray from him, gesturing back to the bedroom door. "I've got this. She needs you."

"I love you too, you know."

"I know. So, go with us to Aunt Marie's."

"I wish it were that simple, honey."

"It can be." I started for the kitchen.

"Joanna?"

I paused mid-stride.

"In this family, your mother is a tough act to follow." His head hanging, he slipped his hands into his pockets and shuffled back into the bedroom.

TEN

A flurry of activity consumed the following morning, setting the tone for the rest of the day. Dad paid triple the rate to have our family doctor make an early-morning house call, insisting on basic check-ups for me and Mom. As it turned out, Dr. Weinstein didn't have to brave sidewalks of panicked pedestrians or gridlock traffic. The streets were quiet, as if the whole city had purged its hysteria and retreated into hibernation mode, hunkering down for an incoming blizzard. Dad was comforted by the shift in energy, celebrating the newfound "peacefulness," but from where I stood, staring down at the street from Mom's studio window, everything about the sudden dormancy felt wrong. On the bright side, Mom and I received a clear bill of health, relieving some of Dad's anxiety.

After Dr. Weinstein left, I made a pitstop to the theater while Mom and Dad drove Helen to reunite with her daughter. By early afternoon, house chores were done, and Mom launched into packing mode while Dad busied himself with promotional strategies for his next release. He tapped away at his laptop's keyboard, glasses perched low on his nose as he scrutinized the computer screen on the living room sofa. Every few minutes, Mom would call something out to him from down the hall about what he did or didn't want packed for the trip to Aunt Marie's. His responses varied, but mostly consisted of some "yes, dears" and absentminded mumbling, until they tapered off and stopped completely. He left the TV news on mute, glancing intermittently at the headlines. So far, no new tremors in the Philadelphia area, but now Boston was in the hot seat, experiencing record-breaking waves of seismic activity. Despite power outage repairs and cell tower service being restored, various oil line disruptions were still a major concern throughout the Northeast, feeding more suspicion that potential terrorist activity was somehow to blame throughout parts of the east coast. More conspiracy theorists had emerged, but each theory sounded more ridiculous than the next, leaving me to believe that we were just grabbing at straws, trying to explain something that could likely never be explained. Accepting the unknown, the reality of unsolved mysteries, was not the human race's forte.

Though its hot brim burned my upper lip, I sipped hot chocolate from an oversized too-early Christmas mug and regarded the sparse stragglers in the streets down below, careening around corners and scurrying over crosswalks like ants on a mission to build their next colony. My bag was packed, and I'd touched base with the theater director. Due to what was happening around the city, Nancy, the director, canceled our remaining rehearsals for our last shows of the season, thankfully buying me some extra time off. They were considering canceling the last performances altogether until they had a better idea of what to expect moving forward. The staff voiced all kinds of mixed opinions on the matter, but I'd walked three blocks to the theater after Dr. Weinstein's visit, tossed in my two cents, then turned right back around and hurried home, eager to be back inside, locked away in our family's concrete tower. Safety was only an illusion, like so many mental constructs in life, but I latched onto it. Until Dad announced his answer on whether he'd be joining us for the trip, our apartment in the clouds was a life raft.

"Jo, your turn, my darling," Florence's voice echoed from my parents' bedroom.

"Already packed," I called back.

"Tell your father to get in here, then."

I sipped the chocolate. "He stopped listening like an hour ago, Mom. I'm sure whatever you packed for him will be fine."

"Any word from Helen?" Florence strode into the studio, hands perched on her hips. "What's next on the list?"

"Helen's fine. She called Dad on his cell twenty minutes ago to thank you again for getting her to her daughter's. Now they're just trying to locate her granddaughter. And what list? You mean the imaginary convoluted one scribbled onto your overactive brain?"

"No, smart mouth, the actual list I wrote down this morning, after Dr. Weinstein left."

"I know of no such list." My lips puckered as my stare swung from the little ant people in the street to my mother's preoccupied pout. Her eyes were sharp and focused, but somewhere else, as if she were operating on some subterranean level in another universe.

"Have you seen my thingy-ma-bob with the whatchamacallit?" she said.

"The red one with the blue thingy?"

"*Mhmm.*"

"Nope."

"Drat."

"Mom?"

"Jo?"

"Do you want to talk about it?"

"Talk about what?"

I blinked at her over the mug's rim. If she didn't get a grip soon and talk about this morning's newspaper, I'd have no choice but to drag it out of her, as much as I hated to be the one to do it. Dad, in typical Asher fashion, had offered consolation by smothering her with affection and accolades, but she escaped the flattery and slipped away to the workout room for a kickboxing session. The paper, mostly littered with reports of yesterday's alarming events, was blemished by a calloused column in the Arts and Culture section, reminding the public that my mother's days were numbered on the orchestra's board of trustees, as her replacement quickly moved in to boot her out. A photoshopped image of Marilyn 2.0 sat next to a portrait of my mother onstage, displayed side by side, Marilyn's showcasing tighter skin, fewer wrinkles, an unnaturally large bust, and a bouffant, beauty queen hairstyle that would be considered big even in Texas. The feature now stuck to our dining room table, pinned in place by a single arrow from Mom's quiver bag. The issue's other sections sat crumpled up in the recycling bin.

As Florence's punches, kicks, and grunts sounded from the workout room after Dad's failed attempts at solace, I'd plucked the arrow from the table. Eying the column with disdain, I thought how grateful I was that it was the baseball bat she'd taken with her the night before, and not her archery bag, or the dude who tried to hijack our car would be dead right now.

My mother and her hobbies.

"You don't need the orchestra board, Mom," I said, lowering the mug. "The members who voted you out are ageist elitists, and the reporter who wrote the feature wants to have Dad's babies. They're parasites. Ignore them."

"Ignore who?" Florence's brows drew together as she scanned the room, searching, searching. For something, anything. "I don't know what you're talking about, darling."

"You want me to storm into their next meeting, guns blazing? I don't have your archery skills, but I know some of your kickboxing moves."

A glint of humor tickled her upper lip.

"You're always the one telling me to keep things in perspective," I said. "I'm telling you right now, you're not seeing clearly. You know what? Bow out early. Just peace-out, with no warning. Don't let them have the upper hand. Reinvent yourself. That's sort of your thing."

"There you go again." With an affectionate grin, she strolled toward me and stroked the side of my cheek with the back of her hand. "Trying to fight my battles. That's *your* thing, not mine, sweet girl. I will bow out gracefully, and on time. I will give them exactly what they want."

"Why? Why would you?"

"Because it's who I am."

"They have no idea what they're giving up."

"Oh, but they do. They just don't care. I know that part is hard for you to digest, but the sooner you do, the sooner you'll realize that the frustration, the anger, the resentment you feel —it's simply not worth it. For you, this is a battle, but in their eyes, they've already won the war. We can't change their perspective, but we can demonstrate our own. We can make statements. That's all."

I studied her quietly. "It's a battle for you, too. I know it is."

"It's a loss. A wound. It's many things. But not a battle, no."

A light knock from the doorway pierced our exchange, my father's knuckles rapping against the frame. "Pardon the interruption, ladies. Thought you'd might like to know that I've left Todd a message about the building video footage. Also contacted the dealership about replacing the cracked car windshield. I made an appointment for the repair two weeks from now, so we can take it in a few days after the return from Marie's. Now I'm going to slip away for a few hours to get some more work done on this launch campaign. Taking a walk down to The Nook for some fresh air and espresso. Want me to bring anything back? Your almond croissants?"

Florence pivoted around and crossed her arms. "You're asking us about almond croissants?"

"I'd like croissants." I raised my mug in approval.

Dad crossed his arms to match Florence's. "Dare I ask? What did I just walk into?"

"Mom packed for you," I replied. "We're leaving for Aunt Marie's at six AM. So, don't drink too much espresso or you won't get any sleep tonight and then you'll be grumpy all morning, and that'll make Mom grumpy, and then I'll be miserable, so . . ."

Florence grinned sweetly. Too sweetly for Dad's good. "Yes, you're all packed, sweetheart, though your input would have been appreciated. I don't want to hear a word about your green flannel or corduroy pants. If you don't like them, don't wear them. They're packed, along with every other piece of flannel you own, and that's final."

"Yes, Your Majesty." Dad sauntered forward, a bounce in his step, and gave her a lighthearted peck on the lips. "I didn't offer input because I'm still not sure I can make it, babe. I'm waiting to hear back from John's assistant, and as soon as I do, I promise I'll let you know."

"It's almost dinnertime," Florence warned, grabbing him by the collar. "Asher, please. Don't do this."

"Come on, Dad. Seriously?"

Imploring us both, he pried Mom's fingertips from his collar, then kissed them. "Things are calming down out there. If I honestly thought you wouldn't be safe going without me, I would cancel Seattle. I told you John wouldn't go for the online meeting. He shot it down. I asked him to reconsider. I should hear from him soon." Lifting his hands in defense, he took a step back. "Please, just be patient. I'll go get some work done and by the time I come home with croissants, I'll have an answer. Maybe I can drive out and meet you at Marie's when I get back from Seattle and spend the rest of the week with you. Maybe we can compromise."

I shook my head. My gaze dropped to the floor. How easily he archived the reminder that less than twenty-four hours ago, Mom and I were *not* safe. How easily persuaded he was by a quick report from Dr. Weinstein and the tug of blind ambition.

"Bring bear claws, too," Florence conceded, waving him off. "We can take them on the road for breakfast tomorrow."

"You got it." Immobile and waiting, Dad's expectant gaze settled on me. Silence trickled across the studio. I had nothing to say. Everything I'd wanted to say, I'd already said. A few more seconds ticked by until he walked out, carving a stretch of uncertainty in the center of the room.

"He'll make the right choice," I said, taking my hot chocolate and resuming my position by the window.

Florence remained fixed on the doorway, lingering in the space Dad left in his wake, grasping at an apparition. Wordless and contemplative, we sojourned there in our quiet space, our high, hidden tower amidst Philadelphia's skyline.

"Will you help me find that list?" Florence asked a few minutes later, breaking the spell. "Need to make sure we're not forgetting anything."

Before I could answer, the irritating strike of the landline rang out from the kitchen and rushed into the studio.

"Joanna?"

"I'm on it." Taking the last sip of chocolate, I jogged out of the room and toward the kitchen to silence my mother's dreaded nemesis. Sliding the empty mug onto the counter, I grabbed the phone from the wall, but I was too late. The ringing stopped the moment my fingers touched the handle. Taking a cue from Mom, I felt along the wall for the cord and gave it a gentle yet satisfying yank, unplugging it from the outlet, not at all in the mood for prank calls today. Swinging around the corner, I hurried down the hall to return to the studio. The sooner I helped Florence find this imaginary to-do list, the sooner the trip prep would be done, and we could focus on unwinding and figuring out dinner.

A faint knock came from the front door, hindering my stride. I paused to listen. The sound was so light, I wondered if I'd imagined it. Another soft series of taps confirmed my sanity and kickstarted me back into motion, spinning me around toward the main entryway.

"Jo?" Florence's apprehensive tone sailed down the corridor.

"Yes, Mother, I've got it . . ." Flipping the lock, I opened the door, unable to disguise my surprise when my line of sight dropped about two feet to land on a pale freckled face. Frizzy, rich brown curls, almost black, framed the little girl's cheeks. We made eye contact and I waited, watching her dainty lashes sweep down to stare at her feet.

"Um . . . hi," she said with a shaky voice.

"Hi back. Can I help you?"

"You're Joanna, right?"

"Last time I checked." I laughed. "And you are?"

"Your last name is Kowalski and you work at the Bluebird Theater on 5th and Madison. You design costumes and props. Your mom's name is Florence, and she's a famous musician." Her tone, like her knocks on our front door, lacked power and strength. She glanced up and watched me carefully. Small, fidgety fingers lifted from her sides to rest against the straps of her olive-colored backpack.

"Yeah, sounds about right. Sorry, do we know you? Have we met before?"

"No, but I know you." The muscles of her throat tensed as she swallowed. "Me, my sister, and my mom know all about you."

Wrinkles tickled my forehead, my brow scrunching in confusion. "Okay, you're gonna have to help me out here because I'm so lost. What's your name? Are you here all by yourself?" I poked my head out into the hall, glancing around for an adult. She couldn't be more than seven or eight years old. "Usually visitors use the bell to ring before they can come up to the floor. How did you get up here?"

She cast a side glance to her left, down the hall. "I'm not alone. Not this time, anyway. My sister agreed to bring me. I skipped school a few times and came here by myself, but then I got scared and changed my mind and left."

"Your sister?" I followed her gaze, peering down the hall in search of the mystery chaperone. "You were scared? I'm not sure I'm following you."

Pointing to the end of the hall, the little girl gestured to what I hadn't seen before: a taller, tanner, curly-haired teenager hiding around the corner. The teenager's black ringlets glistened beneath the hallway's fluorescent light. "That's Niambi, my sister. We snuck in with a delivery . . . It's worked for me a few times before."

Niambi, the little girl's older sister, watched us warily from the end of the hall as she moved out of the shadows, taking a hesitant step forward. Though I hadn't spoken, the little girl signaled permission to join us with a nod to her sister. "I found . . . well, stole . . . your house phone number, and I've been calling, too. But every time you answer, I hang up. I never know what to say."

Taking in Niambi's cautious approach, I blinked and waited, my mind tripping over itself to piece together whatever the little girl was trying to say.

"My mom made me swear to never come here," she said.

"And your mom is . . . ?"

"Your dad's mistress," Niambi replied flippantly, saddling up to her little sister's side. "This is Carolyn." She patted the girl's head and cocked a hip, looking me up and down. "Your half-sister. Don't worry, me and you aren't related. I have my own daddy, I'm not after yours. I'm just here for Carolyn. She wanted to meet you, and with the world probably ending and all . . . no time like the present, right?"

A metallic flash rippled sharply in my skull, retrieving an older yet spitting image of the teenage girl before me: a raven-maned woman draped in a lush, scarlet gown, observing from above, her blank stare raining down from a theater balcony, lancing something inside, something buried within the deepest pit of my spirit.

My lips parted. "That's not possible."

"We came all the way from Havertown," Niambi said dismissively. "Your dad visits a lot, but Carolyn doesn't get him in public the way you do. No ballet recitals, no walks to the school bus. Our mom does all that. He pays her to stay quiet, has her convinced it's in the best interest of the whole family. Nice, right? We should nominate him for Father of the Year."

At last, I found my breath. "Look . . ." I stepped backward. "There must be some mistake. I think you have the wrong apartment."

"Is he here? 'Cause he's not with our mom today." Niambi wedged herself in front of Carolyn. "Or is he on another one of his business trips?" She lifted her fingers and drew air quotes. "He conveniently ignores our calls on the days he isn't with us. Comes up with all kinds of lame excuses. Sorta makes you wonder if he has a third woman, ya know? Like if he has two families, who's to say he doesn't have a third? A whole other life that none of us know about. Then again, he's already a busy guy, it must be hard enough to find the time to write those books of his—"

"Stop." My limbs moved on their own accord, legs stumbling back inside the apartment, arms fumbling with the door to shut them out. "I don't know who you think you are, but you have it all wrong. You need to leave. Right now."

Niambi's palm slapped the center of the door, landing with a sharp smack. Slipping her foot in the doorway, she cut me off, keeping it propped open. "Oh, no. We're not going anywhere until my little sister gets what she came here for. Do you have any idea what she's been through, to get here and finally meet you? Do you realize how royally effed up this is? She's gotten detention for missing classes, she's been grounded because she wouldn't tell my mom where she's been. She's scared the crap out of me, disappearing for hours at a time, sneaking cab rides and bus rides, lying and making excuses to drivers, teachers, babysitters. She could've been abducted. Need I say more?" Swiping a piece of paper from her jean pocket, she shoved it at me. "Here. See for yourself."

Behind her, Carolyn sniffled, the beginning of a series of quiet sobs. Niambi's hand reached behind and squeezed Carolyn's. Unable to confront the piece of paper now in my fist or the plaintive sound of a crying child, I focused instead on their bond, on Niambi's protective stance and the level of trust she'd built with Carolyn. I was an only child, but the dynamic was a familiar one; it was the bond of motherhood, of sisterhood, of women protecting women, because the world regularly stamped us out, discarded us when we were no longer useful, told us we didn't matter.

I released my grip on the other side of the door, yielding to Niambi's force, and looked at the object in my hand. A crumpled image, a photograph with teddy bear stickers in the corners. Huddled in the center of the picture was Asher, my father, surrounded by a fireplace and Christmas stockings and a beautiful family not my own. Carolyn, Niambi, a golden retriever, and the raven-haired beauty in the scarlet dress from the theater balcony surrounded him, smiley and blinded by love. My fingertips went cold and my breath turned shallow. "Come on in," I managed. I allowed the door to swing wider, inviting them inside, our paths suddenly merging into one lane on an unknown highway.

Eleven

"When was this taken?" I whispered as I stared down at the photograph. My eyes brimmed with hot, silent tears. I blinked rapidly, as if the motion could somehow banish them. Tears? What tears? They didn't exist.

"Does it really matter?" Niambi rolled her eyes.

"Why . . . why did you come here? What is it you want? How long have you known about us?"

"Jo?" Florence's bare feet echoed on the floors as her voice carried down the hall. She appeared from the end of the corridor, moving to join us. "Who was on the phone? Oh!" With a warmhearted grin, she greeted our visitors. "Well, hello. Who do we have here?"

Carolyn hid behind Niambi, latching onto the back of her jacket. Niambi's jaw hardened as she studied my mom, watching her like a contagious animal liable to infect her little sister with a deadly disease.

"Mom." My limbs were moving on their own accord again. Somehow, my hand landed on her forearm—to steady myself or hold her back from what was coming, I didn't know. "We should sit down."

Registering the dampness on my cheeks, Florence's grin faded. "Darling? What's wrong? What's going on?" Like rapid fire, her green irises jumped between me, Niambi, and what little she could have seen of Carolyn, settling on the picture in my hand. Carolyn's muffled sobs collided with the rustling sound of the paper image as Florence loosened it from my ice-cold grip.

"Your husband is my little sister's father," Niambi said, voice pricking like a thousand bee stings. "Her name's Carolyn. We tried to keep her from all this, but she found out about you a while ago and decided she wanted to meet you. Your husband's been living a double life. Sorry to spring it on you, but there it is."

Florence's fingers clamped onto the photograph, staring at it like a riddle that needed to be solved. "No. You're mistaken, I'm sorry."

"Afraid not. I'm Niambi, Carolyn's half-sister. We live in Havertown. Our mom's a schoolteacher, and your husband is the one who got us the dog. Five years ago. We named him Max."

"No," my mother stuttered, voice bouncing aimlessly around the room like a missile without a target.

"You didn't answer my question," I said, wiping my tears with the edge of my shirt sleeve. I inched forward, shielding Mom. "What is it you want? To meet us? Okay, well you can cross that one off your list. You must have something else in mind. You said this wasn't your first attempt to come here, so you must have some questions, some kind of plan, right?" I needed something to drown out Florence's pain, to cushion her shock and realization. I needed noise and answers and motion. "Please," I pressed. "Tell us what you want."

Niambi's eyes popped wide, jaw dropping as she tumbled over her own words. "What we . . . *what we want*? We don't want your stupid money, if that's what you're getting at. We have enough of that, thanks to your dad's ridiculous bribes."

"No. I mean, what were you hoping to get out of this meeting? You've known about this; you probably know more than any of us. Until you walked through our door, my mom and I knew absolutely nothing. We have literally nothing you want. Zero information. *Nothing*."

"Look, if I had any say in this joke of a family, I would've told the whole world your dad's secret years ago. The only reason I haven't is for her sake." She jutted her chin at Carolyn. "She's a good kid—the best—and the last thing she deserves is to be thrown into a public scandal, constantly under the limelight in some freak show media circus. It was only a matter of time before she started asking more questions and wanted answers. She's older now, she's ready to know more. So, maybe you should ask Carolyn. She's the one who wanted to meet you." Slowly crouching down, she dropped to one knee and swiveled around to face her little sister. With a gentle hug, she coaxed the little girl from hiding, whispering against her ear, "It's okay, Care. Say whatever you came here to say. They're listening. You're safe, I won't let anyone hurt you."

"No, no, no," my mother's voice played on a repetitious loop as she talked to the photograph, trying to change its mind. Unresponsive to my plea to sit down, she began pacing back and forth. The woman who the night before had driven through a disaster site and took a baseball bat to a crazed car thief seemed unable to cope with what she'd just seen and heard.

Dumbstruck, rabidly defensive, and buzzing with the need to understand, I slid down to the floor next to Carolyn and Niambi.

Carolyn's bottom lip quivered as her gaze found mine. In those eyes were fresh linens, spotless and untouched, carefree merry-go-rounds and effortless honesty, undeniable and unavoidable. "I just . . . wanted to know . . ."

"Go on." Niambi rubbed her back.

"Wanted to know if . . . if you're my sister, does that mean we can be friends? Can we all get along . . . be a family together?"

The little girl's words struck the center of my chest, splintering like a shrapnel-infused shell. Burning coals raked over my nerves, igniting feelings I didn't even know could exist. She wanted to be a family? She wanted to know me? What did she expect, campfire sing-alongs? Cozy movie nights on the couch with her cute dog, our mothers, and our dad sandwiched in the middle? This sweet little kid wanted to be my friend, and I wanted to rewind to ten minutes ago, before I knew she existed. Whatever twisted *Brady Bunch* dream she envisioned wasn't going to happen. That would require mutual love and respect between two families, two families who knew what they were getting into, two families who wanted to come together and live happily ever after.

"Do you know why Dad kept us a secret from you?" she continued with the questions, so sincere, so full of curiosity and longing.

"Well, I can answer that one," Niambi spat, eying me as if I was the culprit. "Because your daddy is a liar and a complete—"

"I think you need to be asking our dad that, not us," I said, curbing the edge in my tone for Carolyn's sake. Damn him for putting me in this position, for having to break this little girl's heart even more than it was already breaking. Niambi had every right to carry a chip on her shoulder, but she needed to channel that anger where it belonged.

"So?" Contempt burned in Niambi's eyes. "Do you want a relationship with my sister or not?"

"I . . . I'm . . . I don't know." Glancing over my shoulder, I looked back at Mom. She was watching us now with a hollow, haunted stare, as if a nuke just dropped and she'd stumbled upon the charred, desolate aftermath. I turned back to Carolyn. "Carolyn, you're so brave. Braver than I could ever be. But I'm sorry, I can't make those kinds of promises." More unwanted tears obstructed my vision. "I need some time to think, to figure things out."

Carolyn leaned into Niambi's embrace. "Can I see our dad?" she asked, peeking over at Florence.

"I'm so sorry, sweetheart," Mom replied, voice dry and raspy, "but that won't be possible. He's not here at the moment."

Adrenaline zapped my veins, sending me back up into a standing position. I wobbled as I rose, fighting to restore my equilibrium. "We'll call him. I'll call him." And when I got hold of him I'd obliterate his ego, level him syllable by syllable, until his shame and pride had nowhere to hide.

Florence snatched my wrist, holding me still. "He's boarding a plane to Seattle. We can't reach him right now." Shooting me a warning to remain silent, she held my frantic stare. When she was certain I'd received her message, she released me. With quick, nimble movements, she floated toward the foyer accent table and picked up a pen, notepad, and some crisply folded cash. Ink raced against the paper with sharp, elegant strokes. "Here, Carolyn," she said, her gravelly tone deepening as she bent down to her level. "Listen very carefully, okay? I want you—or your sister—to call this number or visit this address anytime you want to talk, or anytime your mother wants to talk. This is the number for a woman named Marie. This is where Joanna and I will be from now on. You are welcome to ask questions. Our door will always be open, do you understand? But right now, I think it's best for you to let your sister take you home, where your mom knows you're safe. Your father will be back from Seattle in a few days, and I'm sure you will all have time to talk then. Please use this money for your bus fares." Tenderly skimming Carolyn's chin, Florence exhaled. Casting a pleading look in Niambi's direction, she rose to her feet and gave her the photo back. "Can you please take her home? Joanna and I have a lot to discuss."

"We came all this way," Niambi seethed, eyes darting between me and Mom. "You really have nothing else to say? Don't you have any questions for us?"

"I'm so very sorry." Florence's words cracked as they bled from her lips, her irises darkening, shifting into smoldering, emerald specks. "Sincerely, from the bottom of my heart, I am sorry this is happening to you, and I'd give anything—truly anything—to take away your hurt and disappointment." Her patient glance panned my way.

"Same," I said, summoning what empathy I could amidst my swim in a sea of hysteria. "I'm sorry for you both. For coming all this way, for having to go through this. For all of it. I wish there was something else I could say to make you feel better, but I honestly can't."

"Yeah, well," Niambi huffed, squeezing Carolyn closer to her side, "kinda sucks for you too, I guess."

With a solemn nod, I reached for the back of the sofa to stabilize my wobbly knees.

A heavy quiet descended on the room and the girls started for the exit, flinching when an impatient, persistent knock suddenly sounded from the other side of the entryway. Niambi cast a glance at us, tucking Carolyn behind her as she opened the door and came face to face with Todd, the building security manager.

"Hi, Todd." Florence sighed. "This really isn't a good time."

Tall, husky, and austere, Todd greeted me and Florence, shooting Niambi and Carolyn an accusatory glare. "I apologize, Mrs. Kowalski. I've been away from the office since all the commotion yesterday and just now reviewed the video footage your husband requested. May I speak with him? I just noticed these two on today's delivery entrance playback and rushed up as soon as I could. I think it's best to discuss these matters in person." Gesturing to Carolyn, he adjusted his shiny black belt, flashing his silver badge and credentials. "It turns out this little girl here is a regular stowaway on the freight elevator. Would you like me to escort them off the premises and contact their guardians and the authorities?"

"Heavens, no," Florence replied, rubbing her left temple. A vein throbbed and jumped beneath the skin of her fingertips. "Asher's not available. No need to walk them out or call anyone. They're welcome here any time. Please allow me to handle it from here. Thank you."

Todd stationed his hands on his hips, exuding his very best tough-cop impression. His fingers tapped at his badge and he surveyed the living room like a fresh crime scene.

Florence cleared her throat.

"Right," he said, straightening his navy tie. "Of course, Mrs. Kowalski, if that's what you'd prefer. I'll be on my way, then."

Niambi pinned him with a glare. "Please, after you."

Striding quickly out into the hall, Todd disappeared. Niambi and Carolyn hung back, giving him a head start. Without another word, Niambi ushered Carolyn out after him, away from our tower in the clouds, away from our perfectly crafted fine-tuned existence, the one we'd spent the last twenty-something years cultivating. Mom stepped forward to turn the lock behind them. Pivoting around, she homed in on the clock on the adjacent wall, whispering something I couldn't make out.

"Why did you send them away? Why lie about Dad not being here?" I smashed the silence, completely unsatisfied with the outcome of whatever just unfolded in our living room. "We didn't even get their full names or their address."

In fact, where were all our answers? Why weren't we confronting the man who was brazen enough, reckless enough to pay his second family to be his dirty little secret while he played doting husband and father to the other? An entire genre of Elizabethan plays revolved around the very notion of retributive justice. This level of deception not only called for the same magnitude of vengeance seen in those revenge tragedies, it also proved that though Mom and I called the stage home, Dad was the true actor in the family.

Florence spoke at the clock. "I sent them away. And wasn't truthful. Because we don't have much time."

"We need to call him. Now."

"We have ten minutes."

I followed her gaze to the minute hand. "Ten minutes for what?"

Her deft fingers rose to her favorite teardrop diamond necklace, smoothly unclasping it from the back of her neck. "Joanna?"

"Mom?"

"First take a deep breath."

My frenzied gaze dropped to the necklace, then back up to her mesmerizing green irises, the windows to her soul—still haunted, still hollow, but charged by a dim spark. Despite everything, my tensed muscles, sweaty brow, and trembling fingertips, I did as she said. Dragging in a long, deep stream of air from the very core of my diaphragm, I prepared myself for whatever was next.

A weightless phantom, she glided toward me, necklace draped delicately across her palm. "Do you trust me?"

"Always."

"I'm leaving for Aunt Marie's in nine minutes. The bags are already packed, but if you'd like to go with me, go collect anything else that means something to you, whatever you can carry, from your bedroom and the studio, just in case."

"Just in case?"

"I won't be coming back to this place. Ever. Do you understand?"

I clutched my stomach, the air I'd just taken in already locking up again in my gut. "What? Mom, that's insane. This is your home, of course you're coming back here. If anyone should leave, it should be him."

Raising her free hand to my shoulder, she looked right through me, rifling through my thoughts one by one, sifting until she located exactly what she was looking for. "I didn't say *you* can't return. You can come back any time your heart desires. This is your home, and I won't keep you from it. If you'd rather stay here, that's perfectly fine. But you won't approve of what I'm going to do next, darling. This place won't be the same after I leave, so I need you to decide whether you'd like to go with me now or stay here and wait for your father to come home." Her voice, gentle and even, contrasted violently with the festering tempest in my abdomen. "You have a few minutes to think about it." Abruptly, she vanished from the living room and bolted down the hallway toward the bedroom.

"Whoa, wait. Wait, Mom." My heart was already hot on her trail, but my mind held me in place. Metal clinks and the rattling of hangers down the hall flipped a switch in my brain, allowing it to catch up to my heart. I launched in the direction of the unsettling sounds from my parents' room, cautiously circling Mom as she piled some of her finest things on the edge of the bed. Resting on top of her most cherished dresses was the necklace, the teardrop diamond design Dad gave her on their wedding day, and the jewelry box from her vanity table. She scribbled a brief note to Helen and placed it on top of the bed's luxurious treasure trove: *All yours. Love always, Florence.* She took a solid, hard look in the vanity mirror, tore her eyes from the glass, lifted two suitcases from the luggage stand, and soared out of the bedroom.

I raced after her, both enraptured and horrified by what was happening. She couldn't possibly mean she wasn't coming back. Like . . . *ever.* This was just Florence being Florence, lapsing into an extreme display of theatrics to express herself. Mom lived for the show, on stage and off. Everyone, everything was her audience. She knew how to ensnare and manipulate even the most underwhelmed observer, not because the act was so flashy or original or spectacular that we couldn't look away, but because she believed in her convictions. She believed in the performance, driven solely by certainty and possibly a degree of true madness.

"Mom, please slow down and think this through. What about your life's work? It's all here. What about this other family? Don't you want answers? Don't you want to confront him? If you divorce, you'll have to come back. There'll be lawyers and paperwork and a million other things to do. You can't leave all your stuff."

"Watch me."

"Mother."

Stopping in front of the coatrack, she set the suitcases by the door, slid into her coat, then wheeled around me and beelined it for the studio. "You are my life's work," she said over her shoulder as I chased her into the room. "No matter where you are, I can never lose you, remember? Everything I need to know about the other family was in that photograph. It was in those little girls' eyes, in their pain, in their tears. It was all there. It was all I needed. Things are just things. If I never see them again, so be it. As for your father, I want nothing from him. Everything I have to say is right here." Yanking back a sheet from one of the shelves, she scanned the cans of paint until she found an intense crimson. Loosening the lid, she popped it off and walked the room's perimeter, tilting and slowly drizzling the thick, rich color over the tables, desks, and chairs.

Reflex sent me flying to her side to try to stop her, my eyes bulging as I shouted into an empty void. There was no reaching her wherever she was, no talking any sense into her because sense had no place on Florence's stage. I brought my hands to my forehead, raking them across my hairline. I couldn't watch this. I couldn't be a part of it, whatever it was. And yet as she said goodbye to her paintings and the studio she bared her soul to, I moved wherever she moved, mirrored every step, mimicked each painstaking glance around our home as if it was our last.

We moved back out into the living room. Triggering a domino effect, Mom swept a line of family photos from the fireplace mantle, watching as each one pushed the next into a collective crash onto the floor below. Pouring the last of the crimson over the broken shards of glass and mangled frames, she pitched the empty paint can on top of the debris.

"Time's up, darling," she said, walking naturally to the front door. She grabbed the car keys and picked up one of the suitcases. "Have you decided?"

I shrugged on my coat and beanie hat, silently assuring myself that I could be just as detached from my things as my mother. She'd calm down in a day or two, start thinking rationally, and we'd come back to our concrete tower and properly pack up our belongings.

"Of course." I gulped, retrieving my purse from the rack.

Lifting the other piece of luggage, I nodded at the door. "I'm going with you."

"Okay. Just one more thing." She reached around the foyer table to the tall decorative brown basket stationed on the floor. For a second, I thought she plucked the umbrella from the basket, but as she leaned back and straightened up, the glint of the baseball bat came into clear view. Tucking it beneath her arm, she unclicked the door lock and led the way, as always, one step ahead of me.

TWELVE

Bypassing the building's valet option on the ground floor, Florence marched steadily from the elevator into the private garage to our car. The garage, as quiet as the city streets today, crammed me with unease, the click of our heels on the pavement the only sign of life. Depositing our suitcases into the trunk, she dropped her purse and gloves on the driver seat and walked around to hold the passenger door open for me, keeping the bat wedged comfortably under her arm.

"Mom? About the bat."

"Get in."

I slipped her a side glance. "Did you bring your quiver bag?"

"I always do."

"Maybe I should drive."

"Joanna, get in, or so help me . . ."

"Okay, okay, calm down." I ducked into the passenger seat and slammed the door in a huff, eyeing the damaged windshield. Fractured vehicle, fractured family.

Walking back around to the driver side, she pulled the

door wide open, then leaned down to pin me with her don't-mess-with-mommy death stare. "Buckle up."

I snapped my belt. "I'd feel a whole lot better if we left your archery stuff behind. Or just the bat. You know, one weapon is good."

"Don't move."

"Or sure, we could just . . . take all the weapons."

Florence's silhouette flashed in the side mirror as she stalked across the lot to the next row. I squinted, shifting my gaze to the rearview mirror instead. "What the . . . ?" The seat-belt cut into my chest as I craned my neck for a closer look. A silver gleam whizzed through the air as the bat rolled out from beneath her arm. She flipped it around, locking it into a tight grip, her back to me as she stared straight ahead at her target. I zeroed in on the hood of the car. Black and shiny, just like ours. A nearly imperceptible scratch on the far left corner, just above the headlight, only noticeable to me because I was the one who took it out for a spin and tried parallel parking it—a maneuver I failed on the high school driving test. Dad's sparkly, tarnished vehicle, tainted, just like his phony life. I gripped the door handle.

Whack.

Cringing, I flinched in my seat, then yelled for good measure. Not like I could stop her. I learned this way back in Florence 101. When she made her mind up to do something, there was no flicking off that switch. She screamed a guttural, teeth-rattling roar, a cursed warrior summoning the gods. A series of cracks and the smashing of glass reverberated in the garage, one strike after another, the vibrations pulsating through the car's leather seats. Dad's car alarm joined the chorus, an obnoxious, unnerving wail that only fueled the fervor behind Florence's swings. My gaze darted up to the concrete pillars that divided the garage, scanning each one for the surveillance cameras, waiting for Todd and the security team to make an appearance any second. Florence landed two more blows on the windshield, took out the side mirrors, then cruised steadily back to our car, dropping into the driver's seat as if she'd just taken a brisk, invigorating stroll in the park.

She chucked the bat into the backseat. Her seatbelt clicked. "Mind if I turn the music up?"

A garbled gasp lodged in my throat.

"Good." She cranked the ignition, blowing a wisp of hair away from her face. "Loud is good." The engine purred to life and her finger flitted to the radio console screen. Phantogram's "Blackout Days" filled the car, drenching the irritating sound of the alarm. The blaring music cloaked us like warm insulation. Our bodies sank into the leather seats as our skin absorbed the pounding bass. My head smacked the back of the headrest as Florence threw us into reverse and booked it three levels down to the bottom of the garage. Screeching to a stop at the exit, she drummed her fingers against the steering wheel as her intense green eyes bore into the gate's blinking red light. I counted the seconds, waiting for the red to shift to green, but the green didn't come. She glanced up at the camera.

"They know," I shouted over the music.

She studied the vacant city street before us, so close we could almost touch it, just a few feet separating us from freedom. The cogs in her mind silently worked as she considered the gate's arm. "Still trust me?" she shouted back.

Straight-faced, I looked over at her.

Navy blue, white, and flashes of silver spasmed near the mirrored security pavilion, advancing toward us. Todd, two valet attendants, and the security team mumbled into cell phones and radios as they moved in unison. Their composed, focused strides were impressive, but their tense muscles and alarm-stricken bloodshot eyes gave them away.

Self-preservation and the innate instinct that came with being Florence's daughter immediately told me to duck and cover my head. I wasn't sure how much our already banged-up car might do for us in our goal to reach Aunt Marie's safely, but I was positive that the only way out of this mess was straight through. Our inherent mother-daughter synapses fired away between us, Florence's mind reaching the same conclusion just seconds before I'd finished the very same thought. The gears jumped, the car rolled back a few feet, and she gunned it forward, ramming and steamrolling through the candy-cane-striped bar that told her she couldn't pass. It tried and failed, just like my father's attempts to hold and conceal her beneath his web of deceit. The music pulsed, pushing us forward as the car bumped and skidded onto the street. We swerved, dodging an oncoming SUV and then we were in the clear, welcomed by a near-empty stretch of asphalt. The security guards dashed to the edge of the garage and huddled at the end of the sidewalk, flailing around, shouting feverishly at their phones and radios. Their faces blurred, vanishing in the mirrors as we hurled down the highway toward the 5th and Mercer intersection.

"This can't be happening." A glimpse of our windshield, its crack only a touch worse than before, caught my attention before I squeezed my eyes shut, as tightly as they'd let me without rupturing a blood vessel. I couldn't look back, couldn't bear to see the emergence of police sirens behind us, chasing us through the city. Couldn't face all that had transpired in the course of a single afternoon and the irreparable repercussions brought down on everyone's heads, thanks to Dad's idiotic decisions.

The car's acceleration fluctuated as the minutes dragged on, finally punching up to a consistent speed by the end of the song. I peeled my eyes open, thankful to see us zooming around a ramp that led us to the interstate, and no sirens in sight. Peeking over at her, I clawed at my seatbelt to keep it from choking me.

She flipped the radio off. "Are you hurt?"

"I don't think so." A blended swirl of orange and yellow sky melted in the distance as we barreled down the highway, signaling the imminent sunset, one of my favorite and least favorite features of the holiday season. Beautiful to watch, but far too early for nightfall. Prying my stiff body from the seat, I rummaged around for my cell phone. "I should call Aunt Marie and let her know we're on our way."

"Wait until we get closer to Lancaster."

"Let me call Dad."

"You don't need my permission."

"Since when?" An incredulous laugh escaped. "In case you haven't noticed, you're the one running the show here." Surprised by the flare of anger in my own voice, I dropped the phone on my lap and crossed my arms, turning my attention to the dusky auburn skyline. "In the span of what—less than an hour?—we're vandalizing cars and fleeing like fugitives from our own home. I had two whole seconds to decide whether or not to go with you, and now if I call Dad, I feel like I'll be breaking some sort of code or something."

"Here we go." Mom's amused laugh trumped mine. "Miss Drama Queen. It was your father's car, not *cars,* and you did nothing wrong. I told you, I won't keep you from your dad. I'm not holding you hostage. You can go home anytime you'd like."

I swiveled in the seat and pinched the sleeve of her coat. "I'm sorry, this is all just . . . a lot."

"Oh, I know."

She did know, more than I'd probably ever know. Who can possibly begin to imagine the depth of such a wound, unless you've nursed one yourself? I couldn't imagine being married for over two decades to find out what Mom had just discovered. I couldn't comprehend what a shock to the system like that does to a person. From the outside, my mother appeared to be her beautiful well-put-together self, but only my most twisted nightmares could dream up what her insides probably looked like right now. I couldn't pretend to understand what that knowledge did to someone, did to them as a wife, as a partner, and she couldn't possibly understand what it felt like to be not just anyone's daughter, but *her* daughter.

"You're wrong about one thing," I said, voicing the most pivotal aspect she couldn't tap into. "I *am* a hostage. Don't you get it? Your hostage for life. It's a reflex, not a choice. There was no real decision to make back there. Not really. When it comes to you or him, I choose you, every time."

"Well, that makes me very sad." Loosening her grip on the steering wheel, she melted back into the seat, allowing herself to relax for the first time since we jumped on the interstate. "The very last thing I want is for you to feel like you have to choose me or your father."

"Don't be sad. He made his bed a long time ago." As I observed the sun bidding another day's goodbye to the earth I could feel her stare, pensive and pained, studying me from the driver's seat.

She said, "He loves you, you know."

"How are you even able to try to comfort me right now? And how can you say that, after what he's done? He literally took a wrecking ball to your life."

"I can say it because it's true. It's important you understand the difference between your relationship with your father, and my relationship with him."

"Betrayal is betrayal. He demolished both relationships."

"Yes. He absolutely did. But you're his flesh and blood, his little girl. I will never excuse his lies. But I cannot deny that his motives to keep you in the dark are very different from the ones that drove him to keep me that way."

"Yeah, right."

"I speak from experience."

My gaze snapped from the sunset to Mom's sullen face. "You've never deceived me. Never like this, and definitely not intentionally. There's no comparison."

"Maybe not, but I can tell you that a parent's love is boundless. Especially when it comes to fighting to preserve whatever ideal that child has of us. We are not infallible, or superheroes. We're flawed humans and we know it. But we'd do just about anything to have you go on believing we're unbreakable."

"Love implies respect, which he clearly doesn't have. For either one of us. He lost me, Mom. It's over."

"You might be surprised how different you may feel after some time passes."

"I can't believe it."

"Believe what?"

"You're *still* defending him. Even now. Rationalizing, making excuses for him." I fought back a swell of tears, forcing down the muscle contractions working over my throat and chest. There were so many realities, more each day, that unearthed as I learned what it meant to be someone's daughter, to be someone's person. Florence was my person. Someone ripped my person's heart out. Yet here she was, trying to assure me, trying to salvage my relationship with my dad, the man who didn't deserve her. He burned the one person on the planet I'd burn the world down for. "I don't want to know him anymore. You won't convince me otherwise."

A master of silence and knowing when to wield it, Florence said nothing.

My cell phone lit up, filling the car with its annoying bell chime. "It's him," I breathed, grimacing at Dad's photo blinking on the screen.

"Aren't you going to answer?"

"No." I turned the ringer to silent and flipped the phone face down.

"I thought you wanted to talk to him."

"Changed my mind."

"Jo."

"No, Mom."

"Joanna, I'm going to be sick."

Tearing me from my vengeance-filled reverie, Florence's change in tone sent me reaching for the steering wheel. "It's okay, Mom. Hang on. Pull over up here."

I flicked on the hazard lights as she slowed to veer onto the road's left shoulder. Twilight surrounded us now, leaving just me, Mom, the moon and a spray of stars above. Cornfields lined each side of the highway, a sea of burnt sienna rippling in the November wind. She pulled herself up and out of the car, stumbling over the amber grassy knoll, toward the fields. I scrambled after her, bounding from the passenger seat to catch her elbow as she collapsed to her knees, falling over into a dry heave. Tears stung her eyes and cheeks as she coughed. A fierce wind tore across the field and hit her head on, igniting a roll of shivers over her body. Pieces of her low, braided bun unraveled, streaming wildly at the nape of her neck.

Racing back to the car, I rifled through a tote bag in the backseat for a bottle of water. My cell phone vibrated again, the picture of Dad's face on the screen bringing about my own wave of nausea. Leaning over the console from the backseat, I plucked up the phone and shoved it into my coat pocket before sprinting back to Florence's side.

"Try to drink some of this," I said, gently guiding her into a sitting position. "You're probably dehydrated."

She squeezed my hand, gratefully accepting the water. She swallowed a few swigs, catching her breath. "I've been such a fool."

I sat down in the cold grass beside her. "You are the farthest thing from a fool."

"How could I have thought . . . What was I thinking, living in that world? Inviting it in, welcoming it like a wolf into a sheep's den?" She began to rock back and forth, kneading her fingers against her scalp. "I didn't belong. I never belonged. It was his home the whole time. Oh, I'm a fool. Such a fool."

"Mom. Stop. This isn't you. Listen to yourself. Please, stop."

"And those sweet girls!" Half-laughing, half-crying, she dropped a hand to her chest. "You could see their hearts, couldn't you? Crushed and bleeding out, right on the living room carpet. The stories he told. The excuses he made. He's delusional! Thinking he could manage this balancing act. Thinking he had it all under control."

"We don't know what he thought." I rested my hand on top of hers, soothing the ache over her collarbone. Niambi's words circled back around, spilling from my lips. "Does it really matter? He made a thousand wrong turns, and together they all led him here."

"Maybe you should drive."

"Yes. Finally, you're seeing some sense." Relief sent my head rolling back on a sigh. My lungs drew in a big helping of chilly air while my gaze combed the sky's stars. My phone buzzed again in my coat pocket, stealing my shred of serenity. He wasn't going to stop calling. He wasn't going to give up, because giving up meant defeat, and Asher was a terrible loser. A million tormenting visions of his other, gorgeous family pirouetted in my brain, skipping around like some deranged lovesick monster. I entertained each idea, casting Niambi as her high school's soccer star, and Carolyn as the neighborhood prodigy kid poet, excelling in all her language honors courses. Their mom was a regular at the country club, playing tennis on the weekends while Dad hid away in their family den, penning his next bestseller from their homey, blue-and-white plaid sofa. Suburban furniture was always cozier than city furniture. They watched cutesy family movies together; we watched Sundance flicks. They wore jeans and turtleneck sweaters; we wore props. They were a perfectly planned Christmas photo on a custom-made greeting card; we sat around the Thanksgiving Day table with cranberry sauce stuck on our chins. They were kids' crafts calendars and chore charts; we were nonsense scribbled on a sketch pad.

Dad wasn't the only delusional one in the family.

"Okay." Busting through my hypothetical, tormenting daydreams, I forced myself up, wiping grass and a thin sheen of frost from my coat. "Aunt Marie already knew we were coming this week, right?"

Florence continued to sway, still clutching the space beneath her throat, cradling the ball of pain. "Yes. Why?"

"Because I'm done with this thing." Scooping the relentless, buzzing phone from my pocket, I reared back and pitched it far out over the cornfield, holding my breath as I watched it sail into the thick darkness, only the car headlights illuminating the space around us.

"Jo!" Florence stopped rocking. "Why in the world did you do that?"

My face fell into my hands.

"Who are you, and what have you done with my daughter?"

"I just wanted to see what it would feel like," I mumbled into my palms.

"Well?"

"Mommy."

Florence's voice was instantly near. "You and your grand ideas. I wonder where you get those from." Encasing me in her maternal wings, she tucked my head into the crook of her neck.

"I hate him." A whimper surfed along my lips. "I can't go back there."

"You're not going to figure everything out tonight, my darling."

A pang of shame hit me, realizing I'd cut myself off from everyone else too. Including Niambi and Carolyn—should they ever find a way to reach my cell—who Mom had promised could contact us anytime. But they had Marie's number and address, which was something, at least. I pulled back to peer up at Mom's earring-free lobes and tousled bun, her windblown bangs stirring around her, a shining, luminescent halo. I wanted her to assure me she'd change her mind, that a few days from now, she'd agree to go back to the city with me, just until I finished out my contract at the theater. We could still go to Ireland in the spring. After that, we could leave Philly for good. We could go anywhere, do anything, conquer everything, as long as we stuck together. We'd figure it all out, though Florence was right; the answers wouldn't come tonight.

Walking back to the car, a sinking sensation curdled within, highlighting an inescapable truth: I couldn't exist in a place void of my mom's presence. It was one thing to live twenty minutes away, or to be separated by a long vacation, a temporary hiatus from one another. It was something else entirely to live life apart. It wasn't enough to know she was simply out there, somewhere other than in the city, while I resumed my day-to-day routines in the concrete jungle on my own. Forget moving abroad or out west—those were no longer options. I needed to be near my person. Especially now, as our family crumbled.

Florence's lavender and honey aroma, a life-giving umbilical cord that trailed dependably in her wake, grew fainter by the second, evaporating as we drove on into the night. The corn fields yielded to the pressure of the autumn winds and lured us deeper into the countryside. Clocking the mileage on the dash, the odometer towed my mother's soothing presence farther and farther out to sea with each turn of its white, rolling digits.

THIRTEEN

The scratch of static rustled quietly on the radio, tickling my senses. News anchor reels, chronicling reports of another round of earthquakes, somewhere south, near Virginia's Chesapeake Bay. I perked up in the passenger seat, wrapping my coat tighter around me, as if I could crawl farther inside its warmth. Unsurprisingly, I hadn't lasted in the driver's seat for long; Florence hated being carted around. She did all the carting around in the Kowalski household. Now that Dad was being removed from the picture, were we still the Kowalskis, though? More heavy, intrusive questions made my temples throb.

"Mom?" I asked, groggy.

"Jo?"

"Are we close?"

"We're here." Gravel crunched beneath the tires as she took a right turn, and a pitch-black horizon greeted us beyond Aunt Marie's property. A bright beacon in the twilight, the stark, weathered white and gray farmhouse guided us along the dirt drive to the edge of the porch. Always barefoot, even on the cusp of winter, Aunt Marie rested shoeless in her wicker rocker, watching as we rolled up to the front door.

"Hey lady, there's this thing called frostbite," Mom jabbed, stepping out of the car. "You should look it up."

Aunt Marie's saucy glare shifted as I joined Mom approaching the porch. She rocked steadily, until rising to meet us at the top step. She quietly appraised us, flinging her wild, waist-long hair behind her shoulders. Pale streaks of gray highlighted her mane's reddish hue. "Well, don't you two look like hell." Something tender flickered in her dark brown eyes, a well of mixed emotions that moved me to stretch up on my tippy toes and smother her in a half-hug. "Okay, I take it back," she said. "Not this one. This one's kinda cute."

"Missed you too, Auntie." I dropped a playful smack on her cheek, then pulled her periwinkle cashmere scarf tighter around her neck before releasing her. "I'm freezing just looking at you. Wear some slippers at least, will ya?"

Coming head-to-head, Mom and her sister paused in an affectionate standoff, eyeing one another as if they hadn't seen each other in centuries, when in fact it had only been a few months since our last visit. They both sighed, then moved in for a long, relieved hug.

"He's called about a thousand times already," Aunt Marie drawled over Mom's shoulder. "You can't run from it forever, hon. But you sure can put it off until the mornin'. Let the bastard sweat it out."

"She says she's never going back," I said, jogging down the steps to grab our bags from the car. I didn't have to see my aunt's face to know she was already on the same page as me. "And she destroyed his car. All caught on camera. So that was fun." Lugging the bags up the porch steps, I let them plop at my feet. "It was unreal. She was like a ninja, off her meds and on the warpath."

Marie chewed over my words, studying Mom's face. "Ya don't say."

Mom rolled her eyes and leaned down to pluck up the bags, sidestepping us both. "Oh, bugger off. I haven't even made it through the front door yet, and already you two are ganging up on me."

Marie jiggled the doorknob and pushed it open for her, shooting me a wry grin. "Ah, well. It's good to know your mother's defense mechanisms are still perfectly intact." As soon as Mom was fully inside the house, Marie's head jerked in my direction. Her jaw dropped. "Destroyed his *car*?"

"Totaled it," I whispered back. "Baseball bat."

Marie snorted.

"I heard that," Florence's voice trailed from the house.

"Not like your daddy didn't have it comin'." She tucked me into a squeeze, ushering me inside. "How ya holdin' up, kiddo?"

"Feel the way I look."

"*Mhhmm.*"

A wave of fresh-baked peanut butter cookies teased my nostrils when I entered the living room, awakening my need for real food. "Aunt Marie . . ."

"On the kitchen counter, hon. Snack on those until I sort out some dinner for you."

"Oh, it's way too late for dinner. Don't worry about it." I zipped toward the kitchen anyway, hunger pangs leading the way.

"*Ha.*" She ruffled my hair as I whizzed past her. "You know by now there's no such thing as *too late* for a meal in this house. Besides, if I don't get some meat on those skinny bones of yours, you're gonna vanish into a puff of nothin', and then what? I'm stuck eating all alone again, night after night. You came all this way, the least you could do is give your spinster aunt some company for pancakes."

The clunky oak island welcomed me in my hunt for the cookies, laden with a hodgepodge of pots, pans, and mismatched multicolored utensils. I scanned the cluttered counters, lifting piles of aprons, cookbooks, and vintage issues of fashion magazines. I never did understand how Marie found anything in this house, but there was always a method to her madness. A trait that clearly ran in the family.

"Okay," I huffed. "I can smell them, but I can't see them."

"On the tuxedo rooster tray, hon." Marie shuffled in behind me, nudging her chin toward the opposite end of the island. "Over there, on the other end of that counter. The marble one with the stuff on it, right there."

"Yeah, still not seeing it."

She jabbed her finger in the air, more pronounced, as if that would somehow make it materialize before me. "Well, it's under that do-dad there. I covered it, to hold some of the heat."

I leaned over the counter and splayed my hands out, banging my forehead against a pile of newspapers. "I'm too exhausted for an egg hunt, Auntie. I just want a damn cookie."

"Whoa, now." She shook with a hearty laugh. "Do I need to bust out the swear jar? Breaking out the big-girl words, are we? Here, hon. Auntie to the rescue." Strolling leisurely, she wandered to the far-right side of the island and picked up a rusty drum cymbal, revealing a plate of peanut butter cookies atop the gaudy rooster tray.

"Of course, why didn't I think to look under there?"

"You disappoint me, kiddo. Thought you'd learned to think like your ol' Aunt Marie by now."

"I'll get there one of these days."

"So, are you ignoring your daddy's calls too? I unplugged the landline, and I can't find my cell phone for the life of me. It's 'round here somewhere."

"Probably in the freezer. Or the oven. Sure you didn't bake it with the cookies?"

"Ya know your mouth gets smarter and smarter every time I see ya?"

I bowed. "I learn from the best."

"Yes, you are truly blessed to come from a family so well-versed in the smart-mouth department."

I stuffed a cookie into my mouth. The crumbs collected along the corners of my lips. "Yes, I'm ignoring his calls. I tossed my phone in a field somewhere along the highway."

"And how are we feeling about that decision now?"

"Utter regret."

"I bet your mom was thrilled, though."

My full chipmunk cheeks stretched with a smile. "I'm sure inwardly she was doing happy dances, yeah."

"Are you going to be able to get a hold of your friends? Your boss? Your boyfriend?"

A stabbing sensation lanced me square in the gut. My chewing slowed.

Marie winced, head rolling to one side. "There I go, inserting my foot straight in my mouth again."

"It's okay," I mumbled.

"No, I'm sorry. It's not. I completely forgot for a second how much of a sore spot that still is. Forgive me?"

The stinging pain in my gut traveled up to my throat, rallying a batch of fresh, hot tears.

"Oh!" Marie wrangled me into a mama-bear hug, rubbing my back. "Oh, honey, this is why you can't tell old people things. We forget what you tell us and then we say stupid crap. Don't hold it against me, pumpkin." Pulling back, she took my face in her hands, watching as my shoulders shook and chest heaved with the waterworks show.

"It's just been a really hard day." My lip quivered through the sobs, and I was sure I looked like an eight-year-old crying at camp because someone stole her cookie. Only, I had a crap ton of cookies. I was the cookie monster queen, and I had to be strong for my person.

"*Aww*, of course it has, honey. And I'm sorry about the boyfriend. I know how much you loved him. That's the hardest pill to swallow in life, isn't it? When something just doesn't work out and love can't glue it all back together, no matter how much of it ya got."

"I hate it."

"Me too!" She wiped the tears from my cheeks and kissed the tip of my nose. "Pisses me off. I just want life to do what I tell it to do. Sit, stay, behave."

"Don't we all?"

"Go on, honey." She stepped back and patted my shoulders. "Eat your feelings. I'm gonna go find your momma. Use my laptop if you want. It's in the big blue basket under the coffee table."

I eyed her skeptically.

"It really is in the big blue basket. And by big blue basket, I mean the kinda-sorta fuchsia one stuffed with the potpourri jars we made last Christmas."

"Maybe we can use them this Christmas."

"Maybe. And maybe I'm next in line for the Queen of England." She moseyed around the corner to begin her search for Mom.

I sighed and picked up the plate, shoveling another cookie in as I trailed along. "I'll come with you."

"Darlin', you're already fragile. I'm afraid what I'm about to find won't be too pretty. How 'bout you sit this one out?"

"No. I can handle it."

"All right. Suit yourself."

Loud, heavy thumps accented by explosive fits of rage led us straight to Mom. We found her down in the den, terrorizing the punching bag. The metal rung anchor rocked fiercely from the ceiling under the brunt of her assault. Her fists drove relentlessly at the leather, each slug remorseless and unyielding. She was a sight dangerous and beautiful, pummeling the bag barefoot in her loose, chic black trousers. Her cream ruffled-neck blouse, torn and untucked, hung limp at her hips, her coat strewn across the floor. Her messy low bun, which unraveled hours ago, was now a flowing mass of hazel dangling down her back, swaying at her waist. Aunt Marie and I hovered near the doorway, watching the lioness pulverize her prey. The sound of the impacts suddenly changed in tempo, and my facial muscles contorted as Florence's lean, strong hands slammed into the leather in a new series of short bursts, on the verge of knocking the stuffing clear out of the bag.

"Florence," Marie commanded.

Another smack, another cry.

"Florence."

Knuckles cracked. An anguished scream.

"*Florence!*"

Shoving the cookie plate onto the pool table, I rushed over. Mom's weight collapsed against the bag. She wrapped her arms around it, hugging it tightly, smashing her sweaty face onto the black canvas. I latched on, hugging her from behind. "*Ssshhhh*, it's okay Momma. It's all going to be okay. I promise."

Marie appeared beside us, a still, strong pillar, lending another set of comforting arms. We all held on, clinging to the punching bag, our buoy against the squall.

———

The sunrise peeked above the earth, competing with the thick layer of fog that rolled in over the farm. Aunt Marie sipped coffee by the bay window.

"What's she doing out there?" I asked, my voice groggy

from sleep. Tying my fluffy fleece bathrobe around my waist, I wandered over to the window beside her to watch Florence. Bundled up in sweatpants, a thermal hoodie, and a beanie hat, she jogged along the perimeter, breath visible in the frosty air.

"She's been up since four AM. Out there since five."

"Jogging?"

"Yep."

"She never jogs."

"I know."

"She hits stuff."

"Yep." Marie exhaled over her coffee. Steam rose from the mug's brim. "You seeing her break down last night is killing her almost as much as your daddy's double life."

"Did she tell you everything?"

"Just about, I think. We talked after you went to bed. Talked some more this morning, before she started this." She nodded to the window. "Filled in the gaps for me, the parts your daddy didn't tell me on the phone, before you showed up."

"I tossed and turned most of the night. Couldn't get the image of her crying out of my head. I've seen her angry, stressed, but never . . ."

"She means it, you know. She won't be going back to the city. She's moving in here with me."

"She just needs a few days to clear her head."

"Your momma might be an enigma, but when it comes to her heart, there's no mystery." She cast a glance my way, one filled with wisdom and a tinge of pity. "When she's in, she's all in, hon. And the moment she's out, she's out for good. You don't have to decide today, but soon it'll be time to start thinking about where you wanna go from here."

"I won't leave her. Not now."

"She told me you finally told your daddy about Yale."

"I did."

"I imagine that went down well."

"Oh, yeah. Big hit at the dinner table."

"Your life is in the city."

"Yeah, but I was planning on leaving when my contract was up anyway."

"What about your friends?"

I shrugged. "I can still visit them, and they can visit me. I would've had to make friends in New Haven. My future is in theater, not in Philly. I can go anywhere."

"You say that now, honey, but leaving Philly or going to New Haven is one thing. Moving to the middle of nowhere to live with your eccentric mother and loopy aunt is something else. If you put your life on hold for her, I guarantee you she'll find a way to push you out."

"No." My raspy voice jammed in my throat. "She wouldn't. If she had it her way, we'd be together forever. I'd be her Norman Bates."

A soft chuckle crinkled the corners of her eyes. The humor disappeared when Florence swung back around for another lap. A machine on autopilot, my mother powered on, refusing to check the fuel gauge. "When your momma went away to Julliard, she had a cat."

"A cat?"

"That surprise you?"

"I know she loves animals, but she said no anytime I wanted to adopt one. She always said it wasn't fair to the animal because of how busy we were and how often we traveled. She never told me she had a cat back then. "

"Oh, yes. When she first came here, all the creatures followed her around. The chickens, our ol' boy Shiloh when he was just a pup, and the cats out in the barn. This one, though, this goofy gray and white furball, wouldn't leave her side for nothin'."

My sleepy eyes flared. "Jasper? Your Jasper? The one who died a few years ago?"

"That's the one."

"*Aww*, I loved Jasper. He was her little shadow."

"He sure was."

"I wonder why she never told me he was hers."

"When she closes a door, she can't leave it propped open. Not a hair, not an inch. It haunts her. She hates ghosts. Her dorm building didn't allow pets. I took him in when she went away and made sure he was a fat, happy cat, yep. But it wasn't as easy as all that, believe me."

"What do you mean?"

"She cried and cried. For days. Hysterical. She knew what it meant to be left behind. To be lost, then found again, just like Jasper the stray. When she first showed up here, when we were reunited, I was here, married to Bob. We had a pack of animals, a farm full of love. Your momma had been on her own for so long. Saw so many things. Things children her age should never see. When she got here, when Jasper found her . . . he needed a home. She needed a home. She didn't know me well then. Or Bob. We had to get to know each other all over again after those years of separation. She didn't trust me, and she sure as hell didn't trust Bob."

"Poor Uncle Bob." I laughed, recalling his steadfast, easy-going personality. Always so patient with us. Always up for the challenge, willing to go head-to-head with our family's brand of crazy.

"You can say that again." Aunt Marie shook her head with a big, affectionate grin. "That man was made of strong stock, brave enough to take me, you, *and* your momma on."

Florence finally rolled to a stop at the far edge of the barn. We both paused.

"Jasper trusted her, and she trusted him," Marie continued,

watching as Florence turned back for the house. "Saying goodbye to him, even though it wasn't a permanent goodbye, tore her up. She couldn't visit him once she left for Julliard. She didn't. Not for a long, long time. For your momma, striking him from the equation was the only way to mend her heart."

"But . . . Jasper was here with us for years."

"Yes, but the switch was flipped, and Jasper was mine, not hers. She convinced herself that he'd never been hers. She created a new record of the story, committed it to memory and then believed it."

"Maybe so," I murmured. "But it's not like she erased her feelings. She loved Jasper, you know that. I saw it firsthand. She's way too sensitive of a person to just turn it off. That's not Florence."

"Well, you're right about that, honey. Once she loves you, you have her heart always. If you hurt her, like your daddy did, you'll never lose her love: she'll just conceal it. But there's something else you might not know about your mom."

An incredulous smile swept over me. "I love you, Auntie, but I know her better than anyone."

"Careful, kiddo. You know her better than me. Better than your daddy, I bet. But not better than she knows herself. There's a version of her none of us have ever known, and I do know one thing about that version."

My mother's silhouette appeared at the bottom of the porch. A soldier approaching the front line, she ascended the steps.

"Tell me."

Marie's gaze roamed to meet mine. "No one before you and me lasted. We were the only ones to make it this far, to know her and keep her, to live to tell the tale. Your father had the privilege, and he threw it away." With a sphinxlike smile, she lowered herself onto the bay window seat. "There's nothing more dangerous than a woman who isn't afraid to be alone, and the Florence we don't know? She's the most dangerous woman we've never met."

Catching her breath, Mom wiped her sneakers on the mat outside the front door, watching us watch her, eyes aflame.

"They say no woman is an island." Marie acknowledged her sister through the window with a tip of her mug. "But they're wrong. Your momma's living proof."

FOURTEEN

A spicy, heavenly aroma lured me up off the sofa and into the kitchen. Aunt Marie stirred something in a pot with a wooden ladle, tossing in a pinch of this and a dash of that as she adjusted the music's volume on the old boombox by the stove. I'd caught up on emails and contacted people back home to let them know I was phoneless. After Mom's uncharacteristic morning jog, I'd gone out for some air myself, then retired to the living room for the remainder of the afternoon, doing my best to avoid the news headlines and invasive reel in my head that rattled off a million different things I wanted to say to my father. None of those things were helpful or positive or productive in any way, and they definitely couldn't change anything, but it felt good to think about them, to imagine Dad's face as I reamed into him.

Aunt Marie had spent the day scrubbing the floors, running into town for supplies, and taking care of the horses. Mom hid away in one of the guest rooms upstairs. Every now and then a sequence of crashes would rumble from above. Either Florence was knocking furniture around or she was passionately redecorating. Whatever was happening up there,

Aunt Marie and I had an unspoken agreement to refrain from interrupting the process.

"Panang curry for dinner?" I snuck up behind Aunt Marie with a hopeful grin, folding the laptop closed and tucking it beneath my arm.

"With extra fresh tofu, just the way you like it."

I smiled at the memory this brought. When Uncle Bob was alive, this was a meat and potatoes house. He grew up in Alabama and loved nothing more than loading us up with meals that clogged our arteries and triggered sugar comas. Mom and I didn't eat meat, but we had zero self-control when it came to his okra, cornbread, and fried green tomatoes. Nowadays, it was all about Aunt Marie's coconut curries, and my tastebuds weren't complaining.

"You're an angel, Auntie. Thank you. I'm starving."

"All that thinking makes a girl hungry. Give yourself a little break from that computer screen, kiddo. It's been a long day."

"Agreed. I'm done, I promise. Just wanted to touch base with a few people." I still hadn't heard from Tony, not even by email, and it took everything in me to extinguish the memory of my run-in with Olivia after his party. Their faces loitered around my overloaded brain, and I made a mental note to give the catering company they worked for a call later to see if I could track either of them down. If that was a dead end, I could call around to the local hospitals. "You think Mom will come down and eat?"

"She'll come down when she's ready. Grab us some bowls, will ya?"

"Of course." Collecting some dishes from the cabinet, I glanced over at the piano. Stationed near the front of the living room adjacent to the fireplace, its glossy black lid donned a thick layer of dust.

"Think she'll play by the end of the night?" Marie asked, stirring the curry pot like a magical cauldron.

"She has to. She can't survive one day without touching the keys."

"There's a first time for everything." Marie switched the boombox off as a news broadcaster's voice took over the local country bluegrass station.

"What do you think?" I asked, setting the kitchen table. "About the quakes?"

"I have my theories." Aunt Marie set the ladle down and grabbed a potholder, carried the pot of curry over, then returned to the counter for the rice. "There are some rumors circulating around town. Heard some things today at the tractor store."

"Oh? Like?"

"Some things the three of us should probably discuss." A rowdy crack drew our attention up to the ceiling. "Definitely not tonight."

"What do you mean? What's there to discuss?"

Spooning rice into the bowls, Aunt Marie rolled a shoulder. "From the sound of it, this might not be something that's going to go away anytime soon. Might even get worse before it gets better, and we need to be prepared, that's all. Make sure me, you, and your momma are all on the same page."

"They're saying there might be more tremors?"

"They're saying these aren't normal earthquakes. That there's something else going on."

"Wait. Are we talking about the news, or about whatever you're hearing around town?"

"What's being said in town is what *isn't* being said on the news."

I folded our napkins and placed the sets of silverware down. "I don't know what you're hearing, Auntie, but I'd be careful what you listen to. People are just talking, you know? Don't go falling for any crazy conspiracy theories. Wait until we have some facts."

"And where do you suppose we find those facts?"

"You know I don't believe what the news tells us. But I do think there's some truth to be found in it . . . usually somewhere in the middle. All I'm saying is, I think we need to give it a little more time. Wait for more details to surface."

"I love ya, honey, but I disagree with you there. The time to act is *before*. Now. Not after whatever's brewing boils over. Always better to be ahead of the curve."

"Oh, no." I stilled. A half-smile crept up. "You're one of them, aren't you?"

"One of who?"

"You've already bought into one of these theories." A soft laugh escaped me. My half-smile shifted into a full-blown smirk. "You got Mom started on the prepper kick, didn't you?"

"I beg your pardon?" She pinched my hip as she maneuvered around the table, pouring portions of curry over our rice. "Your momma started that all on her own, thank you very much. Months ago, for the record."

"Auntie . . ."

"I gave her some tips. So what?" She stuck her tongue out at me.

"Oh, man. It all makes so much sense now. How did I not piece this together before? Your cellar storage is out of control. I should've known."

"My cellar. *Ha.* If you think that's out of control, you should see my other one."

"Whoa, whoa." I gawked at her, grinning ear to ear. "Other one?"

"Yes, darlin'. You've never seen the bunker."

"The *bunker.*"

"*Uh-huh.* Not far from the barn."

My butt dropped into one of the kitchen chairs. "You have an underground bunker."

She swiped at my nose with the ladle. "Catch up, Miss Ivy League. What do you think I do out here all day? I can only make jam and pies and sing to the sheep for so long before I get bored. This is what happens when you leave your ol' auntie by herself."

Astonished, my body slumped back. "Okay. We really need to get you a new hobby. One aboveground."

A distant slam marred Aunt Marie's retort, causing both of us to glance toward the living room bay window. A polished white four-door sedan sat in the driveway, parked next to the farm's gargantuan oak tree, the one with my favorite swing.

"Jo." Aunt Marie's cautious voice brought me to my feet.

"Well, look who didn't go to Seattle after all." My jaw clenched when I spotted my father making a hesitant approach toward the front porch. My chair scraped the floor as I pushed it back.

"Hon . . . take a deep breath."

"I'll handle this." Dismissing Marie's wary look, I zeroed in on the one-and-only Asher Kowalski, infamous actor and master manipulator. Steam billowed from our dinner on the table, fanning the burgeoning flames within me. Adrenaline steered me to the front door. The day's consuming thoughts broke the dam, rushing forward in tumultuous, hungry waves —all the things I wanted to say to the man who took an ax to our family. I hurried outside and down the front steps, fencing him in between his car and the porch entry.

"Hi, Jo." He'd stopped in front of me, slipping his hands into his coat pockets. His freshly shaven cheeks made the bags beneath his eyes darker.

"Don't move," I said, leering at his pale, sleep-deprived face. "Don't even think about going near her, Dad. Don't you *dare* go near her. Not one more step."

He raised his hands, ambling backward. He was a coward, but he was a smart one. "I'm just here to talk—"

"*Hi, Jo.* Really?"

"I know the words are empty air right now, but I'm sorry."

"Nice ride." I gestured to the sedan. "Let me guess. It's *hers.*"

"Rental."

"*Ah.*" My feigned venom-infused smile stung as it stretched my face. "Too bad about your car."

His jaw hardened. "You can hate me, Joanna, but you're not going to keep me from your mother. And you're going to respect the fact that no matter how monumentally I've messed up, I will always be your father."

"You said you came here to talk. Sounds like you came here to make demands. If that's the case, you drove a long way for nothing."

"Take me to your mother."

"No."

"I want us to talk. The three of us, together."

"Not gonna happen."

"I have to see her, or I won't be able to live with myself."

"Tough."

"I'm your father and you'll do as I say right now."

"Get over yourself."

Nostrils flaring, neck muscles throbbing, he stalked forward. His conflicted arms reached for me, extending in a desperate plea for a hug or an attempt at a swift smack across the cheek. Maybe both. "It was something that was never supposed to happen, but it did." His voice boomed around me, thick and strained. "That's all there is, all right? That's all you need to know. It was a mistake that cost me everything, and I'll live with the consequences for the rest of my life. Nothing I say would take away your hurt, could ever change your mind about me now. We both know that, so please just let me inside so I can talk to her—"

"You had your chance. You had *years. Years* to talk to us.

Years to tell us. And now here you are, showing up after all that time, demanding to see her *right this second*. You want to talk to us right *now* because you want what you want, when you want it. Your agenda, your timeline. The way it's always been."

Bustling forward, he tried to veer around me. "Move aside, Joanna," he choked. "I have to see her."

"She said no," Aunt Marie's voice took shape behind me, a raw, threatening entity. A sharp *click* echoed over my shoulder, stunning my dad still. I glanced back, eyes widening as I saw the barrel of a shotgun. She aimed it at her target.

Dad slowly lowered himself to his knees, a strangled cry breaking in his throat as he lifted his hands, pleading with us both. "Please. I know I can't make this right. That's not why I'm here. I don't expect to ever make this right. I just want to say I'm sorry. I just want to see her. Hold her one last time. Say goodbye. I don't want it to end this way."

Moisture pooled along my eyelids. "You should've thought about that."

"I did. So many times, sweetie. So many times." He squeezed his eyes shut and shook his head, as if he could banish the reality staring us all in the face. "Please. Please, God. Forgive me. Joanna, I need you to forgive me. I love you both. I love you more than anything in the—"

"Don't!" A flock of birds darted from the oak tree. "Stop lying to yourself! You're a liar. Accept it. Hold yourself accountable. It's time, don't you think?"

The gun barrel drew closer as Aunt Marie moved to my side. "Asher, they'll talk to you when they're good and ready. Right now, you have ten seconds to get your sorry ass back in that car and get off my property."

A solar flare sparked, then dimmed in my father's eyes, flickering out like a shot fuse as they wandered aimlessly, hopelessly. He searched the house, the sky, the fields, but none of it could offer him anything. No solace, no answers, nothing but the desolate valley he'd carved for himself and would now travel alone. He stumbled to his feet, pulling in spurts of air, and the burning embers wedged in my gut betrayed me, extinguishing the very moment I needed them the most.

"I forgive you," I whimpered, startled by my own voice as I took an involuntary step in his direction. My body caved, on the brink of imploding. "I do, Dad."

"Joanna, I love you so much—"

"But you lost us, and we're not coming back."

A sob cracked his chest wide open, and the sound and sight of it branded an eternal emblem into my memory.

"You need to leave."

The gun's weight shifted in Marie's hands. "You heard her, Asher. Go on, now. Head home, where you belong."

"This is my home. My wife and daughter are . . ." Slicking back his hair, he wrestled with himself, mumbling words mixed with spit and more tears, rejecting our warning. He turned in a half-circle, wavering like a lost, drugged victim in a state of feeble delirium.

Images of Carolyn, Niambi, and their beautiful mother thumped at my temples. If Mom and I were home, what did that make them? What were they to him? An ache for the other family, their second-class rank, balled up and festered in my chest like a loose cannon with nowhere to go.

A rusty creak, metal turning on its hinges, resounded in the air from the second floor of the house. Dad blinked, his lashes batting rapidly as his glassy eyes roamed up, behind me. Aunt Marie lowered the gun and we both turned around, following his gaze. The breath stalled at my lips. Florence's sallow face, dark shadows under blank eyes, stared down at us through an open window. Remote, listless irises drilled straight through my father to the oak tree behind him as if he were transparent. A crossed-over spirit, already gone. Limp arms, dangling lifelessly at her sides, suddenly raised, lifting a bow. With effortless poise, she moved into full draw position. An arrow sliced through the air, nearly skimming the skin of my father's neck as it whizzed past him and struck the tree trunk. He flinched with a winded gasp. A sharp smack bounced back at us as the arrowhead made impact with the wood, splitting our nerves clean in half.

Not anymore, the arrow said. *This is not your home anymore.*

FIFTEEN

Freshly lit firewood made my nose twitch. I blinked through a drowsy haze, looking up at the ceiling. The bedroom's darkness enveloped me as I snuggled up tighter to the quilt. Hot perspiration pricked my forehead, but my skin froze. A hum, my mother's familiar lullaby, filled my brain, spilling out into the bedroom. The melody's volume deepened, morphing into a bass record on repeat, skipping over the same track. The quilt's heavy warmth tied me to the bed, but my antsy, icy skin coerced me out of the comfy bubble and over to the window. I held onto the blankets, keeping them wrapped around my shoulders. My flannel PJs clung to the sheets, inciting a scratchy static sensation along my spine.

Scanning the front yard, I blinked, encouraging my eyes to adjust to the inky blackness. I searched for the farm's horizon in an attempt to guess what time of night—or morning—it was. No sunset, no sunrise, just the innate inkling that the rest of the world wasn't yet awake. I peeked over my shoulder at the nightstand, rubbing at my blurry vision. The red digits on the alarm clock read 3:33 AM. A faint light called my attention back to the window. A sliver of moonlight glowed brightly now as a clump of clouds passed over, clearing the way for a crisp, star-filled sky.

Florence's hum continued to float around me, a lulling drone that tempted my heavy lids to fall shut and return to sleep. I fought the urge, rewarded with a breathtaking glimpse of my mother, a celestial siren, swaying peacefully in Aunt Marie's handmade hammock down below, her smooth, wavy golden-brown locks cascading over a crocheted pillow. A pearl-colored, layered chiffon nightgown covered her stately silhouette, emitting a candescent luster in the moonlight. Her hum, crystal clear from where I stood, vibrated from the hammock. She flicked a lighter in one hand, singing to it, the comforting melody that belonged to my childhood and the infinite, promising possibilities of my dreams.

The lighter's flare intensified, burning brighter as the hum dragged on. The ropes of the hammock lit up, dancing in tandem with the flick of the lighter, heat and smoke trickling along their edges. I called out to Florence, tapping the window glass, my voice sinking into oblivion as the flames grew, lapping at the edges of my mother's feet, kissing the ends of her glossy hair. Consuming the hammock, they spread, reaching for her ivory skin. I screamed, pounding at the glass to warn her, but she didn't move, just swayed and sang, transfixed by the snap of her thumb against the lighter's wheel. Vertigo swamped me, and my knees snapped like brittle sticks, crippling me as the fire engulfed her from head to toe. She didn't fight it; there was no struggle, just an easy back-and-forth swing of the hammock as she lounged with the lighter, singing to the fire as if she'd been waiting her whole life for it to claim her. She swayed and smiled and burned, while I screamed into a void.

Crumpling to the floor, I landed on the throw rug at the foot of the bed. Dark sunbursts, black little stars, exploded in my peripheral vision, and the image of a raven-haired woman donned in an elegant scarlet gown perforated a tunnel view. The opening to the tunnel narrowed, its round cutout winding closer and closer together, until it shut me out completely, submerging me in midnight. Dad was there, waiting at the end, and then he wasn't. A razor flash fed me figures of Carolyn and Niambi, walking their fun-loving golden retriever toward a sunset, toward the ball of fire that devoured my mother. We all converged, my mother and her lullaby, Dad and his happy family, surrendering to the tunnel's blazing furnace.

"Joanna," a familiar voice punched a hole in the distance. "Joanna, can you hear me?"

Sunlight assaulted my eyelids, reaching in to pull me from the midnight, to pull me from the furnace. "Mom?"

"It's me, honey." Aunt Marie's voice drew closer. The edge of her clothing—maybe the ruffles of her apron—tickled my shoulder. "Talk to me, kiddo. Open your eyes."

"It's so cold," I whispered. "Even in the sun."

Something clinked nearby. "Come on, honey. Sit up for me. You need to eat some breakfast."

My eyes fluttered open. I wasn't on the floor rug, but still safely ensconced in the bed, beneath the quilt. Fresh, beautiful daylight poured in through the window. "Breakfast?" I lifted my head from the pillow. "What time is it?"

"Ten thirty. You were having nightmares, darlin'. You were screaming. Scared the living death out of me."

"Ten thirty? How? Oh, no." A breakfast tray rattled to my left as Aunt Marie slathered some jam onto a piece of toast. "Did I wake you? I'm so sorry."

"Don't you worry 'bout me, hon. Here. Eat." Shoving a piece of toast at me, she watched me carefully, wrinkles bunching above her brow. "You're gonna need your strength today."

"I was up earlier . . . I thought."

"You fell back asleep."

"I did?"

"You had a rough night."

I scrubbed my hands over my face. "Where's Mom?"

"In town."

"Is she okay?"

"Come on." Aunt Marie wagged the toast. "Take a bite, please."

I pushed the toast away and sat up. "What's she doing in town?"

The doorbell rang, and Aunt Marie sighed. "Errands. You eat and then we'll talk. That's Jared with my delivery." Shuffling to the bedroom door, she pointed sternly at the glass of orange juice. "Juice too. I don't want to see a crumb left on that plate when I get back."

Groaning, I propped my pillow against the headboard and downed the orange juice, my shaky hand returning the drinking glass to the tray. Still muddled, I winced as I dodged the sunlight. As pretty as it was streaming in through the window, it added to the disorientation. I tore the toast into little chunks, chewing slowly.

"I still see fruit on that plate," Marie warned, returning to my side a few minutes later.

"I'm trying."

"Try harder."

"What's going on?"

Aunt Marie lifted her apron over her head, dropped onto the edge of the bed, and started tying her loose ponytail into a tighter knot. "It's been a busy morning." She averted my gaze, turning to look out the window.

"Are you going to tell me, or am I going to have to go on a research mission and figure it out myself? Because I'm gonna be honest, I feel like crap, and I'm officially overwhelmed."

Her deep chestnut eyes rolled toward me. "Well, yeah, hon. Your life has just been turned upside down and inside out. You've been served a major curve ball. I'm aware of this, which is why I'm tryin' my damndest to spoon feed you little bits at a time. It's hard to see you—both of you—like this, ya know."

"Seeing him didn't help." I forced the last bit of toast down.

"I think down the road, you'll be glad you confronted him, but right now . . . no, probably not the best timing. It's all too fresh."

"So, go ahead. Lay it on me. What's up?"

"Let's see. Where to start?" She reached over and plucked an orange slice from my plate, popping it in her mouth. "Your momma got herself a job. So, there's that."

"Come again?"

"She drove into town, walked into the tractor store, and asked for a job. They hired her on the spot 'cause they're short-handed after Billy's granddaughter ran off and married the preacher's son last week. They eloped and took off down to Georgia. Your momma called me from the store to tell me the news."

The little piece of bread I'd forced down my throat got stuck. "A *job*?" I coughed. "She already has a job. Multiple jobs."

"Yes, but they're all back in the city."

"True, but it's not like she has to give up her music or her art just because she's decided to live here."

"Well, she won't be going to the theater, the gallery, or any of the museums any time soon, hon. What else did you think she was gonna do out here in the boondocks?"

"You're okay with her trading in her life's work for a cashier job at Randy's Tractor Supply? I mean, nothing against Randy or the farm community out here, but Mom's career, her hobbies, her entire life is in the city. She's not going to be happy selling fertilizer."

"Believe me, kiddo. You and I are on the same page."

"Then help me talk sense into her. We have to. She can still compose and paint here, visit the city once in a while to meet with buyers or play with the orchestra. Just because she's retiring from the board of trustees doesn't mean she can't perform anymore. The choice to move here doesn't mean it has to be all or nothing." Aunt Marie's silence woke me up faster than a cup of coffee would. "Auntie? You have to help me get through to her somehow."

"For you, it doesn't have to be all or nothing," she finally said. "For her, I think it does. Right now, anyway. Maybe not forever."

Completely bewildered, I stared back at her, mouth agape.

She offered a stern stare in return. "I agree that she doesn't have to—and shouldn't—give everything up. But right now, this is what she wants, and our job is to support her, whatever she thinks she needs. She has a long road ahead of her, hon. Just as you do. A lot to process, a lot to recover from, before she can even think of returning to that life. Try not to think of it as something permanent, but a transition."

"If she doesn't play, if she doesn't paint . . . if she doesn't do any of the things that make her who she is, we'll lose her. And she'll lose herself. I refuse to watch that happen."

Squeezing my knee through the thick quilt, Aunt Marie's iron-willed gaze drilled through me. "I know you still need time to wrap your head around everything that's happened, and I understand it'll be hard for you to accept. But with time, you'll see there are some things we can never come back from."

"I don't buy that." I crossed my arms, neck stiffening. "She'll make it through this. I won't let her lose everything."

"I never said she won't make it. If anyone can survive this, it's your momma. And I don't doubt for a second that she'll emerge stronger. But she's not going to be the person you and I knew before. That person is gone, and the best we can do right now is stand beside her. Let's get through today, first, okay?" She rose and gathered up her apron and the breakfast tray. "Let's focus on getting through Thanksgiving week and then figure out your next move."

"My next move?"

"You have to return to work after Thanksgiving weekend, right?"

"I guess."

"*Joanna.*" She set the tray back down with a gentle yet firm slam. "Remember what I told you about giving up your goals and dreams?"

"Maybe . . ."

"Now more than ever, you have to let go. You can't save her, and you can't give everything up, either."

"I know."

She leaned down and swept my hair back with a pained, kind smile. "You really want to save your momma?"

I nodded.

"Live your passion, and live it well. Brush up on your skills. Learn new ones. See yourself through her eyes, and let that guide you. She needs to know you're going to be okay. She needs you safe and happy. Stay focused. Do that, and you'll help each other."

"Aunt Marie?" I stopped her as she started for the doorway. "What else happened this morning?"

A rooster crowed as a beat passed.

"Get dressed, hon. There's plenty of time for all that." Her words soaked in as she disappeared from the bedroom. My broken sleep and groggy mind made it tough to get out of bed and face the day, because it wasn't just another day. It was a brand-new frontier, something vast, untamed, and unpredictable. I didn't know this new Florence that Aunt Marie spoke of, and every part of me resisted the idea. I didn't want to know the new Florence at all. Aunt Marie was right about so many things, as always. I knew I couldn't control whatever was unfolding, but I'd be a fool not to at least try and salvage the remnants of my mom's life, for both of our sakes. Without the woman I knew, the one I called Mom, I was adrift. Homeless. If home really is where the heart is, what happens if we can't find our heart?

After a long, hot shower and shimmying into the coziest hoodie and sweatpants I could find, I ventured downstairs to await Mom's return home. Aunt Marie paced the kitchen while she rambled away on the telephone, working on a fresh batch of pecan pies. I roamed over to the piano and swiped at the lid's layer of dust. The windows framing the space offered the perfect vantage point for Florence's arrival. I rested on the edge of the bench, tapping my foot against the pedals. The second Aunt Marie's pick-up truck appeared on the drive, I dashed to the front porch and hustled down the steps to help Mom carry whatever she might've picked up on her errand run.

"Well hello there, Sleeping Beauty," she said, climbing out of the truck. "Marie said you slept late today. I'm glad. I'm sure you needed it."

My hurried stroll rolled to a stop when she reached forward to cup my cheek. "Mom, what did you do?" Her wavy, usually elbow-length mane was now a short, choppy bob, barely grazing the tops of her shoulders.

She winked and gestured for me to follow her to the bed of the truck, as if she hadn't heard me. "Lend a hand? I picked us up some clothes. I don't want us to use up Marie's entire wardrobe. And I got those yogurt-covered pretzels you like from Frank's stand at the market. He has a new cherry-flavored assortment—"

"What did you do to your hair?" Waiting for an answer,

my attention fell to her flannel hooded jacket, frayed jeans, and hunter green wellies. Bare-faced and jewelry free, she glistened like morning dew on a freshly cut lawn. The visible creases along the corners of her eyes and around her mouth, mixed with a smattering of pale, soft liver spots on her cheeks, rendered her more lifelike, more accessible than ever before. With disarming confidence, she'd walked straight off one of her own canvases, raw cuts exposed for all to see.

She walked to the back of the truck with a pep in her step, answering me with a serene smile. Dropping the truck bed's gate, she started unloading a handful of brown bags, passing me one after another. "Just needed something more practical," she finally said, slamming the gate closed with her hip. "I love it. What do you think, darling?"

The words fumbled on my lips. "It's different." Juggling three of the bags, I offered to take one more off her hands. She declined, readjusted her grip, then headed for the porch. "You look great, Mom."

"Don't hold back, Jo." She laughed so lightheartedly, I tripped on my way up the porch steps. "You hate it."

"No. It's just going to take some getting used to, I guess." I watched her with care as we entered the house and set the bags down on the coffee table. Aunt Marie's slow, vigilant look stretched across the room from the kitchen. She muttered something into the phone and hung up, wiping her hands on her apron. "If you love it, I love it."

"Okay," Mom replied cheerfully, diving into one of the bags. "What about these?" Rosy, alert, and energized, she held up some cozy-looking oversized sweaters and plaid button-ups, waiting. "I figured whatever you don't like or don't want to keep, you can just leave here with me."

Widemouthed and stupefied, I glanced at Aunt Marie for backup. "Sure, okay. Yeah, those are great. Thanks, Mom. I won't be leaving, though. I'm staying here with you."

Sensing the need to rescue me from Mom's reply, Aunt Marie appeared at my side and rifled through one of the bags, casting dubious looks over Mom's wardrobe choices.

"Staying with me?" A gloomy fog dispelled Mom's sunny glow.

"Yes." I took the oversized sweaters and folded them back up. "I decided I'm not going back to the city if you aren't."

"Give it a few days. You don't have to make any decisions yet. See how you feel after Thanksgiving."

"I know how I feel. I made up my mind the moment he showed up here."

"I'm not suggesting you move back in with him."

"As if that's even an option. For all we know, he's already moving the other family in. Giving the girls my room." The thought turned sour in my stomach. "Or maybe the other way around. Maybe he's moving to live with them in the suburbs. Either way, I'm not leaving you, Mom."

She swept right over my comments. "You have a contract with the theater."

"I'm only there a few days a week during rehearsals. I can commute, renegotiate the contract terms. I'll make it work."

"You have friends, and now Tony. A life."

I managed not to flinch. I'd had no luck finding Tony or Olivia. The hospitals knew nothing, and the catering company hadn't heard from either of them. "Nothing's happening with Tony. Friends visit. They find ways to see each other. Don't bother trying to talk me out of this, because it's a done deal."

"I can't force you to go back, but I can't support you in that decision, Joanna. I'm sorry, but I can't."

"I'm not asking you to. I'm not asking for anything from you, Mom. From now on, I go where you go, and that's all there is to it."

The paper bags rustled as Aunt Marie picked them up and shoved them in my direction. "Please take these and put them in the wash? Flo, why don't you play me something while I finish up these pies? Got the next batch nearly ready to come out of the oven." She tapped Mom's elbow and nodded over at the piano.

Florence's indifference rendered me motionless. No sign of life colored her makeup-free complexion. Cool, passionless, and unaffected, she ignored the instrument, instead tucking her new bob cut behind her ears as she headed for the stairwell. "I need to get my dresser organized and rearrange my room a bit," she said, voice lukewarm and somewhere on another continent. "I'll be down later to help with supper, though." Smacking a quick kiss against the side of my head, she casually walked away, leaving me bereft.

"Chin up, buttercup," Aunt Marie said, ambling back over to the kitchen. She tended to her pies the way gardeners cared for their most prized azaleas. Her gaze lifted from the counter, resting an astute stare heavy on my shoulders. "She'll play again."

The empty space, where she stood only seconds ago, filled me with restlessness. "I hope so."

"She will." Reaching for an oven mitt, she cleared the batch of pies from the counter, making room for the next. "You'll see."

SIXTEEN

Taking Aunt Marie's advice, I spent the following days throwing myself into a design frenzy. It was an ideal distraction from the sitting around waiting for another tremor to hit; the sudden lull in quake activity was a welcome, though unsettling reprieve. Being phone-free helped too. No distractions, no complications while I hunkered down to work. On Thanksgiving morning, it was just me, the sewing machine, and the drafting table in what used to be Uncle Bob's library. Tucked away upstairs in the farthest corner of the house from the front, it was the ideal place for curling up with a good book or for creating. The light was just right—plenty of sun, not too dim in the late afternoon. Compact, cozy, and quiet enough to actually hear your own thoughts. Not always a good thing. Every now and then, I'd play one of Uncle Bob's vinyl records to avoid the truth that surfaced in the quiet. Like the fact that my dad had dropped completely off the radar. No more calls to Marie, no more attempts to visit. On one hand, I wasn't surprised. Yet the nagging desire for him to relentlessly pursue the family he claimed to love—even more than his other family, as sickening as it all was—lingered. At the end of the day, we all just wanted someone to never give up, even when we pushed them away. Even when they pulled away and sabotaged it themselves.

A pronounced knock on the library door pulled me from the creation zone.

"Hey, Jo." Florence popped her head into the room, terse and aloof, just as she'd been all week. "I need to pick up a few last-minute things for our feast today. The market closes early on holidays. You need anything? Want to drive into town with me?"

I studied the desk, considering my fabric supply. Over the last few days, I'd taken intermittent breaks from the Singer, sifted through my neglected flood of emails on Marie's laptop, prioritizing and breaking out our theater's remaining season line-up list. Then I'd dug through piles of scripts, printing them out and scrutinizing every line of dialogue for revealing clues about the characters, translating those interpretations into visuals with an obsessive array of sketches. I'd picked every costume design apart, tracing each delicate curve, ruffle, and asymmetrical feature. After drafting, demolishing, and reconstructing them piece by piece, I'd scrapped a handful of the designs and started over, using whatever fabric Aunt Marie had lying around the house. I'd also picked up materials from the town's quilting shop, but it couldn't hurt to look for more.

"*Mmm*, not that I can think of, but I'll come with you anyway. Might see something I can use for the next project." I'd managed to assemble nearly a dozen mock designs in a week's time. I wasn't sure, just yet, when I would drive to Philly and deliver them to the theater, but figured if I could just get my footing with work, everything else would iron out. The logistics of our new life in Lancaster, the timing of our trips to the city, the way forward—the designs would help light the way. The stage was dependable in that way, always inspiring change and movement.

"Okay. I'm getting ready to leave. Just want a fresh cup of coffee first." She flitted away from the door, barely finishing her sentence.

"Hey, wait." I jumped up from the armchair and hustled after her, following her down the stairs and into the kitchen.

Rooting through the cabinets, she mumbled, her back to me, "Know where Marie put the filters?"

Still catching my breath, I pointed to the highest cabinet above the stove.

"Since when does she keep them up there?"

"Since she changes her mind every other day," I laughed dryly, slipping around her to fill myself a glass of water at the sink. "Last week they were in the refrigerator, remember?"

"Not really, no." She fidgeted with the filter bag.

My natural inclination was to make some wisecrack about the possibility that maybe she should skip the extra caffeine this morning, considering her already antsy state, but I didn't. My sarcasm hadn't been well received over the past week. Most of my conversations with Florence since she'd chopped off her long hair and started working at Randy's consisted of lunch breaks, the weather, and the latest flannel jackets to grace the tractor supply store's shelves. Encouraging her to paint, compose, or even discuss our spring trip to Ireland was futile. She wasn't up, but she wasn't down. She wasn't anything, other than busy and disinterested. Motion was her new thing, with five AM ritual jogs. Gone was her penchant for kickboxing, but after her morning shifts she retired to the frigid fields with homemade targets for archery practice.

Back home in Philly, her morning routines were on time, though never entirely formulaic. There was always room for a detour, a chance of improv. This morning, as I watched her jittery search for coffee filters, it occurred to me that even her days off were finely calibrated now. She needed the coffee before she did the driving-to-town thing, to make it to the market by whatever perfectly appointed time she'd devised in her head, to be back at the house precisely by eleven, when Aunt Marie would begin cooking the side dishes. I was tired just watching her brew a dark roast.

"Okay," I drawled. "I have to ask. What else do you need for the meal? I think Aunt Marie's got us covered. There's enough food to feed an army. Or a very famished family during the zombie apocalypse."

"You found out about the bunker." For a split second, I could've sworn humor teased her lips.

"Why was I just now being let in on this little, big secret?" I saddled up beside her while we watched the coffee drip, feeding her a sardonic grin in the hopes that this might be the moment, the one where I catch a glimmer of the Florence I knew mere days ago. "On the other hand, how can I be surprised, considering your secret closet back home?"

"It wasn't a secret. You just never asked."

"Oh, I see how it is." I lightly jabbed her hip, but she didn't respond in kind. My grin faded.

"You're right. I don't need much. I'd just like to get a few small things, some kind of gift to thank Marie for cooking today and for giving us a place to stay."

"I like that idea. Where is she, anyway? Kinda late in the morning for feeding the animals breakfast, isn't it?"

"She left a while ago. Had a meeting with some of the farmers at the market. If we run into her while we're there, I could use your help distracting her while I shop for the gift."

"Sure, I can handle that."

"And I'm going to cook us breakfast tomorrow morning. Give you both a break from the stove."

"You? Cook breakfast?"

"I cook sometimes."

"No, you supervise while *others* cook. You hand us ingredi-ents. Talk our ears off and distract us while we're trying to read recipes and figure out measurements."

"Your mother's evolved. She cooks now."

"I prefer my prehistoric mother."

"Well, she's dead." Pulling an empty travel tumbler from the cabinet, she filled it with a long, dark pour. "Let the dead sleep, darling."

Pushing away from the counter, I finished the last of my water and turned back for the stairway. "Going to change. I'll be ready in ten minutes."

"I'll be waiting in the truck." Her keys jingled and the door slammed before I made it to the second floor.

———

The ride to town was quiet and bumpy apart from the radio's numbing murmur. I allowed the music to carry on for a few minutes before I killed it with a flick of the dial.

"Mom?"

"Yes?"

"Maintaining background noise to mask discomfort isn't our thing."

"Who's uncomfortable?"

"Will you please just talk to me? About whatever's going on inside of you?"

"Talk."

"Yeah. Something we're usually really good at doing."

"What would you like me to say?" She cranked the truck's rickety window handle, welcoming a gust of brisk air, and I followed suit, cranking mine.

"Anything you want."

"Where would you like me to start?"

"Okay, your music. Let's start there."

"What about my music?"

"You tell me."

Squirming, she rolled her head from left to right and stretched a shoulder. "I don't have the energy for this."

"For what? A conversation?"

"This."

"This *what*?"

"This interrogation. I'm not talking because I have nothing to say."

"I don't believe that. You always have something to say. If you don't say it with words, you say it with music. Or painting, or dance, or sweat and tears. There's always a medium."

"I've been speaking from the moment we left the city. Maybe you're not listening."

"You're shooting targets. Working at Randy's. Running marathons before the sun comes up. Avoidance doesn't count."

"Joanna, stop. Do not dig. Do not pick me apart like one of my paintings. Like one of your designs. I'm not a script, I don't need dialogue. Let's not play this game. It's Thanksgiving. Please, let's stay focused on making it through this meal and this day, okay? It's hard enough, don't you agree?"

"I know what you're doing, and I won't let it happen."

"What I'm doing?"

"You're shutting me out, just like Aunt Marie said you would. Trying to push me away, push me back to my life in Philly because you don't want me to give it up. Push as hard as you want, but I'm not going anywhere."

"Of course I don't want you to give up your life in the city for me." Her lips thinned as she paused. "If I didn't try to send you back home, what kind of mother would that make me?"

"The human kind."

Her left leg bounced beneath the steering wheel. "Aunt

Marie is entitled to her opinion, but that's not what's happening here."

"Then tell me what *is* happening. Please tell me you're going to snap out of this . . . whatever fog you're in, because if we're starting a new life out here, I need to know you're still with me. I can accept Dad is gone, but I can't lose you too. I can't do it alone. I love Aunt Marie, but she isn't you."

"What's happening is I'm grieving. It's that simple and that complicated. There's nothing more to say."

A small fissure ruptured along my rib cage, slick like a hot razor blade. Maybe she was right. Maybe she'd been speaking, and I'd been rejecting each and every wordless statement: every lap around the farm, every wardrobe adjustment, each bout of silence, detached gaze, and dispassionate inflection. Maybe she wasn't giving me the answers I wanted because she didn't have them to give. The burning tear near my ribs brought it all center stage. Florence couldn't be here with me. She wasn't going to offer me her usual comforting words of assurance, tell me everything was going to be okay, because she couldn't. I wanted something from her that she was incapable of providing right now, maybe ever again, and that possibility terrified me.

My tone melted. Softer, like warm butter. "There's plenty to say. You're right, though. You lost him too. We all cope differently. I'm sorry."

We plunged into another silent abyss. The seconds crawled painfully by. Mom's fingernails dug into her knee, scraping back and forth over her leg as she steered with one hand. I waited for her jeans to shred at the kneecap, watched for a loosening of the thread as she picked at the material.

"If you're real, tell me now," she suddenly whispered beneath her breath. "Now would be the time, and make a way out, do you hear me?"

I did a double take. "What did you say?"

"Come on!" she erupted, volume exploding like a spray of glass fragments all around us. She banged a fist on the wheel and the truck pivoted. The seatbelt cut into my chest. "Do you hear me? I won't do it, I can't do it. I can't, I can't. No, no, no."

"Mom?" I grappled with the seatbelt, prying at it with fraught fingers, unable to decipher the string of speech bubbling around her lips. "You're scaring me."

She pounded her knee, the same spot again and again, feverish eyes scanning the sky above.

"*Florence*. Who are you talking to?"

Her voice took full shape. "God, I hope."

I tried to peel my eyes from her, tried to watch the road because someone had to, but I couldn't. "I thought you disowned God." I actually did. I'd heard her in the middle of the night, just a few nights ago, formally declaring to the bedroom walls that she took back every act of devotion, every profession of love she'd ever expressed for her creator.

"Yeah, well. He won't leave. So, here I am." Her bitter chuckle shook me.

My hand moved to the door handle, my mind idling like a getaway car. "Here you are . . . doing what, exactly?"

"Trying the praying thing again. Mumbling like a lunatic into space, because that's what we're supposed to do, right? Have faith?"

I jumped as her palm slammed the dashboard. What had been *in* that coffee? Maybe the extra cup was a bad idea. "Mom, pull over."

She ignored me, turning on the wiper blades to the lowest setting as the crisp fall decided to add a light sprinkle to this morning's mix.

"Florence, stop the truck!"

The blades screeched across the windshield like a dying banshee. We both cringed. The blustery wind ricocheted through the truck again, this time with a menacing howl, and we moved in unison, reaching to roll our windows back up. I rolled mine hard, in a race to cut off the gust's vicious bite, but the glass stalled midway when a startling *smack*, followed by a flash of pure white and the flap of beating wings fluttered somewhere near my head, then dropped like a heavy stone at my feet. My scream fused with Florence's. The truck swerved to the right.

"What is it?" She pumped the brakes. The truck pitched to a stop along the two-lane highway's damp dirt shoulder. Her body ejected from the seat and out of the vehicle like a pilot abandoning a failing fighter jet. She hopped back and forth in the rain. "Joanna!"

The shock had the opposite effect on me. I froze in place like a stubborn icicle. "A bird! A bird. At my feet! It hit its head on my window and dropped dead. That's a bad sign, right?"

"No." Florence covered her eyes. "No, no, no. Don't say it's dead. Please, no. Please don't let it be dead."

I managed to nudge the limp, feathered creature with the tip of my shoe. "Oh, Mom. Please get it! Come over here and get it out!"

"Is it dead or isn't it?"

"Oh, I hope it's dead. Please, God." My eyes drifted up to the truck's ceiling, pleading to my mother's on-again, off-again creator. "Let it be dead."

"Why would you say that?" Florence spun and paced, shoving her fingers through her hair. "Don't say that!"

"I can't watch it struggle! I'd rather it be dead! Cold and gone!"

"I think this is what a stroke feels like." She clutched her chest.

"Mother! For crying out loud, please come get it out! Don't make me do it. I can't look. Don't make me look!" I gripped at the door handle as if it was my only hope. Like a piece of old plastic could rescue me from whatever string of bad luck I'd just unleashed on us. I risked another glance at my feet and whimpered. Of all the birds that could've hit my window, the lifeless one at my feet was a spotless, peaceful dove. Of course it was. Because I was the harbinger of death for innocent feathered things. Leave it to me to manifest this kind of omen.

"This isn't happening," Florence mumbled, still pacing.

"I'm never stepping foot in a zoo again."

"Not happening."

"Can't go near the farm animals anymore. Can't be trusted."

I mumbled. Florence talked to the sky. The rain intensified.

"Mom?"

"Just give me a second," she muttered, gripping her throat. There was nothing Mom and I understood more conjointly than an extreme trigger when it came to the loss of an animal, let alone the potential suffering of one. Cartoon animals made us cry. We were not cut out for witnessing the death of real, flesh-and-blood creatures, which is why Aunt Marie never let us name the chickens and why we stayed a football field's length away anytime Uncle Bob used to make one for dinner.

"Okay." Mom stopped pacing and straightened up. With a resolute nod, her arms steeled at her side. She stalked around the truck and pulled open my door. Cupping the bird with steady hands, she looked away as she relocated it to the side of the road, gently placing it in a bed of tall grass.

The plop of heavy raindrops and labored breathing filled the truck when she returned to the driver's seat, slamming the door and sealing us inside.

A sudden hysterical laugh wove its way through her frantic

breaths. She shook beside me, head dropping back against the headrest.

Like a rusty piece of metal turning on a hinge, my head swiveled toward her. "I'm glad you find this so amusing."

She laughed harder. "You think you killed it, don't you?"

"No," I sulked.

"You do!" She roared hysterically, slapping her hands on her knees. "My daughter, Joanna, the Herald of *Doom*."

The shock of the event momentarily softened around the edges as her laughter, so familiar, soothed my frayed nerves. Relief drenched me. She remembered humor, could still make the connection. Florence was in there. I just needed to draw her out.

"Yup, that's me," I snickered. "Guess I have the magic touch." Florence's contagious delight sank its hooks into me, dragging me straight into her river of pandemonium. Laughter burst from my lips and we both buckled over, succumbing to a crippling state of delirium.

"It wasn't an omen, silly girl," she gasped, pushing out the words as she worked to catch her breath. "It was an answer."

I waited for my breath's tempo to align with the slowing of my laughter. "An answer?"

"Yep." Using the steering wheel as an anchor, she pulled herself upright. "This morning, after I poured my first cup of coffee, you know what I did? Rummaged through Uncle Bob's old journals. You know that trunk, in the den? The one with all his old books?"

I nodded at the memory of the tan leather trunk.

"Well, I stumbled onto this page, a scribbled list—scripture verse after scripture verse—each one talking about fowls in the Bible. Did you know Bob always wanted birds?"

"Birds as pets?"

"Yes. He loved African grays, macaws, all kinds of parrots."

"I don't remember him ever owning parrots."

"He didn't. Marie said he could have any animal in the world except one of those birds. Told him that their lifespans were too long and they'd outlive them both."

"Why did that matter?"

"She knew she'd get stuck taking care of them. Bob provided, but Marie was always the caregiver. Her hands were full enough with the farm animals. She didn't want birds on her hands too."

"Sounds like Aunt Marie." Always in charge, ruler of the roost.

"One verse on the list made me pause. Sister Catherine talked about it one day, on our bench in front of St. Rita's." Her voice, more tranquil than it had been since we came to Lancaster, infused me like smooth honey. I leaned back, absorbing the nectar's flow. "I remember the sun, melting the ice on the sidewalk. We watched this sparrow picking at a branch, and she recited it from memory."

"So? What's the verse?"

"*Who teacheth us more than the beasts of the earth, and maketh us wiser than the fowls of heaven?* Job 35:11." Rain trickled steadily down the windshield. She exhaled. "This morning, when I tried the praying thing, I pressed my finger over Bob's handwriting, over that verse. And I thought, there's no way in hell anything, anywhere could ever teach us more than what the beasts of the earth and the fowl of the sky teach us down here, in this vast, dusty desert. Beasts—humans and animals alike—make us aware of our frailty. Fowls remind us of our limitations, like dependence on others to help meet our needs. I told this God, if you care, if you're there at all, impart some of this elusive knowledge, then. Give me some of that wisdom. If there's something else I need to know, something the birds and the beasts can't teach me, then tell me now. Tell me anything, show me what to do, because there isn't a single drop of water in sight to quench the thirst I've felt since I nailed that arrow to the tree." Her humor dried up like the desert she wandered in, and her gaze fell to her lap like stones tumbling down over the earthy, lush edge of a freshly dug grave. "For as long as I live, I will never forget the look on your father's face at that moment."

I reached for her wrist, squeezing it tight. Who knew how much longer she'd be present, right here in my midst? Her wrist was light and frail, threatening to vanish like a vapor. "The dove was your answer?"

She inhaled deeply. "It was. I know for sure now I'm not alone. There's more to learn, more to do. Life will go on, and I have to keep going."

"I'm so happy to hear you say that, Mom." I leaned over to smother her with a relieved hug. "You have no idea. Just give yourself time to heal. Hang out on the farm, relax, maybe write some new songs. You're right, there's still so much for you to do. Your fans, your supporters, your colleagues—they'll all be so happy to see what you come up with next. Focus on them, not the haters." As I released her I added, "Who knows, maybe by the new year you'll feel up to making a trip to the gallery to showcase a new piece. You always said you'd keep an open mind about doing more theater too. I can cast you in one of our new shows. I already have the perfect lead role in mind for you."

"Lead role?"

I scooted back, giving her space. "Yeah, you'd love the character. I mean, think about it . . . you can reinvent yourself. Have a whole new identity, make a whole new life in the city. When I'm done with my contract we can go—"

"No, Jo. I think you've misunderstood. To keep going means I can't turn back."

"Well, I don't mean back to Dad, obviously. Or to our old place. I just mean do things differently, ya know?"

"Everything already is different, darling."

"I don't understand, then," I stuttered, wiggling back over to my side of the truck. "What more is there for you to do out here? How will you move on with life, cut off from everything that makes you who you are?"

"This is my life now. This is my home. If everything that defined me is back there, in the city, then I don't really exist, do I? We're not having this conversation right now because I'm not really here."

It dawned on me then that I'd been wrong all along. Florence wasn't lost, locked inside of herself somewhere, distressed and disoriented, scrambling to find an exit. She was a shell. An empty shell robbed of its pearl and void of its spark, firmly stationed in the wet sand. She had no intention to find the key to the lock, no plan to restore any faded luster.

She didn't want to be found. Only rebooted.

SEVENTEEN

The farmer's market crackled with excitement as we ducked out of the rain and beneath the entrance awning. Run by Randy's family for over fifty years, it crawled with last-minute shoppers forced to venture to this side of town for their purchases. Most places in the nearby village of Bird-in-Hand were closed today, which meant pickings might be slim, but I was determined to help Mom find something special for Aunt Marie. Randy's vendors were no less authentic than the Amish businesses in Bird-in-Hand, though; their gifts were also handmade, show-casing some of the finest craftsmanship in the region. The warmth and good cheer around the stalls helped dispel the sullen mood we'd left behind in the truck, redirecting my mind away from the conversation I'd just had with Florence. Digging through my bag, I plucked out her pair of big brown sunglasses, the ones we toted around for any crowded public outings. She shunned them this time, tucking them away.

"No. Not necessary. No one out here knows me."

"That's a straight-up lie, Mom."

"Other than coworkers and friends of the family, no one recognizes me."

"Randy's is a gossip mill. I guarantee you those sweet, neighborly coworkers and harmless family friends of yours have already spread your news all over town. You know it's going to be in the papers any day now."

"Good grief, Joanna. When did you become such a cynic?"

"I've been a cynic my whole life," I said glibly. "Maybe you're not listening."

Her green eyes rolled in my direction.

"Just sayin'. Decline the sunglasses at your own peril."

"No one at Randy's cares, believe me. Around here, I'm Marie's sister and nothing more."

"Right. That's why Harlan walks into walls and knocks over coatracks any time you're in his presence. 'Cause you're just Marie's sister and nothing more. That boy is so starstruck when you're around, he can barely formulate a sentence."

"Harlan is just a sweet, accident-prone teenager."

"Well, someone took their denial pills this morning."

"*Ohhh*, back in the knife drawer, Miss Sharp."

The desire to leap forward and hug her sprang up, but died the second I reminded myself that a brief flaring of our old banter didn't change anything. Florence wasn't going back. Not to the city, and not to revive the woman she was before my father dropped a nuke in her white-picket-fenced yard. I couldn't free her, not with wit and not with humor. I couldn't coax a resigned prisoner from her cell.

"Anyway, listen . . ." She skimmed her fingers over a rack of lush, colorful scarves. "I've been thinking. I want you to take the car home for a few days. I know the windshield is cracked and still needs to be fixed, but it's drivable. Marie has her truck, I have Bob's. We'll be fine. Go make peace with some things before you make the commitment to stay out here. See your friends from work, keep searching for Tony, maybe visit your father . . ."

I picked up a jar of chocolate-covered amaretto cherries and placed them in our shopping basket. "Hard pass, thanks."

"Just hear me out, please." She removed the cherries from the basket. "You're going to have to go into the city soon at some point anyway, right? You have to deal with your contract, and after the way things went with Tony at the party —the way he and Olivia vanished—I'm sure it would make you feel better to tie up those loose ends."

"Mom, of course I'll keep asking around and try my best to find them and make sure they're okay. Even if I find them, there is no Tony and me. That ship has sailed, and Olivia wants absolutely nothing to do with me. Yes, I'll eventually need to go to the city for a few days. Not anytime soon, though. My mind's made up, so can we please change the subject? Like why are you putting the cherries back?"

"Marie doesn't need more cherries. What about one of these scarves? What do you think?"

"She doesn't, but we do." I plopped the jar of chocolate amarettos back in our basket. "No to the scarf."

"An apron?"

"She has a million of them."

"You're not helping, Joanna."

"What did you expect? Your sister is impossible to shop for. She has everything and wants nothing."

"Okay, I'm going this way." She gestured to the home decor booths. "You go that way. Go browse."

"You're ditching me?"

"You're slowing us down."

"I didn't realize this was a race."

"I'd like to get home."

"We just got here."

"Jo."

"What's the rush? It wouldn't kill us to slow down for a few minutes."

The tense wrinkles deepening around her taut lips told me it just might. "I'm not going to argue with you on Thanksgiving. Please go look around while I shop for Marie."

"No, no. I really do want to help, I'm sorry. We'll find her something, come on." I linked my arm with hers, the basket knocking us both in the stomach as I surveyed the booth to our right. "Look! Llama placemats."

Unlinking our arms and firmly gripping my shoulders, she spun me around and launched me in the opposite direction. "Meet me back at the entrance in fifteen minutes."

"Rude," I said and pouted, shuffling away.

Shoving a batch of caramel apples into the basket on my way to the other end of the market, I decided to pay for my sweets and skip shopping for design materials in exchange for book browsing. I wandered down to the very last booth, thumbing through crates of used paperbacks, each one of them calling my name. Amidst the scuffle of shoes, the rustling of bags, and animated conversations swirling all around, a bouncing echo called my attention to the nearby corridor, laden with restroom signs and off-limits storage closets. A throng of hushed whispers, followed by more lively, heated debate resounded through the tiled walkway. I abandoned the paperbacks and ambled toward the noise, craning my neck around the corner of the hall. A quarter of the way down, a wooden stopper propped a shabby door open. A janitor sign hung across the single window, a little blackboard scrawled with white chalk. Taped below the window, a piece of paper read *Farmer's Association Meeting in Progress*. I felt my way along the corridor wall, inching closer to peek inside the little room.

"The eastern colonies are already on lockdown," an irritated male voice powered over another woman's, who sounded equally on edge. "As I've said again and again, the only viable options now are the western colonies, and only one is large enough to continue recruitment and intake. There are two others near Victoria, but they're not up and running yet. It could be months before launch."

"What if your intel is flawed, Nate?" the woman shot back. "We might not *have* months, have you been paying attention? We're running out of time, and you know it. You were wrong about Edwards Isle. Why would we send our loved ones clear across the country without hard proof that Burtonshire's still accessible?"

"The intel isn't perfect, but it's the best we've got. And for the last two years it's been reliable, hasn't it? We've heard hundreds of accounts from Burtonshire, each one verifiable, with more trickling in each week. Our contacts are solid, and our network is steadily growing. No one's asking us to send our loved ones thousands of miles on a blind leap of faith, Noreen. Recruitment directors are still on the buses, handling intake assessments immediately upon boarding. If a passenger doesn't make the cut, they're notified then and there."

"Hogwash," a tired, salty man's voice jumped in. "We've had numerous reports over the last few weeks of people gettin' all the way out there, only to be turned away at the boat. Blind leap of faith? It's a suicide mission. I say we keep trying to talk the eastern colonies into reopening admission. Let's meet for negotiations, offer them some incentives."

The next voice, I recognized. Firm, feisty, and all too convincing. "It's not a matter of incentives, Jeb," Aunt Marie said, the back of her peppered-gray head poking out near the front of the gathering. "It's a matter of space. Edwards doesn't have any left, and the other eastern islands hit full capacity weeks ago. The reports from Boston have been pouring in. You already know this, yet here you are, flappin' your gums again about what we can't have. If we don't shift our energy to loading the buses heading west . . . the longer we drag our heels on this, we're risking more and more lives. Burtonshire isn't foolproof, but what is? Nate's right, it's the most reliable intel we've got right now. We're talkin' the largest colony in the west with replenishable resources, highly efficient, devoted residents, and room to spare—the most potential, hands down."

A ruckus of bickering zipped around the room. Aunt Marie threw her hands in the air while Nate, the apparent ringleader, pounded his fist on the table. Chaos ensued. More comments about boats and buses and islands swept the space, followed by some kind of tirade about damage control, exit strategies, and armories. Armories? A whole lot of gibberish that made me wish there was some kind of translator on site, someone who could decode whatever foreign language they were speaking. I could knock. Ask what all the commotion was about. Ask how any of this had anything to do with the Farmer's Association. But even with my trusted aunt's presence, the thought of intruding made me halt. Straining to make sense of the uproar, I ducked out of the doorway. As I did more racket, a swell of surprised shouts and boisterous chatter, blew down the hall from the market, drawing me back in the direction of the booths. Confounded and curious, I paused when I turned the corner and spotted a group of shoppers congregating around my mother.

"Is it true your husband's other children broke the news of his infidelity?" a pushy voice from her left poked its way through the disorder.

Another viper struck from the right. "Was your decision to vandalize your husband's private property a reaction to his affair, or would you say your recent career setbacks prompted you to attack? Was the mounting pressure just too great, Florence?"

Then I registered what was going down. Some shoppers in the crowd weren't shoppers at all. Steam churned at my ears and I bulldozed through the wall of spectators. "No comment," I seethed at the reporters, latching onto Mom. She sputtered uncontrollably, eyes darting around, a frozen doe cornered in the forest. Onlookers gawked and whispered, snapping pictures with their phones.

Then they realized who I was.

"Do you condone your mother's destruction of your father's property, Joanna?"

"Is it true you've resigned from your position at the Birch Theater, Joanna?"

"Do you regret your decision to run and hide here?"

"Do you have anything to say to the woman who stole your father and wrecked your family?"

"Do you feel any remorse for your actions the night of your mother's recent gala, what was likely the final performance of her career? . . . Joanna?"

From the first question, I'd started booking it for the exit, towing Florence behind me. "None of your damn business," I yelled over my shoulder. "Get out of the way."

"Oh, Joanna?" the pushy, high-pitched voice from before trailed on my heels into the parking lot. "How do you feel about your father's girlfriend announcing her pregnancy this morning? Are you aware she's officially gone public with the relationship, now that Asher's ended the affair?" Her minions clamored behind, unloading round after round.

"Are you hoping for a baby brother or a baby sister?"

"Florence, do you approve of Asher, dumping his pregnant mistress? Do you hope to reconcile? Would you take him back?"

A strong, invisible hand punched through my gut, grabbed hold of my organs and pulled, ripping them out and placing them on display. I froze. Mom stumbled, her basket of unpaid goods spilling onto the muddy ground. She tore her hand from mine, swinging around to face the leeches, the rain's drizzle coating her cheeks and forehead. She tried for words, but only a whimper came out. My head's mental dam hit the reject button, sending the flood of horrific new facts bouncing back to where it belonged: not here, not now, and as far as I was concerned, nowhere. Ever. There was no baby. No announcement. This was all concocted by some sadistic reporter, out for her five seconds of fame, a flash beneath the limelight.

"Don't even look at them, Mom." I yanked the keys from her purse, then steered her toward the truck's passenger side. Her limbs cooperated, allowing me to direct her into the seat. I raced around to the driver's side, my feet slipping in the mud as I jumped in. We catapulted away from the market, leaving behind a trail of fumes, fog, and shredded dreams. Mom stared blankly, a drained corpse on the cusp of a zombie's existence. My thoughts were jumping. I wrestled them one by one, strategizing ways to bring her back, to keep her from swimming farther out to sea. Problem was, I needed her to row the oars, or we'd never make it back to shore.

"I saw Aunt Marie at the market," I said, working a different angle. "Overheard some of her meeting. Have you ever been to one of those meetings with her? None of it made sense. It sounded more like they were organizing a special ops mission than talking about vegetables. Didn't understand a word of what they were saying."

I cast a furtive glance at the passenger seat. Catatonic, she'd crossed over the great divide.

"I know this is a lot, Mom. But we're going to be okay. Just think about everything you always tell me, everything you've ever said to encourage me to move forward. Take all of it and apply it to yourself right now. I'm living proof that everything you've always said is true, right? I wouldn't be standing right now if it weren't for your strength—you single-handedly transferred it to me. I never would've survived losing

Miguel. Never would've stood up to Dad about my future or been brave enough to say yes to the theater contract. Every single victory I had started with you. Don't give your power away, Mom. You taught me that, remember? Remember the dove. You're not alone. You have to keep going."

Nothingness curled around me, lingering the rest of the drive home. I helped her out of the truck and inside the house, though she didn't really need me. Though slow and mute, she was mobile and aware of our surroundings. She closed herself into her bedroom and I wandered around the kitchen, opening and closing cabinets for no reason at all. My heart stirred at the sound of Aunt Marie's truck pulling into the drive. Fatigue tugging at her countenance, she hurried up the porch steps, catching sight of me through the living room windows. We met at the door.

"What's goin' on?" She dropped her purse on the foyer bench. "Heard the commotion from the meeting room, saw you running out to the parking lot. Got here quick as I could."

"She was ambushed by reporters."

"Well, her whereabouts weren't exactly a secret. It was a matter of time."

"That's what I said. I think."

"You're pale as a sheet. You okay?"

I felt any remaining color in my cheeks drain straight to the soles of my feet. "Dad's girlfriend is having another baby. He ended their relationship and she went public."

"Where's your momma?"

"Locked in her room."

Aunt Marie's strawberry scent enveloped me as she roped me in, folding me into a bear hug. "Listen to me," she spoke firmly against my ear, "and listen to me good. The very best thing your daddy could've done was drive away, you hear me?"

I caved against her, battling with my spine to straighten up and stand guard.

"Not everything we love is good for us. There are things in this life we have to give up to survive. Let him let you go. Or you'll all drown."

"Auntie?"

She reared back, pinning me square in the eyes. "What is it, honey?"

"We're losing her."

"I won't let that happen."

"I don't think it's up to us."

"You're right. But we can remind her who she is, and that's something."

"How?"

"The surest way home is usually the hardest. We have to let her fall, darlin'. Just let her fall."

"I can't do that."

"The harder we push, the farther she'll run. She'll find her way back when she's tired of hurting."

A yawning crevice broke apart somewhere within, a geographical coordinate that couldn't be located. For the first time since we left the city, I shared my mother's desire to run. Not to struggle, fight, or push uphill, but to yield in the direction of the wind, to let it carry me downstream. I wanted movement, forward motion, air whirling past me as I tore on by. If Florence fled farther, I'd flee too. I'd cross continents if it meant I could hang on and never let go. Like the dove, I'd somehow find her obscure whereabouts and crash right into her space, forcing her to face what she couldn't ever escape: my love, devotion, and commitment. My bulletproof role—her daughter, her Joanna.

EIGHTEEN

A no-nonsense voice, poorly concealing its insincerity, droned away on the television as Aunt Marie and I set the dinner table. A red-headed entertainment news anchor woman, hair stiff as a helmet, talked to us, the masses, as if we had a right to be informed about the appalling piece of gossip known as my mother's life. As if the woman's stiff shoulder pads and the station's harsh lighting could help masquerade the information as dire, groundbreaking news.

"These latest developments beg the question," the helmet-haired lady said, "could confirmed reports that schoolteacher Mia Wallace—Asher Kowalski's former mistress—is expecting another child with Asher explain the recently leaked footage of Florence Kowalski, Philadelphia's prodigy pianist, demolishing her husband's car less than two weeks ago? The Kowalskis' building security manager, Todd Baker, declined to comment, but the footage is clear: Philadelphia's long-time beloved orchestra board trustee has not only destroyed her husband's car, but also her marriage and career. Take a look."

My fingers smashed the remote's *mute* button as the video

footage of our getaway car, speeding from our building's parking lot, flashed across the screen.

"Oh, just turn it off," Aunt Marie muttered, loading warm rolls into a bowl. "Makes me sick."

Yet I couldn't. I walked back around to the dinner table, unable to peel my eyes from the images. Seeing them made everything more real, a stark reminder that Mom was right. There really was no going back to our lives in the city. What was back there waiting for us, anyway? Rooms full of fancy things. Plastic and gold and metal and gems. Memories encased in glass and steel frames, no less real or any more forgotten simply by being on display. Art that could never be replicated, yes, but had already been born and lived enough life to die. Our concrete tower in Rittenhouse Square, a skin shed, useless and used. Judgmental glares, social exile, and cesspools of pity. Whispers and camera flashes, digital blackmail and cyber abuse. Piles of charred, once cherished memories, nothing but graves full of ghosts.

"Think she'll eat?" I asked, finally looking away.

"She will," Mom's voice appeared from the other end of the room, still and small.

"Hey!" Aunt Marie beamed. "She's emerged from her cave! What'll it be for your Thanksgiving feast, Madame? Your favorite tofu crumble and sweet potato casserole?"

Florence eyed the table. Dark shadows moved along the chiseled edges of her cheekbones. "A little bit of everything, please."

"That's what I like to hear." Aunt Marie pinched my elbow as she swung around, dropping dollops of each dish onto a plate. "Time to get some meat on those bones."

A mute wraith, Florence moved toward us, as shapeless and lifeless as the sweater that hung over her form.

"Did you get some rest, Mom?" I pulled out a chair for her and waited.

"A little. Thank you, darling." Accepting my invitation, she sat gently, allowing me to push her in like a cherished guest. Being tucked away in her room all afternoon while Aunt Marie and I cooked, I'd hoped the morning's events had worn her out enough for her to catch a nap. Between waking up at four AM every day and being constantly on the go, it was inevitable that her mind and body would crash, but trying to convince her of that was pointless. She wouldn't listen. Not to me, not to Aunt Marie.

My gaze flicked to the TV. I hurried to grab the remote, and turned off the news. Florence focused on the bare place-mats, waiting as Aunt Marie and I buzzed around the table, filling plates. Candlelight danced in the late afternoon's dim light, wax hardening around each pillar's edge. We didn't speak of the dove. It was ours and ours alone, a mystical gift buried in the fields on the side of the highway and in the fabric of our recollections. Florence's cooperative, borderline submissive mood set my blood on edge, bubbling beneath my skin in an agitated cry for a way out.

"Is that enough?" Aunt Marie set Mom's plate down, studying it like a delicate artifact.

"Water and wine, Mom?" I hovered with two carafes on the other side of her, poised and ready to pour. "Just water? Lemonade? Cider? We have chocolate milk too."

"She said a little of everything, honey, weren't you listening?" Aunt Marie leaned over and snatched the glass pitchers from me, pouring two cups. She wiggled her finger at the cider tray. "Grab that, now. Come on, hand it here." A well-oiled machine, we passed trays and glasses and pitchers, waltzing around Florence like synchronized swimmers. By the time we finished playing waitress, seven different beverages surrounded her, forming a semi-circle around her plate. She stared down at the billowing cloud of steam rising from her mountain of food.

"You've outdone yourselves," she said. "To what do I owe the pleasure?"

Aunt Marie and I took our seats. "Well, let's be real, shall we?" Aunt Marie stabbed at a cluster of green beans, plopping them on top of her mashed potatoes. "I think it's fair to say this morning was pretty craptastic. I for one think the events that took place warrant a feast fit for queens, not to mention it's Thanksgiving. You deserve a nice meal, so dig in."

Florence raised her silverware, cutting her tofu crumble into even smaller, baby-sized bites. I watched with Aunt Marie as the globs on her plate morphed into a pile of mush.

Aunt Marie's fork clinked her water glass. "I'd like to say a few words. Say grace first, Jo."

Florence stopped dicing her food. We all joined hands.

My eyes flitted shut and I silently prayed to find the words to say on what had to be one of the most painful days of our lives. I allowed one eye to open, glancing at Aunt Marie. She peeked back, knowing that a simple dinnertime prayer was akin to dismantling a ticking explosive. How did we navigate Florence's latest make and model? I decided on short, sweet, and to the point. "Thank you, Lord, for this meal and for this time together."

To my relief, a unified *amen* circled the table.

Holding a glass high above her head, Aunt Marie smiled. "I propose a toast to us, the ladies of the court, who, together, have had a long, trying year. Big changes, big loss, big pain. May the three of us lean on and uplift one another, draw comfort from one another's presence, and eat lots of cake."

"Here, here." I contributed a playful *clink* to my glass.

"I'm thankful for you both, kiddos. You're survivors. My heroes. My inspiration. Now eat, before it gets cold." Marie lowered her glass and dug in, mumbling through stuffed cheeks. "You know, Flo. I don't think I've told you yet, but I

love your new haircut. Edgy and earthy, a blend of old and
new. Suits you. Doesn't it suit her, Jo?"

"Yep," I lied, sipping cider from a tall, cobalt blue glass.
"So you, Mom."

Florence resumed cutting her mushy tofu.

"Joanna," Aunt Marie changed gears, "how are your
designs for the next show coming along? Find any interesting
materials at the market this morning?"

I swallowed hard. "They're coming together. No, I didn't
have much time to browse before . . . everything."

A quiet hum vibrated in Aunt Marie's throat.

"I did find something interesting, though."

"Yeah?"

"Your meeting. Sorta eavesdropped. I thought you said
you were meeting with the Farmer's Association. Who were
those people?"

"Oh?" Marie's chewing slowed. "I did. They were
farmers."

I laughed, sliding a bite of potatoes onto my tongue.
"Really? What were you guys talking about, then? Colonies
and islands and something about . . . buses?"

"They are farmers," Aunt Marie repeated, wiping a napkin
over pursed lips, "concerned about our community."

Florence's head tilted slightly, eyes lifting from her plate.
"Did you say colonies?" Her astute tone caused us both to
pause mid bite.

"We were talking about off-grid communities. We call
them colonies, yes. They're governed differently. Virtually
unacknowledged by the government, not official by law, but
recognized by the residents, and that's what matters."

I mulled over the memory of the scene as I blinked in her
direction. "What are you all concerned about?"

Aunt Marie smiled wryly. "Just our self-sufficiency, especially in light of all that's been happening around here. Pipe-

line hacking, cell towers going down, social media network interruptions . . . these new shakes. What you overheard was a discussion about how to manage these communities. We're trying to be proactive, that's all. Nothin' that would interest you ladies."

"Why's that? Try us." Amused, I leaned back.

Marie cast a careful glance at me, then at Mom. "All right, well, these off-grid towns have been filling up. They're mostly experimental, or at least they have been, for the past few years. They've cropped up around the States, bringing like-minded people together. Some are inland, but most are off the coast, island establishments . . . private real estate purchases with multiple co-signers, groups of people investing in land. Each colony has been gradually identifying what works and eliminating what doesn't for their community—classic trial-and-error methods, basically. Managing population wasn't an issue in the past, but there's more interest in these places now. Space is running out. So, we were debating how to handle it."

Florence's fork tapped her plate. "I thought that sort of thing was illegal."

"In some states, some regions, yeah, it can be. Certain areas allow it, but enforce strict building codes. There can be many hoops to jump through, but also many loopholes, depending on where you're tryin' to live. Generally, growing your own food or generating your own power doesn't break any laws. It's how you do those things on your property that gets tricky. Zoning restrictions and local laws tend to complicate things." Aunt Marie shrugged nonchalantly and slathered a roll with butter.

"Okay," I said, "but what does all this have to do with the farmers around here?"

Marie gulped down water and scraped some food around on her plate. Mom's fork continued to tap away. My gaze bounced between them. Mom appeared mildly curious, but I was dumbstruck by how much my aunt knew about this movement.

"We're part of a small, regional group that supports these off-grid colonies," she continued. "We partner with other groups nationwide, work together as a network."

"So, you and this group of farmers help build these colonies? How do you support them?"

"Not exactly. That's the founders' job. Each colony has a founder's council; they build the communities, decide how things run from the inside. Groups like the one I'm a part of just help others join them. We help our loved ones and neighbors within our region make the transition, make the move to their new colony."

Florence set her fork down. She leaned forward, resting her elbows on the edge of the table. "Your guess was right on the money, Jo." It was faint, so dim you almost couldn't catch it, but a smug grin rippled over her lips. "Your aunt is one of them."

Marie narrowed her eyes. "One of *who*?"

"You know very well *who*."

"No, I don't. So, please. Enlighten me."

Florence cocked her head in my direction. "The bunker says it all."

Marie's spoon jabbed the air. "Plenty of people have bunkers. Plenty of people prepare for storms and disasters. It's practical, common sense, Madame Sassy Pants. And if I'm one of the pod people you're poking fun at, you might as well count yourself in. Need I remind you about your little pantry closet project?"

I cupped my mouth to smother a grin. Florence wasn't the least bit flustered or touchy, but she wasn't coolly indifferent, either, so I counted her subtle, glib humor as a small victory. "Wait, wait," I couldn't help but giggle. "So, are you thinking of going to one of these colonies yourself, Auntie?"

"What? Heavens, no. I'd never leave my farm. You couldn't pay me to walk away from this place. Besides, I could never live entirely off the land. Not fully. Too extreme."

A laugh sounded from Florence, knocking us both back. The winning scoreboard was on fire tonight. "Newsflash, Marie," she chortled. "You *are* extreme."

A sparkle of hope, mixed with a dash of surprise joy, drew a big, goofy smile across my face, and I instantly wanted to slap it away. The joy wouldn't last long, because any second, Florence would remember the weight she was dragging around, but I'd bask in it as long as I could.

"Oh, laugh all you want, little sister. I didn't say I wouldn't *like* to live like these people, I said I *couldn't*. I'm boring these days, ladies, and one hundred percent okay with that, thank you very much." She stuck her tongue out at us, eliciting another wave of cheer around the table. "Getting too old and too set in my ways to go on some grand new adventure. I don't have the energy to make that kind of change. Besides, Bob's spirit is here. Leaving our farm would be like cutting off one of my limbs. No-can-do."

I swiped some crumbs from my lap. "If you have no plans to join one of these off-the-grid towns, why are you so involved? How long have you been a part of this?"

"Like I said, darlin'. To help loved ones and neighbors. My group counsels new colony residents. We offer them resources, then help get them to their new homes. It's rewarding, showing people a new way to live, how to improve their quality of life. Started doin' this after your uncle died. As much as I love being involved, it can be tough sometimes. Like right now."

"Yeah, I didn't understand a word of what was going on, but your meeting sounded tense."

"Sometimes the less you know, the better."

"Well, Mom and I are going to be a part of this community now too. What if we want to help? Maybe you should fill us in."

Florence slid her untouched plate forward. Clasping her hands together, she rested her knuckles beneath her chin, studying Aunt Marie. Shadows flickered from the candlelight, lapping at her face. "I'm curious, Marie," she mused. "Who exactly does your group share this information with? Who are these new residents, and where are you finding them? People right here, in town? They're agreeing to pack up and go to these unplugged, isolated camps?"

"They're far from isolated, and I wouldn't call 'em camps. They're villages. Thriving, independent, happy villages. We're talkin' alternative living for those who've lost confidence in the way things have been runnin' around here. For those wanting refuge. Yeah, we recruit people right here in Lancaster, and throughout the northeast."

"Alternative living?" I gawked.

"Define *refuge*." Florence's brow furrowed.

"Hold up." I tucked my hair behind my ears. "Are you saying you've been blindly shipping people off to these communities based purely on word of mouth? How do you know what these places are really like?" The debate over reliable intel resurfaced in my mind, and the scene from this morning's meeting streamed across my memory like a vivid roll of film.

"Not blindly, obviously," Marie said, taking another sip of water. "Of course we have some photos, some video. All kept under tight wraps, mind you. At this point we have a system pretty much down. This thing didn't happen overnight. These groups have been in the making for years now. They've had to build, toss out plans that didn't work, and rebuild again and again. Within the past year or two, they've really come along. The island colonies have been the most successful. They're more stable than they've ever been, and we have verifiable, first-hand accounts. These communities are like living organisms: they evolve, and can be revised. It's been a lot like a game of telephone. Sometimes the messages and the wires get crossed, sometimes the reports aren't exactly right, but the core details, the nuts and bolts are solid. Our sources are credible."

Like a slow balloon leak, lightheartedness seeped from the room.

"Like I said, not a topic that would interest you." Aunt Marie rubbed her forehead, befuddlement coloring her gaze as she met our silent stares. "Why do I get the feeling you're about to read me my rights? Should I be consulting my lawyer now?" She released a hearty laugh. It rolled right over us. "Okay. Maybe you just want me fitted for a straitjacket, then."

"This isn't a joke, Marie," Mom said. "How underground is this thing? Why didn't you tell me about this?"

I clenched my fingers on my napkin as the electricity snapped between them like a broken rubber band. "Take a breath, Mom. Apparently it's not too underground if they're holding public meetings about it."

"Masquerading as Farmer's Association meetings," Florence quipped. "Marie, these people are conspiracy theorists. More than theorists, they're actively living out these ideas. Have you signed something? Taken an oath? Made some sort of secrecy pact?"

"Whoa there, Nancy Drew, slow your roll." Marie laughed as she said this, but her face fell as she registered my mother's austere, angry irises boring into her from the other end of the table. "Florence, I didn't sign my name in blood or offer them my firstborn, for heaven's sake."

"Maybe not, but this could still be dangerous, Marie. These kinds of groups have expectations. When you're privy to this kind of information . . . once you're in, you're in. You break their trust, they retaliate. They're not your friends. They're conditional allies, have you thought about that?"

"*Okaaaay.*" I rose from my chair, taking in the massive feast sprawled out before us, barely touched. "Mom, this isn't the mob she's talking about. Auntie, you're right. We're better off not knowing. It's your business. See, Mom? No need to get worked up. Let's enjoy the rest of our dinner. Who's ready for pie? I'll get the pie."

"Good thinking, kiddo," Marie lightened her tone, delivering an encouraging smile that didn't quite reach her eyes. "I'll take the pecan spice, please."

"Your involvement with these people implicates all of us," Mom pressed, an unshakeable gaze trained on her sister. "Do you understand? I knew you're into prepping, Marie, I am too, but this? I had no idea you were so deep into this world. These are things I need to know if I'm going to be living here, now. If Joanna's going to be living here. That's great you're some non-conformist renegade, devoting yourself to the protection of your fellow man from the system, but what about those living under your roof? Whatever you get tied into, we get roped in, too. I have a daughter to protect here."

I dropped my napkin on my plate. The blood thudded against my veins. Just when I thought a glimpse of the mother I knew came to the surface, her cyborg replica reappeared. "Mom. I really think you're overreacting, here—"

"Jo?" Aunt Marie's chin tilted in my direction, but her eyes held onto Mom's, patient and unperturbed. "Can you grab that pie for us, hon? Your momma's just looking out for us. Aren't you, Flo?"

Picking at the corner of her placemat, Mom lowered her gaze.

"We can talk through it all tomorrow, after this lovely meal. After lots and lots of pie. Sound good, sis?"

Florence nodded, looking through us, somewhere into outer space. "Fair enough."

The pie buffet was a hit. We sampled Marie's classic recipes and tried some of her newer flavors, then forged on through the remainder of our holiday feast, avoiding all talk of my absent father, his pregnant ex-mistress, the morning scene at the market, and Aunt Marie's controversial hobby. I didn't share Mom's resistance to Aunt Marie's prepper-friends circle. In fact, I kind of liked how my kooky aunt was spending her free time, even if it was off the wall and ranked a little high on the creepy scale. She was passionate, interested, and seemed genuinely invested in the effort, and that was more than I could say for both me and Mom, who had virtually no idea what to invest our energy in moving forward. There was more than enough to mull over right now. My family was in pieces, our future was uncertain, and at some point, we'd have to venture out of this farmhouse and make some decisions. Thankfully, it was Thanksgiving. Thankfully, "some point" was not now.

My lashes fluttered as I stirred from sleep that night. Bright, blinding light cracked through my bedroom doorway. My sense of time slid sideways. After our Thanksgiving meal, we'd resorted to hokey board games around the coffee table and hot chocolate, just long enough for my mother to grow increasingly somber as the evening dragged on. She finally retired to her room, once again declining Aunt Marie's suggestion to play something on the piano for us to all sing to, and I followed suit, ready to collapse into intoxicating slumber.

"Mom?" I mumbled into my pillow, straining to make out her silhouette against the stark light.

"*Ssshh*, go back to sleep." She moved to the window curtains and parted them, allowing the moonlight to stream in.

I smiled against the pillowcase as the moon kissed the top of my bed quilt. "Thanks."

"My little moon baby."

"Can't you sleep?"

"I did. I will. Just wanted to tuck you in." She breezed toward me and pulled the blankets as high as they would go, to the tip of my chin, then tucked the edges of the sheets tightly around my shoulders. She resumed her stance, a spectral presence, lithe and looming, standing tall beside me. "How hurtful all of this must be for you. I haven't said it yet. I'm sorry. I'm so sorry you have to go through this."

"What could you possibly be apologizing for? You didn't ask for any of this, Mom."

"How did I miss it?"

"How did we both?"

"I shouldn't have missed it." A surreal puff of breath materialized against my forehead, depositing itself against my skin as she dropped a kiss from that high pedestal, suspended above me, the place I couldn't reach.

Before I could respond, her figure sank away, back into the room's shadows. The light pulled her through the doorway, and sleep reclaimed me.

NINETEEN

A tremor arrived with the force of a freight train, knocking me from dead sleep. Untied shoelaces lashed my ankles as I wrestled to tie my bathrobe around my waist. The stairwell walls pounded in my eardrums like an explosive stampede as I bounded down the steps, two and three at a time. Whether my footing and pace were due to accelerated speed or the uncontrollable loss of balance, I wasn't sure, but with each uneven stride, I told myself I was one step closer to reaching them, the most important women in my life.

"Auntie?" My voice was a living thing, outside myself, bouncing aimlessly around the living room for its owner.

"Here! Front hall!"

The kitchen cabinets rattled as the ear-splitting sound of shattered glass, a sound I was all too familiar with lately, fractured around us. "Where is she?"

"Where else? Running."

Terror snagged in my throat. I slammed into Aunt Marie. We braced ourselves beneath the sturdy frame of the foyer entrance, eyeing the front door. The seconds were spitfire in my head; I counted them as I could catch them, bottling them up in hopes of measuring the time it would take for Florence to burst through the front door, unbloodied and in one piece. "We have to go find her." I sprang for the door, but Aunt Marie caught and hurled me back like a slingshot. "Let me go!"

"Not killin' yourself. Not on my watch. It'll pass. Stay put."

A raw bellow tore through my windpipes and I tried again, this time feeling the wind bumped from my lungs as Marie power slammed my shoulders. "Look! There." I gestured behind her, catching a glimpse of Florence through the living room windows. A speeding bullet ripping along the fence, she charged toward the porch. "Come on, she needs us!"

Marie reluctantly released me, hobbling over to the door to drag it open. Mom's precision was uncanny in contrast to the ground's pitch and roll, her arms churning mechanically as she propelled herself forward. She staggered but regained balance, tearing across the farm in choppy sprints and spurts. From the doorway, I could make out her pupils, enlarged and black, drowning out the magical green specs from her irises. Her gaze remained on target, focused and unyielding. The taut air stung my ears with a high whistle, a teapot kettle overblown. Florence powered up to the porch edge, grasping for the stair rail, feeling her way along the jagged wood and pulling herself upright. Marie teetered back through the doorway, allowing her room inside.

"Oh, thank God." Florence's breath hit my forehead as we collided. Her long, graceful arms latched on to my frame, and the three of us moved together like magnets, ducking and covering one another as beams split above our heads. Our huddled bodies crawled beneath the foyer table and lowered to the floor. We held on, rocking with the weight of the earth, my mother mumbling a string of repetitious Hail Marys. A montage of images pelted my vision, even as my eyes squeezed tightly shut, triggering stars and pops of color and light: My past love, still a present love. New friends and former friends, my father and his other family. Years of accumulated belongings, which mere weeks ago, lined my bedroom shelves in our city home. A glistening string of perfect pearls, given to me by my father on my twenty-first birthday, chucked somewhere in the pile of jewelry left behind for Helen. Finally, a narrowing tunnel, shadows circling, closing and shrinking, flooding out the light.

"Joanna," my mother's voice rang out. She pulled back to stare me down, bracing the sides of my head. "Stay with me, okay? It's almost over."

"How do you know?" My teeth rattled. My eyelids grew drowsy, but I did as she said, hanging on to the present moment, refusing my body's attempt to drag me to unconsciousness. Bruises and scrapes smattered Florence's sweaty face, drawing the attention of my ailing mind. She looked as if she'd gotten into a fight with a horde of tree branches and the branches won. A grim reel of all my mother might've endured to incur the injuries struck me like sharp, rusted metal.

"Count to ten with me. Ready?"

Marie joined us as we started the countdown. Our backs hunched as we heaved against one another. Like counting sheep to fall asleep, we remained suspended in time, waiting in anticipation, only it was breath we counted. One inhale, one exhale, each one confirming we were still alive, that much closer to the finish line. The rumbles rolled to a stop. A lingering echo of the porch wind chimes dusted the sudden silence. We peeled ourselves apart but kept our hands linked, sprawling out across the floor.

I shuddered. "That was the worst one yet."

"I need to calm the horses," Marie panted. "Check on the barn."

Florence winced as blood trickled down her forehead, over one eyebrow.

"Mom, we have to clean you up." We released hands and I scrambled to action, rising wobbly to my feet. Aunt Marie followed suit. I helped her up and she reached for her coat from the toppled-over coat rack. She wrapped her favorite Southwestern Native American patterned shawl over her coat shoulders, shaky hands fishing out gloves from the pockets.

"After I check on the barn, I have to get to the market," she said.

"The market?" My mother asked, voice muddled. "Now? But the aftershocks . . ."

"Yes, now. I have to talk to Jeb."

"Jeb who?"

"Farmer friend. He'll be meeting with the others. They'll have some updates."

I returned my attention to Florence. "I'll go with you after I get Mom bandaged up."

"No. You take care of your momma and I'll go. Stay here. Try to use the battery-powered radio by the stove to tune into some news. Find out what they're telling us. The generators should tide us over for a while, but you've got that for now, just in case."

"You're not driving over there yourself," Florence said.

"I am and you're not gonna give me a hard time about it. Let Jo fix you up. Use the first aid supplies beneath the sink." Her eyes flicked in my direction. "When I get back, it's time to have that talk we haven't had yet."

"Talk?" Florence accepted my hand and stood, grasping my forearm to steady herself.

"I won't be long." Marie brushed Mom's hair back, eyeing one of the swollen scratches on her cheek. "Get some ice on that forehead." Car keys jingled and she was gone, entrusting Florence into my care.

"What happened out there, Mom?" I carefully led her over to the kitchen, beginning my search for the first aid kit under the sink. "Does anything feel sprained or broken? Any bumps on the head?"

"No. Some sore muscles, but I've been running all morning. The cuts burn. Ducked into Mr. Tenney's shed when it started."

I glanced over at Mr. Tenney's place through the kitchen window, the closest neighbor for miles.

"Didn't last long there. Axes, shovels, jagged metal." She pointed to her bloody face with a wry smile. "Clearly the right choice for shelter. Great for the complexion."

My still trembling fingers tore open an alcohol swab. I tended to her cuts one by one, patting her skin with a warm, damp washcloth before applying the bandages. "Something's wrong."

"What do you mean?" Florence felt her bandages, as if one was out of place.

"These quakes, I mean. The news just keeps telling us the same things over and over. Just slapping different headlines on the same recycled reports. Aunt Marie said something to me one day, when we first got here. Said this might keep happening, that things might get worse."

"How ominous."

"I'm starting to wonder if she's right."

"It's possible. She usually is."

I discarded the bandage wrappers, stepping over a pile of broken dishes. Glass crunched beneath my shoes. "She mentioned the three of us having a conversation . . . about being prepared, or something. Making sure we're all on the same page. Whatever that means."

"*Ah.*" Florence meandered around the counter and pulled

out a chair from the kitchen table. She took a seat, first swiping away a layer of drywall dust and chunks of a shattered cookie jar. The pieces fell to the floor, the sound echoing throughout the house. "The talk."

"I'm not sure how I feel about these farmer friends of hers. I liked the sound of them at first, liked that she's passionate about all this disaster preparedness stuff, but now I'm wondering if they're filling her mind with the wrong things, ya know?"

Florence laughed dryly. "Now you're thinking like a parent."

A lopsided smile crept up. "She's like a perpetual twelve-year-old."

"With the wisdom of a ninety-year-old."

"Exactly." I chuckled. She'd taken the words right out of my mouth. Florence, the mother I knew back in the city, once had that special gift. I reveled in the awareness that she still did.

"Well, darling, if there's one thing I know about your Aunt Marie, she isn't easily swayed. These friends of hers might be feeding her ideas, but if she chooses to believe them, chances are she has good reason."

Digging out an ice pack from the freezer, I wrapped it in a fresh dish towel and pressed it against her bandaged forehead. "I thought about him. About *them* too." My voice came out in a whisper, as if speaking at a higher volume was betrayal. "When the tremor hit."

Florence's eyes—pupils still dilated, green hue still faint specks—rolled up to meet me as I kept the ice pack firmly on her skin. "You want to know they're okay."

I shrugged.

"I meant what I said yesterday at the market. I'd like for you to go home and make peace with some things before you commit to staying here, Jo. Visit him. Go see your sisters, if that will help you somehow. Try to find some closure."

"What about you?"

"What about me?"

"Don't you want to say goodbye? Say you're angry? Say something? Some last words?"

She didn't respond, but she didn't have to because I already knew the answer. I just wanted to hear her admit it, as if saying it out loud made it real and not just some nightmarish truth sloshing around in my head.

"You don't want to say goodbye to anyone? Not even Helen? Or Sister Catherine?"

"Sometimes silence is the only goodbye." Her indifferent stare returned like a hazy spell, casting itself over her features. "Not everything needs to be tied up with a pretty ribbon and bow. I wish those I love farewell every minute of every day, right here." She placed a hand over her heart. "Distance can't separate us or change the love, and words don't always equal closure. You and I are different people. Which is why I think you should go after those goodbyes you're craving." She gently removed my hand from the ice pack and took over, holding it to her head. "Whatever you feel you need to do, go do it, and do it soon."

My arm fell to my side like dead weight, lost and purposeless. I wandered over to the stove and switched on the old boombox. Adjusting the dial, I watched as it surfed over the radio waves, searching for a clear station. Static screeched and groaned, ebbed and flowed, leveling out on an AM news channel. Two broadcasters debated animatedly, their voices rising and falling as they fought to be heard over one another's convictions and the rustle of surrounding street noise. It took me a moment to make out their words, but eventually one reporter yielded to the other, allowing them to complete full sentences.

"As they say, this is not a drill," a broadcaster's solemn voice announced. "If you're just tuning in, I'll be perfectly clear for anyone listening. Events we've learned about today off the coast of the Atlantic Ocean, as well as in the Gulf of Mexico, have ignited a wave of excitement and intense curiosity among NASA officials, marine biologists, and military experts alike. Machines composed of materials yet to be identified have emerged from the ocean floor, containing what are believed to be extraterrestrial marine lifeforms, and seem to be headed inland. According to reports we've just been handed, their ascent to the surface was detected just days ago, though officials believe their sudden appearance is not a new development, but rather has gradually been working its way from the depths. Scientists claim harvesting our resources is not likely their motivation, though we do not yet know the intent of these lifeforms, or what they hope to accomplish by moving ashore.

"Surely many questions will continue to arise as the event unfolds, but what we *do* know is that we are urged to remain calm, identify areas near us for safety and shelter, seek the comfort and support of our loved ones, and await further instruction and guidance from our commander-in-chief and trusted experts. While there's a great deal we don't yet know, this marks a global, historical change. This unprecedented discovery might well signal an irrevocable turn—perhaps the beginning of a new era for the human race. Once again, ladies and gentlemen, I repeat: this is not a drill. May God be with you all."

Street noise, alarms, and sharp, rapid pops drowned out the broadcaster's voice and then hypnotic static trilled, washing out the commotion. My mother's silent presence—motionless, warm body heat—was suddenly beside me. I switched off the radio. Numbness circled, clamping down like the jaws of a great white. Another musical whisper of wind chimes swayed in the distance. An out-of-body experience seized me, the kind that steals your ability to produce speech and paralyzes you with the sensation that you're watching yourself from across the room—your very own supernatural doppelganger. You watch the train wreck, watch it all unravel around you, because you're not really there.

"We should go to the market," I finally said, syllables staccato.

"No. We'll wait." Florence swayed, hand snaking to the counter to hold herself upright. "She told us to wait."

A deluge of faces poured through my consciousness like a gushing waterfall: Tony. Olivia. Helen. Dad. Dad's no-longer-secret family. The theater staff. Security manager Todd. Elise Grayson, our neighbor two doors down the hall and her hellion two-year old, always throwing his toys around, driving the whole floor to the brink of madness. The little terror was so cute, though, it was impossible to stay mad at him. Then, there were images, colorful and acidic, one bleeding into the next like a hallucinogenic trip: pigeons outside my bedroom windowsill, staring back at me while I peered out at the skyscrapers. Shopping for Feliz Cumpleaños decor for Miguel's birthday at the party favor store off Chestnut Street. Mom and me, spinning around the studio like euphoric lunatics celebrating Mom's newest composition. The memories continued to blast away, dousing me in unwelcome emotion I was nowhere near ready to acknowledge.

"Then we'll wait." And we did. For minutes, for hours, I wasn't sure. I only know we both stood the moment Aunt Marie returned from the market.

"Have you heard?" she asked, setting those too-wise-for-her-own-good eyes on us from the other side of the kitchen counter.

We nodded. My mute doppelganger shuddered.

"Okay, then. Time for that talk. Let's go."

In a team effort, my throat, tongue, and diaphragm pushed the words out. "Where are we going?"

"To the bunker."

The neighing of horses echoed outside. We followed Aunt Marie back out to the truck, out into the corrosive wilderness.

TWENTY

L ong, horizontal rows of fluorescent light flickered on above our heads as Aunt Marie led us through a concrete-and-steel door down a flight of stairs, squeezing past us when we reached the main floor. She flitted from shelf to shelf, lifting items one by one, barely giving them a glance, gathering them against her chest in a hurry like a time-crunched shopper with no luxury of grabbing a cart or basket. Dumping the items into piles onto a family-style picnic table as she went, she zipped around like a seasoned chef well acquainted with the layout of her walk-in freezer. Mom and I hung back.

My mouth fell ajar. "You've seen this before, Mom?"

Mom's gaze rolled up to the gray arched ceiling, then back down. "Bigger than I remember."

"So, uh . . . Auntie?" I swallowed hard. "What *is* this place?"

"What does it look like?"

"Death. It looks like death."

"On the contrary, honey."

I glanced back up the stairwell at the fortified door. Claustrophobia bloomed as I half waited for the thing to slam closed and lock us in.

"It's sealed," she said, sensing my unease without looking my way. "Designed to prevent gas, water, and air permeation." She tinkered with a box of batteries, then reached high on her tippy toes and heaved two olive green utility backpacks down from a dusty shelf. "Don't worry. We've got a built-in ceiling escape hatch for a secondary emergency exit."

Somehow, that still didn't comfort me.

Stuffing the bags with freeze-dried food packets and first-aid supplies, she unzipped each compartment, checking every nook and cranny. "Well, from the sounds of it, *this place* is going to be my home soon. In theory, it can help me survive most catastrophic events for at least a good five years, maybe more. Air and exhaust ventilation shaft—NBC filtration system—plus wind power for generator back-up, a well water system, and a hydroponic garden over there." She wiped her hands on her jeans, nodding to the far-right corner of the bunker, where an intricate row of gardening trays, lined with fresh, leafy greens, and crops I couldn't identify sprouted up from a collection of organized bins.

"Oh, is that all?" A sardonic laugh escaped me.

"Not even close." She smiled. "I can keep going, if you'd like."

I blinked. "*Nah*, I think I get the picture . . ."

Florence folded her arms and stepped forward, a beam of harsh light washing her out from above. "NBC filtration system?"

"Nuclear, biological, and chemical."

Mom and I exchanged glances. She inched closer to her sister, rubbing a thumb along her brow. "Marie, why'd you bring us down here?"

Zipping up the backpacks, Aunt Marie exhaled, running her hands gingerly over the cargo pockets. "Jo's right. That was the strongest tremor yet, and they're only going to get stronger."

I tugged at the hem of my bathrobe, still wrapped beneath my coat. "It's them, isn't it? The machines in the ocean. Causing the quakes."

"There's no other way to say this, so I'm just gonna come on out with it. You can't stay here, ladies. You have to go, and you don't have much time." She shuffled over to meet us, peeled off her coat, then rolled up her flannel sleeves, capping them at her elbows. "In a matter of days, maybe hours, things are gonna go sideways. The panic's already setting in as we speak. We have a very tiny window of time—my guess a fraction of tiny—before things go south."

I started to shift from foot to foot, swaying in place. Mom was a pillar beside me, rooted to the cement floor.

"I spoke to Jeb at the market and I've got you two spots out on the next train. Leaves in a few hours and we need time to drive to the station, so let's pack up, attempt to make some calls, send some emails . . . whatever you need to do before you get on that train."

"Train to where?" I stuttered.

Florence's gaze cut to the backpacks. "Where's the third bag, Marie?"

With a definitive shake of her head, my aunt resumed motion, rooting through some drawers. "Told you. I'd never leave my farm or the animals. This captain goes down with her ship." She lifted a finger, signaling us to simmer down, then ventured over to a storage cabinet installed next to a small counter, a fully functional kitchenette area. She presented three mismatched champagne flutes and a jar of chocolate amaretto cherries, sliding everything on the picnic table. Mom and I drifted over to sit. Instead of popping bubbly, Aunt Marie filled each glass with a splash of red wine, dropping a cherry into each one. The cherries landed like stones at the bottom of the glasses, and she raised one of the flutes, affection swarming her irises like bees flooding their hive. "Train's going west. The Pacific Northwest, to be exact. Headed to one of the colonies I mentioned."

"Oh *nu-uh*. Nope." I rejected the glass, pushing it back.

"Let her speak, Joanna," Florence's voice, a wraith's echo, grazed my earlobes, turning my skin cold. Florence, more than anyone I knew, wouldn't normally listen to a second of this. Not because she didn't value Aunt Marie's thoughts, or because she couldn't relate to her sister—they were more alike than I'd ever realized—but because whatever option Marie was presenting was based on fear, and Florence didn't bend to fear. She dug her boots in, rode out the storms in life. Leaving the city didn't count. She wasn't afraid of anything back in Philly; she just refused to live another second in a place that took her for granted. Catching the blunt edge of her new haircut from the corner of my eye, goosebumps sprang up, reminding me that this wasn't Florence I was dealing with anymore. Remnants of the mother I knew before we left Philly were still embedded—I'd caught glimpses of those elusive pieces—but as I sat there, watching the green hue in her eyes flare with interest, I shivered. Who was this nervous woman, emboldened with curiosity, eager to hear my crazy aunt's idea to ship us out west, less than an hour after we learned that a new life-form had been discovered?

"The safest option is the Isle of Burtonshire," Aunt Marie said. "Before this news turned official—before it became public knowledge—other colonies were already turning people away. Too many crowded colonies, filling up too fast, like I told you before. Burtonshire's gate is one of the last to close. I secured you both admission. You'll be in the final batch granted permission to board the boat to the island. If you have any chance, any chance at all, Burtonshire is where you need to go. Immediately."

"Like yesterday," Mom mumbled, understanding in a way I wish I could.

This was utterly insane. I shoved the jar of cherries back. "Hold on. I don't understand. These things are coming from the ocean floor, right? They're invading from the water. Then settling on an island is suicide. Hello? What about right where we're sitting?" My hands waved frantically around my head, gesturing to our creepy, oversized hidey-hole. "This is exactly where we need to be when things start to go bad out there, not on some random train that's going to take us to some rock out in the ocean, where these things are coming from. You just said it yourself." I slapped my palm on the table, eying my aunt. "This is going to be your home, right? You're staying in the bunker. So, this is the safest place for all of us. What makes you think we'd be better off going to live with some delusional fearmongers on some freaky island?"

"Hush, Jo," Mom said hoarsely. "Go on, Marie."

I blanched. Her words were a smack in the face. How was I the only one seeing this clearly? "Seriously. What are you two smoking?"

Marie's presence moved in like a thick, rolling fog, ensnaring me from across the table. "You need to understand this, hon. It's not the monsters in the ocean you have to worry about. They're the cause of the commotion and the upheaval, but they're not the immediate threat."

"But the news said—"

"What did I tell you about the news? It doesn't tell us the whole picture. The reality is we know very little about these creatures. When something on this scale happens, the monsters on land—they're the real danger."

"Okay." My jaw flexed. "So then please help me understand why you don't want us to stay here, in your bunker?"

A lump shimmied down Aunt Marie's throat. She took a sip of wine, glancing down at her fingers splayed around the glass stem. "I'm not gonna lie to you and say it'll be easy or perfect, but I know one thing for certain: whatever waits for you on Burtonshire will be a thousand times better than what's coming here. Jeb gave me some new intel. These things, coming from the ocean . . . turns out they don't like heights. Won't go near steep mountains, high altitudes. Burtonshire isn't just one of the last island colonies on the US West Coast to have its doors still open, it also sits on the highest point in Rosario Strait, second only to Mount Constitution in the San Juan Islands."

"Who *are* you?" Florence's voice twirled on a breath.

"I'm your sister, Flo. The same woman you've always known."

"Then how do you possibly have this kind of information?"

"I'm nobody special, just have connections. A lot more these days, more than I ever did before Bob passed. As soon as he was gone, I needed to stay busy. God knows I love our animals, and I love this damn farm and the house and all the life Bob and I tucked away in its walls over the years, but when he died . . ."

"You became someone else," Florence finished for her.

"That's how it always happens, isn't it? Another chamber unlocked. Illuminated a part of me that was always there. Bob's death helped light the way."

Mom's fingers floated across the table, linking with her sister's.

Aunt Marie's lips set in a thin line. "This network of people I've befriended over the years . . . they're good people. Run-of-the-mill average farmers, just like me. Only with more knowledge than the average civilian, thanks to our sources. We have people all over, infiltrated just about everywhere. We've been keeping an eye on this thing, preparing for the inevitable.

Working with them, I'm useful. I'm a part of something bigger."

"What thing? Preparing for what?"

"What all preppers get ready for: disaster." Her shoulder rolled. "We weren't sure what, exactly, or how it would look when it arrived, but we knew something was coming. Our society's been entirely too vulnerable, too dependent on fragile systems for far too long. We knew it was only a matter of time. As the colonies were gradually developed, our network sharpened its focus, narrowed down its mission. We've seen so many signs over the past year, hints of change. Incidents that didn't look like much at the time. Not when they were strewn apart and lost in the shuffle, lost behind the next news headline. But as they all strung together over time, it became clear something was shifting."

"The creatures . . . " My neck muscles tightened. "Do you know what they are?"

"No idea." Marie scooped another cherry from the jar. "But the word is, they've been buried inside the earth a lot longer than any of us want to think about. Watching? Waiting? For what, who knows? We do know their ascent to the surface isn't new. They've tried to make contact before. We suspected they don't like elevation, but we couldn't be sure. Jeb confirmed this morning that there's more evidence of this now. 'Bout six months ago, they showed up at night, off the coast of La Push, Washington state. Some surfers camping out swore these things tried climbing the cliffs. The higher up they traveled, the more they hesitated, fell back. Released this sound, this ear-piercing scream, some kinda high-pitched wail, whenever they lost their footing. Scrambled right back down the cliffs and disappeared into the waves. No one believed the surfers, of course. News wrote 'em off as some dumb kids tellin' ghost stories."

A shudder rolled across my collarbone, eliciting another frigid bite along my flesh.

"Sure enough, as this news spread through the network, the western island colonies became a hot commodity," Aunt Marie continued. "Especially Burtonshire. It offers the highest elevation—a natural safety net—plus plenty of distance from the mainland and from other islands. It's the most isolated of them all, another layer of protection."

"How do you figure?" The chill on my skin suddenly somersaulted into a heat wave. I unbuttoned my jacket, tugging at the neckline of my bathrobe.

"Well, the elevation should keep the creatures away, and the isolation will keep *people* away. It's more difficult to get to, giving it an added advantage—not like you can just drive a car there. Being surrounded by miles of nothing but water is helpful for spotting incoming threats. More time to prepare to defend the territory."

Florence released Aunt Marie's hand and sat back, lapsing into a pensive gaze. "More difficult to leave too."

"You won't want to leave," Marie said. "Not with readily available resources and support. No creatures, less people. Harder to find, harder to get to. Greater chance of survival all the way around."

A whiff of Bordeaux and chocolate teased my senses, but I still wasn't biting. "What about when those resources run out?"

"You'll cross that bridge when you get there, just like everyone else. Burtonshire has reserves. It's my bunker times a hundred. When it comes time to replenish, you'll have people to forage with, strategies in place to find what you need. You can't think that far ahead right now."

"I wonder why these things were drawn to the islands out west," Florence mused. "Why they tried climbing the cliffs."

"Maybe they're attracted to the terrain, the climate, the

vegetation . . . we may never know. There was another sighting two or three months ago, somewhere near Algeria. They ventured pretty far inland, then retreated back to the coast, slipped into the Mediterranean Sea."

"You're sure it has to be this colony." Mom ran a finger along the rim of her glass. "If we go, it has to be Burtonshire."

"There are inland colonies in the mountains. Some in Tennessee, Montana, Colorado. There's one right in our back-yard, up in the Poconos. If I thought I could send you there and trust you'd be safe, I'd drive you there myself in a heart-beat. But the inland colonies are locking down too. Gates are closing. We're out of time. And after talking with Jeb this morning, I'm more certain than ever you don't wanna be there, anyway. Better you not be landlocked. If the creatures do turn out to be aggressive, I'd rather you be trapped in a remote, elevated environment with a dependable team of defense, not stuck somewhere inland, at the mercy of too many desperate, unpredictable men. You can't beat Burton-shire. I got to Jeb just in time. A lot of people would kill to be on this train."

"Are you two involved?"

"I'm a married woman."

"You're a widow, Marie. Are you seeing one another?"

"Bob is my husband." Her voice dropped an octave, dry and cracked. "My husband is dead. Jeb owed me a favor, and I called it in. That's all."

My brain thumbed through everything she'd told us like a computer calculating its results, sifting through and orga-nizing the data. I one hundred percent understood not wanting to leave this place, especially from my aunt's point of view. But wasn't this an exception to the rule? Alien lifeforms, invading from the seas, on the verge of throwing our planet into inconceivable chaos. "Look." I licked my lips. "If this Burtonshire place is as safe as you believe it is, then you're coming with us. Isn't there a farmer friend of yours who can look after the animals until—"

"Until we come home?" Aunt Marie snorted softly. "Until we make it back?"

Florence expelled a breath. "I'm with Jo on this, Marie. You're coming with us."

"You're not gonna win this one, Florence."

"Make an exception."

"No. Even if I did, the last train is full. There's nothin' more to be done about it."

"You're a part of their network, they'll find you a seat."

"Doesn't work that way. If it did, they'd have to make allowances for everyone."

"I bet Jeb will be on that train."

"He's staying too. You're beatin' a dead horse."

Mom flicked a finger between us. "Fine. Either Jo and I stay here with you, or I'll take Jo out on my own, find another way to live. If you insist on kicking us out, I'd rather take our chances on our own. I won't put our lives in these strangers' hands."

"Don't even try playing that card with me," Marie warned.

"Who's playing?"

"Don't turn my words around. No one's kicking you out. I'm telling you to choose life. You should know by now manipulation won't get you very far under this roof, little sister." A hard glare passed between them, and in it was years of unspoken history, foster homes and abandonment, separation and trauma only they understood. "Sometimes we need people, Florence. This is one of those times. You just have to make sure you pick the right ones to have in your corner. Staying here with me isn't the answer. I know you want it to be, I know we all want it to be, but I won't be able to protect you the way Burtonshire will."

Color drained from my mother's complexion.

"The same goes for you," I spoke up. "You need people too."

"I have lots of people, darlin'."

"Yeah, and all of them will be underground. We can protect each other. We have everything we need right here."

"You're not hearing me, kiddo. There won't be anything left here to protect."

Florence shifted. "You don't know that."

"Enough," I said, standing. "We're not leaving you here on flat land, around a few measly rolling hills. If everything you're saying is true, then living in this bunker means nothing if these things do attack. Who knows what they're capable of? Not to mention what people will do when they find you down here. You'll have to come up for air eventually. They'll wait until you're weak and vulnerable, they'll find a way in. You don't honestly expect us to throw you to the wolves."

"This is the way it's meant to be." Aunt Marie straightened, sealing the words with a resolved glare. "Someday you'll understand."

"Tell her, Mom." I touched Florence's elbow, pinning her with an emphatic stare. "Demand she goes with us."

Florence's glass flute shifted between her fingers, from palm to palm. She watched the untouched red wine roll back and forth, hazy and unresponsive to my plea.

"Mom?"

"What happens when we get off this train?" she asked Marie, voice featherlight. "How does it work—getting onto the island?"

Mouth agape, I sucked in a breath. She couldn't seriously be entertaining the idea of leaving without her sister. Not possible. My fingers raked over my front hairline, head falling forward into my hands.

"Come on," Aunt Marie replied, sealing the cherry jar shut. "Let's finish getting you ready. I'll give you the rundown." She stood, loaded the packs onto our shoulders, and led us to the stairwell toward the fortified exit. Like a paper doll, a mere prop in one of my stage shows, Aunt Marie dressed me for the part. My mother followed wordlessly on her trail, while my own consonants and syllables died in my windpipes. The backpack weighed me to the floor. Raw, festering terror sliced through me, a ball of disbelief, denial, and numbness demanding to be felt, to be heard. Somehow, a decision had been made. I couldn't pinpoint the moment it materialized, but Florence made the call for us. Reduced to invalid, invisible words floating around the picnic table, my concerns were smothered down in the cement bunker. The sealed, blast-proof steel door locked them tightly away as I adjusted the backpack straps on my shoulders and ascended the stairwell behind the women holding my destiny in their hands.

TWENTY-ONE

" There will be one, maybe multiple buses after the train," Aunt Marie said, pointing at plates of finger sandwiches and potato salad on the kitchen counter. She'd insisted we eat real food before starting our journey west. "Don't be afraid. Just trust where the Intake Guards direct you. They'll route you to the right buses. The train is a private railcar with clearance arrangements with Amtrak. The atmosphere will be dicey with everything going down, but hold your ground and stay clear, stay focused." Following her own advice, Aunt Marie zipped around the kitchen with sharp, purposeful precision, intermittently sweeping plaster and glass into piles, collecting the aftermath of the quake into a dustpan. "The guards will make sure you get to where you need to go. Make sure they see your regular photo IDs, along with these IDs right away, and name-drop as much as you need to. Tell 'em you're there on Jeb Hadley's direct order. Lancaster County, Alliance District 307. It's all right here." She rested the broom against the counter and retrieved two faded IDs akin to vintage library catalog cards, with the alliance district number and destination stamped across the lines.

"What about weapons?" my mother asked, gobbling down one little sandwich after another. I hadn't seen her eat this much since before we left Philadelphia.

I picked pieces of celery from the potato salad, stabbing them with my fork. "Weapons? Heaven help us."

"It's a valid question," she mumbled through stuffed cheeks. "How are we supposed to defend ourselves?"

Shooting my aunt a look, I dropped my fork, giving up on the whole eating thing. "Hide the bat, please."

"Your momma's right. It's a valid question. But an unnecessary one. That's part of the intake department's job: to protect you. The guards will handle anything that comes your way."

I cringed at her response and considered protesting again, raising all the same points I'd tried to raise down in the survival bunker, but I knew better. The effort would be fruitless. Why bother questioning the decision, as if I had any real choice in the matter? The answer was alarmingly simple. Wherever Florence was, there I'd be, and all three of us knew this, even if our destination seemed like an asinine one to me.

"No," Mom said, flicking the remains of a croissant onto her plate. "Not good enough. We have to be able to defend ourselves. The bat goes with us. As does the bow."

"The bow can go," Aunt Marie agreed. "It's a skill Burtonshire will want. When they learn you can shoot, you'll be even more valuable to them. That's another major asset. Pack up your case when you're done eating. The bat stays." She cut me a glance, winking as she resumed working the broom over the tile.

"Not like we can carry anything else anyway," I said, watching Mom intently. Wrenching my hands together, I shifted in my seat. "What about me?"

"You want to carry a weapon?" Florence met my gaze.

I couldn't believe we were having this conversation.

"No, I mean, how will I be valuable to these people? I don't shoot bows or kickbox or have a superpower . . . what if they don't want me?"

Mom leaned forward. "Is that how this works, Marie? We have to prove we're assets?"

"Yes and no." She stopped sweeping, stumbling off into thought, as if siphoning the words into a funnel to formulate a response. "In essence, the colonies believe in the survival-of-the-fittest mentality. Those most prepared, the healthiest, naturally increase their chances of survival, but everyone should contribute what they can. The focus is to enrich the livelihood of the colonies as a whole. They're interested in skill, natural talent—your gifts. They recruit residents based on what they'll contribute to the community, to society."

My brows rose steadily. "And if you have nothing to contribute?"

"We all have something to give, hon. You and your momma already have an advantage. Between your design skills, your momma's musical talents, and your celebrity status, you have more than enough to offer."

Once again, privilege to the rescue. "Wait. What, am I gonna make them costumes for their next Shakespeare production? I doubt my design skills will be useful to a bunch of off-the-grid island-dwellers. My celebrity name is by association." I glanced over at Mom. "What good is a famous name to these people if all I can do is dress up a set?"

"Sometimes you surprise me, kiddo." Aunt Marie tossed me a saucy look. "Just when I thought you think as outside of the box as your momma, you go and say somethin' like that."

"They need clothing, don't they?" Florence's hand suddenly touched my elbow, a warm, maternal contact that

calmed my heart rate. "Blankets, quilts . . . all kinds of necessi-
ties, I'm sure."

"You sew, hon." Aunt Marie leaned over the kitchen
counter and nicked my chin with her thumb and forefinger.
"Sewing supplies are in the third pocket of your backpack. Tell
'em you know your way around a Singer. While you're at it,
run upstairs and grab your sketch pads, so you can show 'em
your work. You'll both need to demonstrate your skill in the
admission ring."

"Come again?"

"The admission what?" Mom and I blurted simulta-
neously.

Aunt Marie slowed, propping the broom against the wall.
Gaze suddenly downcast, she leaned into the counter. A pause
bounced between the three of us.

"When you arrive at the ferry dock, you'll be expected to
demonstrate your skills." She spoke the words carefully, as if
playing a relay race with us, passing a ticking bomb from her
hands to ours. "Don't let that send you into a panic. This is
how they verify your claims, test that you're able to deliver
what you promise to bring to the community before entry."

Jumbled questions, far too many than my mind could
process in the span of seconds, rushed forth. "You're saying
they're gonna make me sew for them? Right there on the
spot? Like an interview?"

"Like an audition," she countered. "You show them what
you can do, and the judges will grant or deny you access to the
final round."

My eyes, wide now, roamed over to Florence, then back.
"Define *round*."

"Admittance. Your place on the boat, your golden ticket to
the Isle."

Florence's lithe form suddenly towered beside me as she

lifted herself from the barstool. "You're saying none of this is a guarantee."

"I'm saying this is the process. The colonies put this protocol into place for a reason, and we have to abide by it, but it's not something you two need to be concerned about, because you'll meet their requirements. Your reputation alone secures your admittance, Jeb is sure of it. Burtonshire wants and needs people with influence, charisma. They need leaders, strong residents. You offer all of that and then some. Just demonstrate your skills, do as you're told, and you'll be fine."

Florence pinched the bridge of her nose. "Back up a minute, Marie. This is a lot. You're asking a lot of us. I don't even recognize you. I don't know who you are anymore."

"I could say the same about you, Florence."

A vein throbbed like lightning across Mom's forehead. "This is not some warm, cozy, tree-hugging off-the-grid community you're selling us here. Now you're talking admission rings? Auditions? Winning tickets? What are you getting us involved with? How can you assure us these people are safe? Or even sane? How do I know we can rely on them for this support and protection?"

"Well, I'm sure some of them are off their damn rockers. Obviously I can't vouch for everyone on the island, and I can't guarantee you won't run into problems along the way. The point is the people who make up this community share the same goals, have the same vision. They're all after the same thing. You'll be in this together. No one's telling you to throw common sense out the window, Flo. Keep your wits about you. Stay alert. Don't let your guard down. But give these people a chance. You just have to take my word for it. As I said, it's a process. Yes, it's sterile. Meticulous. Regimented. It was created this way for a reason. The entire system was designed with the possibility of a catastrophic event in mind. Structure and regulation are a must in order for the system to work. Please try to keep that in perspective."

Mom began to pace. "And you trust this Jeb, no questions asked? Why? Because he did you a favor, getting us some seats on a train? How do we know his people won't toss us out on the streets once we make it to the ferry terminal, to this admission ring? What if they decide they don't need whatever we have to offer? What if they kidnap us and sell us to the highest bidder? These are things I need to know before we galavant across the country, Marie."

Aunt Marie cleared her throat. "Yes, I trust him, Flo. Of course I've asked questions. Tens, hundreds of thousands of them over the last six months alone. But that's the difference between you and I nowadays, isn't it? I choose to trust. You can only chew something over for so long. Eventually, you choose. Call it blind, call it crazy, call it whatever you want, but it always comes down to a choice. You have to weigh your options and decide whether or not to jump."

Something passed between them, scorching embers, my aunt goading my mother into some sort of challenge.

"Forgive me if I'm not thrilled about risking our livelihood based on a hunch of yours," Florence's gruff voice pushed through clenched teeth. "Jeb may be your friend, but he's a stranger to us. This network is yours, not ours."

Another wave of electricity sparked within. There was still an *us*. We were still a unit. Florence might not be the same woman she was before we got to the farm, but she was still my mom, and I was still her sidekick.

Marie's frame drifted forward like a spirit rising from its tomb. "A hunch backed by plenty of research and tangible proof, and no less of a hunch than your decision to leave the city."

"Excuse me?"

Gliding around the kitchen counter, Marie aligned herself

head-to-head with her sister. "When you drove away that day, was it just a *hunch* that leaving your cheating, lying husband was the right thing to do? Or did you drive away knowing it was the *only* thing to do?"

A tight breath rattled in my throat, pushing me to move between them, but my legs turned to jelly.

"Well?" Aunt Marie pressed. "Come on, let's hear it."

"How dare you."

"You drove away without question, and why do you think that is, Flo?"

"There's no comparison here."

"You left that life knowing full well that if you stayed, it would eat you alive and there would be nothing left."

"Of course I knew that," Florence seethed, muscles popping along her neck. "Here I had safety. A place to rest, a place to breathe and thrive."

"You call selling overalls at the tractor store *thriving*?"

"There's nothing wrong with this life, Marie. It's a beautiful life."

"Oh, it's a fine life. But it's mine, Florence. It fits me. It's my beautiful life. You're more than this town, you're someone else, with an entirely different purpose. No matter how safe you thought my farm was compared to the city, you were still walking into a big ol' gaping hole of uncertainty the minute you smashed up Asher's car. Out here you're left with the quiet and your thoughts and all the muck built up inside of you that you gotta face. Face it here or face it in Burtonshire, it's gonna follow you wherever you go, and you were kiddin' yourself if you thought it was gonna be any easier here, while you were shoveling horse manure. Damn it, Florence, this is your new reality. You really wanna fight to the death, trying to ignore it?"

Florence ground her teeth. "I'm not ignoring anything."

"The hell you're not. If you wanna rob yourself of the

chance to be happy again, to have peace and joy, spit out a million reasons why you shouldn't believe what I'm telling you, then knock yourself out." Her long hair swung over her shoulders as she threw her hands up. "But I'm not gonna stand here and listen to it. You're meant for much more than this, and so is Jo. On the island, you have a shot—not just at survival, but at purpose. There, you can give, grow, be who you were always meant to be. You stay here with me, you're lookin' at a future wasteland. You'll throw it all away."

"We're *not* leaving you," I blurted again, moisture pooling along my eyelids. "Mom, don't back down. Either she comes with us or we don't go."

Aunt Marie shut me down. "Jo, go upstairs right now and get your sketchbooks."

My hand moved to Mom's shoulder, hesitating, unsteady. Her body heat rolled off her skin like flowing lava.

"Go on, now," Aunt Marie urged, voice louder.

My body jolted at the command, and I raced upstairs to collect my sketches. Dizziness clouded my vision as I scanned the rest of my belongings. Not that I'd taken much, leaving our life in the city behind, but the few things I'd preserved seemed to wrap a viselike coil around my neck, connecting me to this place I'd just begun to envision as home. The moisture leaked from my eyes. My lashes fluttered. Desperate thoughts, nagging and infuriating, tapped at my throbbing temples: *I want to go home. I want to see Dad. I'm not ready to say goodbye.*

TWENTY-TWO

Rushing back downstairs, I found Florence and my aunt silent and winded, gripping the edges of the counter, as if they'd just called off a duel. I bit my lip, tasting blood. "I don't like this," I said, returning to Mom's side. "Any of it. Everything Mom's saying makes sense. It's all a game. A gamble. Who are these people, these admission ring judges? They make this place sound like some kind of utopia, but who gave them the key? Who gave them authority to dole out the jackpot winnings?"

With a wry grin, Aunt Marie's eyes shimmered with dampness. "You are your mother's daughter, kiddo."

"It *is* a game," my mother said, glancing pensively out the window. "A dangerous one."

Understatement of the century.

The edge melted from her tone, but her next statement pierced my ears. "Marie's right, though. We have to go. We have to take our chances either way."

"Wait. No." I chucked the sketches on top of my bag. "What if we went home first? Checked on Helen? Visited—"

"There's no time," Aunt Marie said softly. "I'm sorry, Jo."

The three of us looked over at the radio, but no one moved to turn it on.

Mom's fingers grazed her lips as her gaze wandered farther. "It doesn't end when we make it onto the boat, does it?"

The metallic taste intensified on my tongue. "Meaning?"

"There will be more tests."

"How do you know that?" I glanced at Marie. "Is that true, Auntie?"

Aunt Marie hesitated. "Possibly. I'm familiar with the admission process, but arriving on the island is only the beginning. Each colony runs differently, and things are changing fast. I admit I don't have all the answers, I can't tell you what comes after, especially now, but . . ."

A taut sting, like the tip of an ice pick, tickled its way down the back of my neck.

"I'm convinced it's where you need to be. Whatever hoops they make you jump through, remember it's all about commitment. The founders are trying to maintain something safe and secure," she continued. "They want to bring in only those who want to support the community. Burtonshire wants everyone to benefit. New residents pledge to protect and defend one another. Once admitted, you make a public declaration of loyalty to the community. Yes, the selection process is exclusive. It has to be, since space and resources are limited. They're attempting to be practical, trying to think long term about the survival of the colony. I don't agree with it all, but I understand the logic."

My words burned as they rolled off my tongue. "We're really doing this."

"Yes," Florence whispered. "I believe we are."

"What do we do for money? How will we pay bills and survive?"

Marie glanced at her wristwatch. "Where you're going, you won't need money, hon. Your talents and skills are your currency. You'll be provided for based on your service to the community." She reached for my sketch pads, folded and stuffed them into my backpack.

"And if we want to come home?"

Aunt Marie slipped her arm around me. "There's no saying how long I'll make it out here, but if I'm still here, you know my door is always open, hon. Always." Her nose buried itself in my hair, and she planted a kiss on my head. Her hold on me tightened, and Florence squeezed her eyes shut, turning away. Silence zinged between the three of us, saying what we couldn't say aloud: The cross-country trek back to Lancaster might be impossible under the potential conditions headed our way—if we could even get off the island once we'd arrived. And only God knew what the mainland would be like if these creatures intended to dominate dry land.

I sank into Aunt Marie's embrace. She could wring the life right out of me for all I cared. I needed someone to hold onto me, someone to extinguish the surreal fog invading the room. Florence's presence moved, but not toward us. It wasn't a group hug she was after. She gravitated to the piano, its shiny expanse of black pulling her like a magnet from the kitchen over to the living room bay windows. Her gaze fell on the keys, motionless fingers hovering just above, barely skimming the ivory.

Aunt Marie straightened, watching. "Would you like to play before we leave?"

"No time."

"We can spare five more minutes."

"No."

"Please, Mom?"

She reached out, touched the lid with her fingertips. "Are you ready, darling?" Her empty stare roamed toward me. "It's time to go."

I'd never hated those words more.

With another glance at her wristwatch, Aunt Marie inhaled sharply. "Okay. Let's get this show on the road. I'll pack up your bow and meet you in the truck. If you wanna try to send any emails, make any calls, now's the time."

Florence nodded, and Aunt Marie released me. My earlier intent to go home, just long enough to say goodbye, drew me back.

"Mom. You're one hundred percent, absolutely sure about this?"

She heaved her bag over one shoulder. "When I try to talk myself out of it, you know what I see?"

A barrage of possibilities filtered through me. Dad, sleeping with the other woman. Dad in the delivery room, welcoming another newborn baby. Countless lies on the telephone, nights away, claiming to be somewhere other than where he really was. Past visions of happiness—were they ever real?

"The dove," she replied with a dry smirk. For a second, a flare of life invaded her hollow eyes. "Landing at your feet."

My parted lips clamped shut, shoving the possibilities back down into the deepest recesses, where they belonged.

"You're not alone, darling. I'm afraid too. Yet I still can't bear to go back. Since we got to the farm, all I can think about is my role in our life, in the city. I was your father's wife. The city loved me, gave me a place to belong. It wasn't just streets and sidewalks. It was a living thing." Shaking her head, she brushed some rogue bangs from her forehead as if swatting away the memories. "But I had it all backwards. I thought it gave me life, but it was really a parasite."

A scream sparked inside that warred with my mind, a need to caution her, to show her how far off-base she'd wandered, but my mind won, pinning my tongue to the roof of my mouth.

A manic laugh snaked its way from her throat. "When I

was thirteen, I got stranded somewhere on Route 66. Stopped in a gas station for water, desperate for my next ride. I said yes to a man in a van, waiting by the fuel pump. He offered to take me all the way to Santa Monica. He took me all the way. I took his wallet. Slashed his tires when he stopped at a diner to use the restroom and escaped. When I made it to the pier, I bought some elote and gave the rest of the cash to some busker violinists. I swayed to the music, waves crashing behind me, and I pictured the man's face, what it must've looked like the moment he walked back to his van to find me gone. That was the best street corn I've ever had." She looked once more at the piano, as if she could still hear the music on the pier. "Once the world takes everything from you, it loses. You win all the power. Once it empties you out and gives you its worst, you're invincible. Joke's on the city. That's how I know we're going to be okay. You'll see."

I swallowed hard, picturing the dove. And just like that, released a silent prayer for God to help me believe her.

———

As if a vacuum had sucked all signs of life from the truck cab, we drove along in wary anticipation. Not even the obnoxious scrape of the wiper blades on the windshield or pieces of tinkering metal in the pick-up's bed could distract us. If anything, the noise only accentuated the vast gulf of wordlessness and eerily lifeless streets surrounding us.

Aunt Marie was first to speak. "There are burner phones in your bags, preloaded with minutes. Not sure how long service will last, but it can't hurt to hang on to them. Take this too." Lifting a hip as she drove, she pried a silver zippered case from inside her coat's breast pocket and handed it to me. "A healthy chunk of my savings. It'll come in handy for the trip, get you what you need until you reach the island. The bag's fire- and waterproof."

Sitting between her and Mom, I glanced at them both then unzipped the case, running my thumb through the stacks of crisp bills.

"That's too much, Marie," Mom said, peering down at the cash. "I already have plenty."

"You'll burn through cash fast, believe me. Take it. You two will need it more than I ever will."

"Not necessarily," I said. "Maybe this is all a big hoax. Maybe we'll all wake up tomorrow morning and realize it's just a really bad dream. Wouldn't that be nice?"

Florence took the case from me and zipped it back up, tucking it inside her coat. "Not really. I'm done with nightmares."

Aunt Marie's throat cleared.

"Look at it as another chapter," Florence added. "A new adventure."

My fingers clenched over my thighs as I discarded her statements, opting for silence like my aunt. We continued west on nearly empty highways, doubly chilled by the absence of air traffic. An ambulance flew past us, then another, followed by a string of police cars and then nothing. Miles of hills sprawled around us, brown and barren. I dozed off, flinching awake every so often, my head resting on Mom's shoulder.

Quiet activity surrounded the rural, neglected-looking train station when we arrived. Small groups gathered, chatting together, congregating in tight cliques. Suitcases swayed as single-file lines formed on the platform. Hopeful passengers stared down the tracks, waiting for the mystery train. Everyone was moving, lips were speaking, but the space was muted, only the scuffle of shoes bouncing off the pavement. I half expected tumbleweeds to blow by in this abandoned ghost town crawling with words understood but barely spoken aloud.

Aunt Marie led us to a woman holding a clipboard near the edge of the platform. The woman blended into the crowds, donned in a parka and jeans, all neutral colors and comfort. Aunt Marie seemed to know her on a first-name basis. She checked the three of us in and then I left them to chat, popping inside the station house. The little brick building's yellow paint peeled inside and out, and a dust-caked, motionless clock was suspended above the entrance. A boarded up, dilapidated bathroom door loomed beside the vacant teller window. A retro cigarette dispenser and creaky snack vending machine were stacked back-to-back, adjacent to the useless restroom. I walked over to the machines and stared into the glass displays. My fingers moved quickly on impulse, depositing all the quarters in my change purse. Packs of cigarettes dropped into the bin. I scooped them up, then stocked up on chips and candy. Murmured surprise lit up nearby, awe that the machines actually worked. A line formed behind me, pushing into my space as I hurried out of the way, jamming the snacks and smokes into my pockets and socks.

Hopping on one foot, I cursed down at my ankle as a pack of menthols tumbled from one sock onto the floor. I plucked it up and turned in circles, hair falling into my eyes as it loosened from my braid. I blew at the pesky strands, pausing when I saw Mom and Aunt Marie watching.

"What?" I asked, shuffling closer to them.

"Planning on picking up a new habit? Or just a bad case of the munchies?" Aunt Marie said with stifled amusement.

Mom's gaze dropped to my puffy, overstuffed boots.

I glared back at them. "Hello? It's called bartering?"

"Learned a few things in prison, have we?"

"Too bad you never started that stand-up act, Auntie. I think you missed your life's calling."

Mom brushed my braid over my shoulder and patted my cheek. "Oh, my darling."

I pulled a bag of chips from inside my shirt, ripped it open, and started munching. Personally, I felt a whole lot better now showing up to this island with more currency. "Laugh now, but you'll thank me later."

A harsh, distant siren blared along the train tracks, drawing everyone huddled inside the station out onto the platform, scurrying to join the single-file lines. My heart hammered away, the salty snack in my stomach turning sour. The three of us turned to one another, arms reaching, eyes searching.

"I'm staying," I suddenly blurted, heart giving out. "I'm staying on the farm. In the bunker."

"Joanna." Mom's hand gripped my elbow.

"I can't do this."

"You must," Aunt Marie's voice laced the charged air, the train's whistle approaching.

"Mom, don't go. Let's stay. Let's fight."

Florence's fingers loosened on my arm. "You stay. It's okay, Jo. I won't force you."

Aunt Marie's voice, fueled with militant urgency, killed my reply. "Your momma won't force you, but I will. You're not splitting up. You're not staying. Get in the damn line. Now. Or I'll wrestle you to the ground, throw you onboard, and strap you to the seat myself."

"Mom was right. I need to go back to the city. I'm not ready. I won't go, Auntie. Not unless you come with us."

"Joanna," Aunt Marie seethed, "there is no going back. There's no room for me. The seats are yours. Get on the train."

Florence's words assailed me from the right, *Stay, darling, stay,* while Aunt Marie's struck from the left. My muscles locked up, lungs tightening. The train roared. The tracks rattled. The woman with the clipboard approached, leading us into the line, asking questions, words I couldn't hear.

Stay, darling, stay.
Get on the train, Joanna.

The station's composed, subdued energy suddenly grew teeth, gnashing violently, nipping at my ears and ankles. Panic pooled in my gut, warming my cheeks and chest. Aunt Marie's words implored me until they drifted into a sea of faces, moving farther away, down the single-file line. Florence mouthed sounds, moving in the opposite direction, away from her sister, off the platform and up onto the train. Forward motion carried me along, my elbow linked with Mom's, but my aunt's muddled words kept drawing my attention backward, over my shoulder. I couldn't see her anymore, but I could hear her, feel her presence. Suitcases bumped my knees as more passengers filed inside the railcar with us, backpacks knocking into my shoulders and chest. A ragdoll strewn into a vicious current, I bobbed aimlessly down the aisle, Aunt Marie and Mom's words thrashing me around at the surface.

I found myself seated, cold and still in a red-and-white velvety seat. There were two more just like it, one on each side of me. Once again, I was in the middle. Always in the middle. I looked out the window for Aunt Marie's face. The chill wouldn't leave my bones. Just as I considered moving to the window seat, Mom squeezed past me, filling the space, chest rising and falling quietly as she settled in.

"Stored our things two compartments down," she said, loosening the top button of her coat. Tugging at the collar, she followed my gaze out the window, scanning the faces for signs of Marie. "We'll call her when we make it to the next stop."

I quit my search and rested my head back against the seat.

"The phones will work," she said, talking to herself. "They'll work."

A voice from an intercom announced momentary departure, instructing us to wait for Intake Officers to make their rounds, whatever that meant. My hands flattened on the armrests. The railcar's energy fizzed while people finalized their bag storage and found their seats. The engine hissed and steam plumed along the platform. A gust of astonished laughter rippled down the aisle, near the railcar's right entry, as a tall guy clad in a baggy gray business suit tripped and stumbled onto the train just as it began to move. Out of breath, he caught his balance on the edge of someone's seat. He carried no bag, just a bewildered grin and a piece of paper, which he presented to one of the clipboard people. A sheen of sweat shone on his forehead when he folded the paper back up and stuffed it inside one of his oversized pockets. Dark, intense eyes roamed the seats as he made his way down the aisle.

"This one taken?" he asked, pausing at the empty space beside me.

I shook my head, gesturing for him to sit.

"Thanks." He nodded politely at Mom and me, his shoulders flinching as he lowered himself onto the red-and-white velvet. "These guys are trippin' if they think they're gonna get me on another train. You wouldn't believe what I had to go through to get here. Already been on one train and three buses. Gonna be honest, I don't even know where we are. Maybe you can tell me?"

"You're somewhere in Western Pennsylvania," Florence said absentmindedly. She remained fixated on the window, still studying, still searching.

"Where were you traveling from?" I asked, taking in the nasty cut on his neck.

"Boston." He winced as he shifted, a small, visible spasm jumping over the skin near the injury. "Lived and worked in the city. Ever been?"

"A few times, yeah."

"It's a good city. How about you two?"

"Coming from Lancaster."

"*Ahh*, okay, country girls. Sounds nice, livin' with all that fresh air and open land."

"It was."

"This place we're goin' sounds spacious."

"What do you know about it?"

"Nothin', really. Heard it was rustic. Some kinda island. You?"

I shrugged.

"This whole thing's a blur, right?" He snickered, shaking his head.

"That's one way to put it."

"Name's Mason." He extended a hand. I offered mine. "Pleasure, Miss . . ."

"Jo. Short for Joanna."

"Real pleasure, Miss Jo."

"Just Jo."

"Right. Jo, just Jo."

"This is my mom, Florence." Mom gave him a half-hearted wave, her distant eyes momentarily flickering in his direction. "We're a little tired. Been a long day."

"*Oooohhhh*, yes ma'am." He exhaled and whistled. "I feel that." Our gazes met. One glance at this guy—all banged up, suit torn—stirred the sour bitterness in my stomach, reminding me it was still there, and that this long day was far from over.

Twenty-Three

We'd barely hunkered down for the trip west when men and women with old-school walkie-talkies clipped to their belts started down the railcar's aisle. They made their way from the front, combing through each set of passenger seats, spewing a list of obviously well-rehearsed, scripted questions.

"You okay?" I asked Mason, who'd gone abruptly quiet since our introduction.

Watching the guards make their way closer to us, he blinked, dazed. "Sorry?"

"No offense or anything, but . . . you sort of look like you might hurl."

"I might. Straight up."

I noticed a slight tremble in his chest, not far from the cut above his shoulder blade. "Everyone on this train has the same look, so you're in good company."

"Not you, though."

"You kidding me? I'm terrified."

"Could've fooled me." His head pivoted as he snuck a

glance at Florence. "You both look like you can handle yourselves."

"We have good poker faces."

"It's just hittin' me, ya know? This morning, I was makin' breakfast, rushin' out the door for work. Next thing I know, more tremors and news of the Turn and then this guy is giving me a ticket at South Station, and *boom*. Here I am."

"The Turn?"

"That's what they're calling it. The invasion, I mean. Haven't you heard?"

"Oh." I shook my head. "Sort of. We've heard bits and pieces. Tell me about it. Just yesterday I was trying to wrap my brain around—"

"Charles Douglas Harvey?" a guard's voice rolled over us. "Is there a Charles Douglas Harvey here?"

"Right here," the guy who'd called himself Mason raised his hand, looking down the aisle toward the guard. Florence's silent presence suddenly reemerged, her neck craning slowly to my right, peeking over at him. I followed her gaze.

He cut us a look. "Mason's a nickname."

The guard approached, a middle-aged redheaded man with a slick comb-over and wiry fogged-up glasses. He pulled the glasses from his nose and gave them a quick swipe across his shirt sleeve. "You're supposed to be in Seat 3B," the man said curtly, sliding the glasses back up the bridge of his nose. "Is there a reason you're not in 3B?"

"Sorry, man. I barely made it in time and just took the first seat I could find."

Peering down at the rows behind us, the guard scribbled on his clipboard. "Well, it seems someone else is in your assigned seat, so no harm done. We'll sort it out. Moving on. Please confirm your destination."

"Uh . . . Burton Island, I think?"

"You *think*?"

"Whatever it says on my paper here." He scrambled to retrieve the ID card paperwork from his pocket. He squinted, rubbing the sweat from his eyes as he pointed to the handwriting, showing the guard. "Oh, my bad. The Isle of Burtonshire. Fancy."

"You don't need to present the paperwork again. Just confirming a few details to ensure we route you to the correct place." The man's pen raced across the clipboard. "Okay, now state your offering."

"My offering . . ."

"What you intend to contribute to the community."

"Right. Okay. Music, I guess?"

"I'm the one asking the questions here."

"Music. I said music."

The guard rolled his eyes. "Define music. In what way will you contribute your skill?"

"Well, I play the guitar . . ."

"Do you read music?"

Mason's eyes dropped to the man's feet.

"I asked if you read music."

"He's not deaf," I piped up. "He heard you."

Mason bristled beside me, hand brushing the armrest. "I play by ear. Is that going to be a problem?"

"It depends."

"On?"

"If you have anything else to contribute."

Shrugging, he released a flustered breath. "Don't we all? I mean . . . I know how to cook. I'm sure there's more I can't think of right now."

"Tell me the primary skill you were nominated for."

"Oh, right. Okay, I thought you meant any skills at all—"

"I do. Any known skills you can rattle off are helpful for your record, but let's start with your primary talent. On what basis were you nominated?"

Mason's fingers twitched, intensifying the trembling of his hands. "Teaching. I'm a teacher."

"What do you teach?"

"Middle school, mostly."

"Subjects?"

"Reading . . . literature."

"Last place of employment?"

Frown lines creased around Mason's mouth as he stared ahead at the back of the seat in front of us, studying it like an invisible textbook. "Wickham Prep—Academy, Prep . . . downtown Boston."

"*Hhhmm.*" The pen scribbled away. "Good. Age?"

"Thirty."

"Marital status?"

"Single."

"Ever married? Any children?"

"Nope."

"Okay, that's all for now. You'll be moving to the number 453 bus when we reach Missoula. You take that all the way to Washington. Listen for the transfer announcement in Montana. Don't miss it. That's the end of the road for this train."

"What if we don't make it that far?"

"We will." Sharply shifting his attention to me, next, the guard asked me to confirm my name.

"But you can't really promise us that, right?" Mason's wary voice cut me off. "What happens if we get stranded before then? Do you guys have some kinda back-up plan or somethin'?"

The guard tapped his clipboard against his leg. "As I'm sure your nominator made you aware when they made you a candidate, there are no guarantees, only goals. Things are changing fast out there, and the number one *goal* is to keep things moving, to get as many people to where they need to be as quickly as possible, before the system breaks down entirely."

"No . . . I wasn't aware. I didn't have time to sit down and have a solid heart-to-heart with the guy who voted me into this seat, so . . ."

The guard's mild irritation suddenly took on an heir of scathing contempt. He cast a furtive glance down at his records. "Ah, yes. Says here your seat was secured thanks to forfeiture. Guess it was your lucky day. Look, man. We all have a sob story to share, but I have a job to do, and we all want the same thing, right? So please just cooperate and make this much easier on us all."

"We do? What do we want, exactly?"

"Yeah," I mumbled. "I'm a little unclear on that myself."

The man glared at me, then back at Mason. "Do you want to be on this train or not? Do you want the chance to outlive and long outlast everyone else on this continent? If you do, then give the questions a rest, because I assure you, if you don't, someone else out there who wants to survive and thrive, who'd kill to have your seat, will know when to shut their mouth. Especially under your circumstances."

My fingernails dug into the skin of my knees, the sting penetrating through my jeans. "Unbelievable."

"Excuse me?" The guard's gaze flicked toward me.

"Joanna," Florence's voice teetered over my shoulder, like an angel tugging me back to goodness and light.

"Here's a thought," I snapped, glaring up at the man. "What you're supposedly offering on this island is a friendly, happy, safe existence, right? Then maybe you should approach this thing a little differently. Ya know, be friendly. Be happy. Make us feel safe, instead of beating us over the head with the idea that we're easily disposable to you. If we're so replaceable, if there really are a hundred more of us out there on the platform just like us, just as special, just as equipped to make your colonies a better place, then why waste your breath threatening us?" I leaned forward, scooting to the end of my seat. "Toss us out, then. Hit the eject button, kick us to the curb. Go ahead—I dare you to find three other warm, healthy bodies out there who have the experience, knowledge, and backbone to bring the very same skills to your precious *community*. Lay off him. He's exhausted and in shock."

The guard sneered down at me like a little wife with little dreams, a woman who only belonged in the kitchen and just had the nerve to tell him there would be no dessert after dinner. A nerve pinched the back of my neck as I held my breath, praying that calling his bluff wouldn't backfire and land us all on the pavement at the next stop. Florence cupped her hand over her mouth. Mason sat up straight.

The guard's disgust bathed our row, landing in a heavy puddle at our feet. He flipped the pages on his clipboard. Returning to the top page, he scanned it, cheeks flushing as the cogs in his brain turned. He shifted his stance. "Miss . . . Joanna Kowalski, is it?"

"Grace," I corrected him. "Joanna *Grace* Kowalski."

"Right. As in, the daughter of . . ."

"Florence Kowalski." With a coy grin, Mom gave him a little wave.

"Of course." He gulped. "How stupid of me. I apologize."

"We're not the ones you owe an apology to." Mom jutted her chin at Mason. "Charles here is a good friend of ours. His mother played in the orchestra with me. Commuted back and forth from Boston to Philadelphia three days a week, for almost ten years."

"Mr. Harvey, I apologize for losing my temper."

Relief swelled as I settled back against my chair. Glory be to all that was holy, our names still carried some weight, even in the midst of an apocalypse. Tension bubbled in my ribcage at my mom's white lie, but I stifled the fear, thankful it had helped diffuse the situation.

"As you can imagine," the guard continued, falling all over himself, cheeks bright red, "things have been stressful around here. It's no excuse, I know."

"*Nah*, it's cool, man," Mason clapped the guard on his shoulder, startling him. "We're all just doing our best."

Florence's nose wrinkled as she smiled, while I perfected frosty indifference, channeling it like a lightsaber.

"Anyway, Mr. . . . ." Florence's tone sweetened.

"Herb," the guard said, puffing out his bony chest. "The name's Herb, Ms. Kowalski."

"Okay, Herb. Do you need Joanna and I to confirm any other details for you?"

"No, ma'am. I've got that covered. Just be sure to listen for the Missoula exit and—"

"Take the 453 bus to Washington, don't miss it," I said.

"You got it," Herb exhaled slowly. "Just . . . keep your admission IDs handy and your eyes and ears open. Oh, and Ms. Kowalski?" Herb looked at Mom.

"Please, call me Florence."

The red in his cheeks spread to his ears. "For the record, I think Asher got everything he deserved and then some. Me and my wife watched the footage of what you did to his car on repeat. Priceless." With a wink, Herb hopped and did a little fist pump. "Stay safe out there, ladies. You too, Charlie."

"Awe, gee. Thanks, Herb," she said, smiling through clenched teeth.

"*Charlie*?" I mouthed at Mason, biting back the reflex to laugh.

Herb regained his composure and moved on to the row behind us. Mason's upper body swung in our direction, alight with curiosity and unrestrained humor. "Okay, don't leave me hangin', now. One of you please tell me what just went down right there." He lowered his volume, moving in closer, bringing with him an aroma of sweat and spearmint. "Orchestra?"

"My mom's a musician."

Mason gawked.

"A professional one."

"For real?"

Florence melted back into her seat. "I used to be, yes."

"Still is," I said.

"You too?" Mason's eyes widened like a little kid at his first rock concert.

"No, I'm just her roadie."

"Don't listen to her," Florence whispered. "She sings. Plus she's an immensely talented designer."

"*Daaaaaamn*, so I'm in the presence of royalty, then."

Florence delivered one of her signature playful grins, and I wanted to shout at Mason, *That's my mom! That's her, do you see her? The one I've known since birth, the one I've known all along. Sometimes I lose her for a little bit there, but she's still around. Do you see what I see? Isn't she incredible?*

I chuckled and hushed him. "In our book, teachers are rockstars too."

Vibrant admiration faded from his face. "Yeah, I agree. They're great."

My grin fell as I watched the brightness dim in his chocolate eyes. "You're going to miss your job, aren't you?"

He resumed his original position, realigning his shoulders with the seat. "Guess I'll miss a lot of things."

I gently nudged his forearm. "Hey, you'll still have the chance to teach. Look at it this way . . . where we're headed, you'll have a whole new group of kids who'll need your help."

"I hope you're right."

"Herb said you wound up on this train because someone gave up their seat, right?"

"Somethin' like that."

"There you go, then. Everything happens for a reason and all that."

"You think that's true, or just somethin' we say to make each other feel better?"

"I think it's true. I think we end up wherever we're most needed. Where we belong."

Mason hummed thoughtfully, his eyes drowsy. I watched him doze off, head rolling limply to one side. Florence moved to rest her chin on my shoulder, her arm threading tightly through mine.

"Keep your distance," she whispered, eyes drifting shut. "He lied about his name."

"That doesn't mean anything," I whispered back. "He said it was a nickname."

"Means something."

I rolled my eyes. Typical Florence, always suspicious. "You're the one who made him our *good friend, Charles*."

"I don't have to like someone to show them compassion."

"How can you dislike someone you don't even know?" I cocked a brow in her direction, challenging my mother and her baffling contradictions.

"Easily. The second they lie."

I peered down at the dark, tired shadows above her cheekbones, the ones the reporters loved to point out in recent months, the sight chiseling and chipping at my heart. When I looked back over at Mason, he was out cold, snoring softly. Both he and Mom swam happily around dreamland, while I stared out the window, watching the miles skate on by.

TWENTY-FOUR

The bizarre burner phone's ringtone blared from my backpack as I sat munching on stale french fries. I regretted carrying my bag off the train with me, but Mom's was still stored away. Someone had to protect at least part of our remaining livelihood. For all we knew, it might be our final and greatest fortune. The train made only a few stops on the way out to Missoula, so when a retro diner near the tracks appeared during our next break somewhere in South Dakota, I'd jumped at the chance to go. The place won extra points for having no TVs. If it were a sports bar, there would no doubt be a million TVs, and everyone would be staring at them, crawling the walls as they watched the world cripple in panic. Here, golden oldies played while customers stared at their greasy menus and spoke in hushed voices over bitter coffee. I wrestled with the zipper on my bag to locate the obnoxious prepaid phone, praying I'd hear Tony's voice on the other end of the line. I still hadn't had any luck finding him, and the phone number the catering company gave me for Olivia had been disconnected. Mom hung over the jukebox, studying the song selection intently, as if making the wrong choice would cause the machine to combust. Tammy Wynette's "Stand by Your Man" suddenly filled the diner, turning heads from all directions.

"Jo?" Aunt Marie's voice drifted through the line when I answered.

"Auntie, thank God."

"How ya holdin' up, kiddo?"

"Uh oh," I mumbled.

"What now?"

"She's deviating from The Supremes to country."

"That can't be good. Dolly? 'I Will Always Love You'?"

"Nope. 'Stand by Your Man.'"

"Uh oh. Where are you?"

"At a diner. Not far from Sioux Falls, I think." I'd spoken to Aunt Marie a few times over the last few days, but each time we tried to cut straight to the important stuff, unsure how much longer we'd have the luxury of phone conversation. "A lot of places are open out this way, operating as usual. What's it like back home?"

"Have you seen any of the latest news?"

"A little. People watching on their phones and stuff on the train. Everyone packs into the diner car and exchanges info, swaps ideas, tries to solve the great mystery over cigars and brandy. I feel like we fell into some 1940s whodunnit film."

"Well, sorta the same around here. Been quieter than I expected. Folks are still trying to go about their business, as if the invasion's just some rumor invented by the press to sell papers."

"Think it's called denial."

"I don't blame 'em, I guess. Not one bit. Though we can't keep our heads buried in the sand forever."

"You're okay, though? Have everything you need?" We both laughed. Aunt Marie was prepared enough for all of us.

"I'm fine, hon. Nothin' I can't handle. Been a ghost town

around here. Everyone's waiting for the next ball to drop. Feels as if a rubber band's been pulled back and it's about to snap. Won't be pretty when it hits the fan. Any word on the admission process? They giving you any more details?"

"Not really, no." I bit the tough edge off a fry, then slathered the rest of it in ketchup to smother the stale taste. "Hoping we'll find out more as we get closer. Maybe when we transfer to the bus in Missoula."

"She's going to have to play, you know."

"Are you sure? The Intake Guard didn't seem interested in having her furnish proof of her skills. He didn't even bother confirming anything once we boarded. The minute he saw our names on his records, that seemed to be enough for him."

"The judges might not let you off as easily in the ring. Your status will impress them, but if you can't—or won't—deliver what they're expecting, be prepared for some kickback. Remember what I told you. Comply and cooperate, and it'll be smooth sailing. How's she been since we spoke last?"

I cast a glance over my shoulder. Mom had moved away from the jukebox and was now dancing to "Stand by Your Man" with an elderly gentleman in a cowboy hat. They laughed as they shuffled around the counter and he cradled her gently, making a sweet attempt to dip her. Nevermind the world was probably ending. Nothing a little country music and dancing couldn't cure. "She's happy right now. Beautiful as always. Laughing. But . . . she lapses into these spells, and it's like . . . it summons a thunderstorm. And she's the lightning."

Aunt Marie hummed. "You're gonna have to be her rock out there on the island. I know it feels the other way around to you, but don't let those feelings blur the reality. You'll have to help her get settled, keep her calm and leveled."

"You mean make sure she behaves."

"Bingo. Don't be those new neighbors, stirrin' up drama. Just try your best to keep the peace, honey."

"I'll do my best. Any more quakes out there?"

"No. Not since you left. Officials are saying the creatures are retreating, which might explain why."

"Retreating? Like giving up?"

"No. Just laying low. Tunneling back into the ocean floor, supposedly. So much BS news, so much hysteria, it's hard to tell. But the White House is backing up this claim. We'll see, I guess. No telling what these things will do next."

"What about your sources? What do they say?"

"That the retreat is a bunch of crap, naturally. Some kinda cover up."

I sighed, pushing away the plate of fries, turning to my chocolate shake. "Sounds shady, even to me. Even if they are retreating, it's not the end."

"You got that right. It's only the beginning."

"Auntie?"

"What is it, honey?"

"Do you think it's possible to hang on, even when the other person lets go?"

"Hang on to what?"

"I don't know . . . memories?"

"What makes you think it's not?"

"At first I thought I could. I mean, memories are the one thing no one, nothing can take away from you. No matter what changes around you or where life takes you, you'll always have them."

"Sounds like you've already answered your question, darlin'. You can keep those memories alive as long as you'd like. Just because someone else leaves them behind doesn't mean they aren't still alive in you. Ain't nothin' stoppin' you from taking them to the grave if you want."

I sipped my chocolate shake, thankful for its familiar

comfort, a simple pleasure from my childhood, which right now felt lightyears ago. "I thought that at first. I really did. But the longer we're on this train . . . I wonder."

"You don't have to give up hope, honey. Never. But be realistic. Eventually you're gonna have to decide how you live your life and who you'll be, no matter what your momma does, or if she doesn't decide to fight for herself. Remember, your momma's seen a lot, she's lived a colorful life. But this? This is uncharted territory for you both. The trick with memories is knowing which ones to let go. Some of them will eat away at you like cancer. Hang on to the good ones."

Silence passed between us. Something rustled on the other end of the line and then Aunt Marie said, "There's something else I need to tell you. I hate to bring this up now."

"I'm listening."

"Your daddy called. Wanted to see you and your mom."

Acid churned in my throat. "What did you tell him?"

"The truth. Told him you were gone."

My fingers left the frosty milkshake glass and moved to my throat, pressing against the acid burn. "I wanted to see him."

"I know. I hate that things happened this way, Jo. I really do."

"How'd he sound? Is he okay?"

"Unhinged. It wasn't an easy phone conversation."

"Does he know where we're going?" The words tangled with anger and heartache, catching in a sticky web. "Does he know how to find us? Have his daughters called you? Tried to reach us?"

"He knows you're headed for the Pacific Northwest, yes. I didn't give him your number. Figured you'd reach out to him if and when you wanted to. Haven't heard from the little girls, no."

"Thanks. If they do call, give them my number."

"You sure about that?"

"Mom promised them they could contact us any time. I want to keep that promise. Especially now."

"Whatever you wish, darlin'." There was a quiet pause. "Your momma doesn't have to know, Jo. If you want to tell her, it's up to you. I just wanted you to know that he tried to reach you, that he hasn't forgotten about you. It's important that you know that, carry it with you."

A timid round of applause sounded near the counter. Mom gave her partner a grateful little bow, and he tipped his hat at her in return. Customers smiled and shook Florence's hand, transfixed by her natural charisma, just as her fans were back home. She made friends, won people over, swayed them with otherworldly magic wherever she went. "You think I should call him, don't you," I replied, watching Mom pick up her quiver bag and walk over to the counter to pay the waitress.

"Can't answer that for you, hon. All I can say is that when a burden's weighing on you, it's better to do something about it sooner, rather than later. Before it's too late to change your mind."

More questions piled up, so many unsaid words desperate for exchange, hanging between us. A wave of nausea triggered me to push aside the remnants of my chocolate shake. I sat back against the blue and white leather booth, the rising volume of a woman's voice calling my attention to the cash register.

"Jo?" Aunt Marie's concerned tone pricked the line. I pivoted around, homing in on the interaction between Florence and the waitress. "What's happening? What's wrong?"

"I don't know . . ."

Tension pooled between Mom and the brunette waitress wearing a poodle skirt. The waitress stiffened behind the register, gaze darting around the room, while Mom's palm slammed the edge of the counter. Mom stared down, counting change aloud, pointing at each coin, repeating each syllable, though I couldn't make out what she was saying.

"I think I have to go," I said hoarsely. "She's causing a scene at the cash register."

"Okay, honey. Hang in there. Call me back when you can and tell me what's going on."

"I'll try." We shared hushed *I love yous* and then I clamped the phone into my sweaty palm and moved to the checkout counter. Florence rubbed her forehead and mumbled in agitation, shifting from foot to foot. Her irises, foggy with affliction, carried her to another place. Where was the free, lighthearted woman dancing just moments ago?

"Excuse me," I cut in, approaching the waitress at Mom's side. "Is there a problem?"

"I'm not sure." Alarmed, the brunette turned to me and slowly stepped backward, distancing herself from the register. "She paid, I gave her change and then she asked for a pie to-go . . ."

"Hey, Mom. What's going on?"

Florence counted the change again.

My voice lowered. "Mom? How about we go get some fresh air?"

Her reply came out in a raspy breath. "I don't need fresh air. I need another fifty cents for the pie."

"Pie? Okay, well we've got more than enough change. Here." I searched my pocket for my coin purse. I didn't want to advertise to the whole diner that we were comfortably swimming in cash, but if it was money Mom was so worried about, there was definitely no need to get so worked up.

"No, no," she insisted, scraping the coins across the counter toward the waitress. "I have it, look. Count it, please. It's all there."

"Ma'am, it's no problem, really," the waitress's shaky voice intervened. She turned to the dessert spinner display and retrieved a pie from the top shelf. "You wanted chocolate silk, I think?" She presented the pie, then slid it into a to-go box. "This one's on the house."

Watching Mom reach over to trace the coins with her delicate fingers, I tilted my chin up, glancing at the waitress. "Thanks, but we'd really like to pay for it." I slid her a crumpled hundred-dollar bill. "Sorry for the troub—"

"I said we have the fifty cents!" Florence lunged forward and sent the coins flying across the counter. They sprayed the waitress's poodle skirt then bounced to the black-and-white tiled floors. Giving the cash register a rock, she released an exasperated shout. Metal and change shook as she knocked it around. Heads turned. Gasps, then silence ensued. I eyed Mom's archery case, the leather strap slung over her shoulder.

"He always has the spare change," she said firmly, releasing the register.

"Who does, Mom?" I clasped my hands over her wrists, eyes wide. "Take a breath. Are you with me? What are you trying to say?"

With bloodshot eyes, her erratic movements slowed as she looked at the stunned waitress. "I swear," she whispered. "I'd never lie about something so petty. I swear, it's all right there. I'd never lie." Her forlorn gaze drifted down. She struggled to find words while I struggled to work over the source of the outburst. Innate suspicion fed the truth to me piece by piece: a hotbed of loathing existed inside her, anger for the parts she played in Philadelphia, the sharply executed roles that were laid out for her like gala cocktail dresses by my father, the orchestra board of trustees, and their minions. It all bubbled and simmered, a cauldron of rage and helplessness, the awareness of what drove her away from the city. That's why we were here right now, out in the middle of nowhere in South Dakota. The Turn was terrifying, but deep down, it was just another reason to exit stage left. She didn't care where we went, as long as we went somewhere else. Somewhere far away from the glittering lights and tabloids, the Botox and mockery. If it wasn't Aunt Marie's farm or Burtonshire, it would be someplace else. Anywhere but Philly.

The decision Florence made to lead us down this path unnerved me, but there was so much validity fueling the choice. Our life in Philly was chock full of all the people we would have been, should we have tried harder and achieved it all. Not only should we have achieved it all, the city wanted us to achieve it all at once, *right now. Keep hustling, keep climbing,* it said, *because damn it, you are a twenty-first-century multi-tasking wonder woman. Don't waste one single second, don't let 'em see you sweat, or they win! Can't handle the heat? Then step aside, 'cause there are ten more in line just like you, ready to jump in. Take care of your man, or someone else will take care of him for you. You're not unique, didn't you get the memo? Just another piece on the conveyor belt, created to be used, created to break. Watch it, now, don't you dare break. You broke? You're broken, and down the chute you go.*

So what did we really have to lose? What were we saying goodbye to that hadn't left us already? Taking the boxed pie, I gently guided Mom out of the diner and walked back over to the train. Some fellow passengers congregated a little farther down the platform, smoking and chatting, casting curious glances our way as we boarded and returned to our seats. I removed the quiver from her shoulder and wrestled with my backpack, flinging them both into an overhead compartment. Florence stilled as she sat, a doll stiff and posed on display in an antique shop.

I plopped down to join her. "You want to tell me about the change now, Mom?"

"Oh, you know me," she said, staring blankly at the

window. "Hating credit cards, preferring cash. Your father always knew."

"My father." I sighed, roping her into a consoling hug. "He knew what?"

"I always lost my change. Never had the right coins. So he carried extra. He always had my back when it came to the little things. The things that matter."

I watched her return to me, the cloudy haze vanishing from her eyes. "You're romanticizing the good stuff, Mom. He didn't have your back with the big things."

"Well, I guess none of it matters anymore."

"Don't say that, because we both know it isn't true."

"I'm sorry, darling." Her listless fingers grazed my forearm. "I behaved badly. I won't embarrass you like that again."

"You're the very opposite of embarrassing. I'm proud to be your daughter."

"Even when I melt down."

"Even then."

"It's sweet of you to say."

"You're going to be okay. I know it doesn't feel that way right now, but you are."

"I'm failing you."

"Stop." I squeezed her fingers. Her rigid stance gave way and she slumped against me. I began to sing "If You Were the Only Girl," resting my head against hers. I nudged her and she took her cue, singing her part. Our voices tapered off and I let the quiet envelop us, let her fall into my hug. The shuffle of feet filled the railcar, passengers trodding along the dated hunter green carpet that lined the aisle. Mason appeared, reclaiming his seat to my left.

"Hope I'm not interrupting anything," he whispered, eyeing the to-go box wedged on my lap, buried beneath our tangled limbs. "Is she sleeping?"

"Just resting." I nodded for him to sit. "Want some pie?"

He chuckled, dropping softly into his chair. Buckling up, he exhaled. "Sure, why not? I'm starving."

"We went to that diner. Did you eat at all today?"

"Nope. I thought about stopping in there myself but really just wanted fresh air. Took a walk."

Florence's eyelashes stirred and she released me, lifting the to-go box from my lap. "Well, *I'm* having pie," she said, peeling one of the plastic fork packets open. "I'm warning you, Mason, I can eat this whole thing on my own." Mason gave her an incredulous look.

I plucked up the other fork packet and placed it in his hand. "Like I said. Don't let us fool you."

He grinned, opening the plastic wrapper. "All right, if you're gonna twist my arm . . ." As he waited patiently for Mom to shovel in a big bite and pass him the box, the tear in the right arm of his suit jacket, just above the wrist cuff, caught my eye. My gaze traveled from the jacket's tear down to the pant hem at his ankles, frayed and far too wide. Excusing myself as they passed chocolate silk pie back and forth, I slipped out of my seat and pulled my backpack down from the overhead storage.

"What are you looking for?" Mom asked, crumbled crust on her shirt.

"This." I squeezed past Mason and back into the middle chair, popping open my mending kit. I snatched the fork from his right hand and shoved it into his left. "Eat with that hand, will you?"

"Um . . . yes ma'am?"

"Don't call me ma'am."

"What do you want me to call you, then?"

"Jo. Just call me Jo."

"Okay, what are you doing to me, Jo?"

"This is going to drive me crazy," I said, taking his right

hand, tugging his sleeve toward me. I threaded the needle. "I can't look at it the rest of the way to Missoula."

He glanced at Mom. She shrugged and held up her fork, pointing at his torn sleeve. "This is what she does. Don't bother arguing."

"I mean . . ." His brows raised. "Thanks?"

"You're welcome. Now stop moving." I could feel his eyes on me, studying me as I worked. His mint scent moved in, mixed with a hint of cocoa. "Is this the only clothing you have?"

"Yup, you're lookin' at it."

"Then you're gonna need a proper outfit. Next I'm working on your pants."

"Wait, don't I have to be standing up for this?"

My lashes drew up with an impassive gaze.

"Careful," Florence mumbled through a mouthful. "You're treading on thin ice, Charlie."

"Hey, I thought it was a legit question." He shrugged and I tugged again, pinching him with the needle. "*Ow!* Damn, woman, watch it!"

"Don't call me woman."

"But you are. A woman."

"Do you want me to stab you again?"

"Distance," Florence reminded me beneath her breath, sliding me side-eye.

"If you can eat pie with the man, I can sew him up."

"Yeah, you know I can hear you, right?" Mason glanced at us.

I gave the needle a hard yank.

He squirmed. "How about I just shut up?"

"Smart man." I worked thoroughly, diligently, stopping only when we sensed a tidal wave of unease surf down the aisle. Passengers rose from their seats, leaning to one side of the car, then moving to the other, scrambling to catch a glimpse of whatever was happening outside. Mom, Mason, and I moved with them, pressing our faces as closely as we could to the window. A unit of fighter jets ripped through the sky above, leaving behind trails of spiraling contrails. Clusters of helicopters appeared in the distance, moving in the same direction as the jets.

"Well, that's comforting," Mason said dryly.

Florence silently watched the horizon. The mending needle nicked my finger, but I barely felt the sting.

Twenty-Five

The announcement of our arrival in Anacortes, our final stop to board the boat to Burtonshire, was a welcome one. Brooding Florence had returned, at moments dreamy and wistful, oscillating between lucid and present to withdrawn and agitated. The bus had been cramped, and after thousands of miles of travel, mental and physical fatigue had worn all of us down. I'd managed to stay in touch with Aunt Marie for at least most of the trip, feeding her updates as I could, hungry for whatever reports she had for us back home, but phone service since then turned spotty, and I hadn't had the chance to charge our burner phone since Missoula. The creatures had vanished, and much of the country had experienced some relief from the quakes, but officials cautioned us to remain vigilant, and the lull in extraterrestrial activity did nothing to calm our country. People were restless, descending into a state of paranoid madness. Were we safe? Would we ever be? Where did we go from here? No one knew, and like acid eating through metal, apprehension seeped into the hearts of the human race.

Our group's desperate need for hot showers, real beds, and

deep sleep, not to mention fresh air and exercise, was hampered by the adrenaline rush from the moment we parked at the ferry terminal. One by one, we collected our bags and hurried off the bus, clumping together like a herd of lost sheep in the empty parking lot.

Florence scanned the sky, locking her elbow with mine. "Haven't seen any more planes or choppers, have you?"

"No. Nothing."

"Where is everyone?" Mason asked no one in particular, somewhere behind us. "Have they suspended normal ferry service to the other islands? How are those people getting around?"

"My guess is they're not," I said.

The last leg of our journey had been a dizzying montage, days filled with late-night card games, cigar smoke, sing-alongs, and arm wrestling in the train's dining car. Mason played CCR covers for everyone on good ol' Herb's acoustic guitar, and Mom cleaned house playing darts while I happily stepped in as her bookie, raking in her winnings at the end of the night. We'd been in pretty good spirits for passengers who were on the road to the unknown, and the bus transfer in Missoula was seamless, which came as an added relief, but the aircrafts' presence back in South Dakota had ignited a fresh wave of nervous energy that traveled with us all the way from Montana to Washington. There, beneath the exterior of rosy cheeks, friendly banter, and hearty laughter, ambivalence brewed, just as thoughts of my father and his other family did. I was relieved to be free, severed from the poison of his lies, but the toxin still lingered, tethering me to him no matter how much distance the miles placed between us. Like stagnant cigarette smoke, Carolyn's little face, so innocent, so pure, clung to me, along with the realization that I'd never meet my new half-sibling.

Mom and I took in the wide expanse of gray, choppy water

spread out to the right of the terminal. A majestic backdrop of snow-capped, evergreen-laden mountains lined the horizon. Mist cloaked the treetops, a cloud invading the rugged terrain. Docked ferries dotted the other end of the waterfront's terminal, unlit and deserted, while dulled sunlight hid behind a curtain of overcast cloud cover. The Intake Guards that traveled with us from Missoula approached us with instructions to move to the other end of the terminal, toward the vacant ferries. We shuffled along, discovering more guards surrounding the empty vessels, dressed head-to-toe in cream-colored garments. They were armed with taser batons, but said things like "Peace and wellness to you" to the newcomers approaching the metal barriers along the landing. The barricades directed us, the fresh recruits, through a winding structure, funneling us into one single line. A tall, olive-green circus-like tent loomed over the landing's ramp, its thick tarp dropped to the ground on all four sides.

One minute, I was sure I'd entered a dream, fully entranced by our surroundings and the astonishing reality of our circumstances, of everything that brought us here. The next minute, I'd pinched myself, sober with the shock that I'd agreed to come here in the first place. This place, a picture-perfect, albeit gloomy postcard, zapped me with the strongest dose of homesickness I'd ever experienced, more than any other state or country I'd visited.

"Stay close," Florence whispered against my ear. She studied the guards as we moved, distrusting yet curious, as conflicted as the war raging between my heart and instincts. Static thrummed in my veins. Our single-file line suddenly merged with another small swarm of recruits. New faces, none of them from our train or bus. They were void of protest, compliant, and most noticeably, eager to move forward with the final step in their voyage, just like our group. I bumped shoulders with two women in front of us, clumsily knocking into them from behind.

"Sorry," I muttered beneath my breath, looking down at my feet.

A tangled mass of copper hair shifted, one of the women turning fully around to deliver an annoyed scowl. A bruised cheek highlighted wide, tired eyes that did a double take when they landed on me. "You have *got* to be kidding me."

My gaze lifted at the sound of the voice. I gently touched the girl's shoulder to make sure she was real, sweeping an incredulous look over her dirt-stained, black-and-blue cheekbones. "*Olivia?*"

Florence perked up beside us.

Olivia crossed her arms and stepped back, rolling her eyes. "Kill me now."

"What are you doing here? How are you here?" I stuttered and pivoted around, eyes darting everywhere for signs of him. "Is Tony with you?"

"Someone hooked me up." She looked away. "No, why would he be?"

"I just thought—"

"Well you thought wrong."

"I'm so glad you're okay. I tried to find you both, I was so worried."

Olivia pulled her coat tighter, sizing Mom up. "Yeah, I bet you were."

"I'm Florence," Mom spoke up, extending a hand. "We know one another, but not officially."

"We've met." Olivia shot a scathing glance at Florence's open palm, rejecting the gesture. "Plenty of times."

"Well, either way, it's good to see you again. To see you alive and in one piece, I mean."

Olivia grimaced as she swallowed, turning her attention

back to me. A raw hurt shined in her irises. "Tony's okay. For now, I guess. Made it to his parent's place, or so I heard."

I exhaled. "I can't believe this is happening."

"Better start believing."

"I just want it to be over."

"How'd you end up here?"

"My aunt set it up."

"You trust these people?" Olivia eyed a pair of guards, passing by.

"Not sure. My aunt says we can, though. So here we are."

More clipboard folk ushered us forward, cutting us off. Olivia disappeared down the line and the guards approached each recruit one by one to confirm the same details we'd already been asked to provide during the first part of our trip. Just as Marie described it, the process was meticulous. Each word, each exchange between guard and recruit seemed a solemn oath, a swear against all things false. Perjury would not, under any circumstance, be tolerated. The guards' commitment to this honesty, this devotion to integrity of character, reflected the title stamped on their uniforms in camouflage patterned, military-style patches: Pledge Officer. An ill disquiet unraveled through me like a loosening thread as I observed the sterile, cordial officers searching my mother for firearms as we drew closer to the tent. One final flash of Olivia's silhouette flared somewhere in the distance and then I lost her.

"Release and surrender, please," one of the Pledge Officers said as he patted Mom down, nodding to her bow and quiver. His cream-colored uniform was ironed and spotless. One look at the finely pressed fabric made my skin itch for a scalding hot shower.

"This is one of my skills," she said. "When will I get it back?"

"In the admission ring," he replied. "Drop the backpack, too, please."

"We have to surrender our bags too?" I asked, unable to hold back. "Are you serious?"

"We wish you no harm, friends. This is for your own safety." The Pledge Officer confiscated Mom's archery case, then gestured again to her backpack. "Release and surrender, please," he said again. "Just a quick search."

Static pulsed.

They promptly rummaged through her bag, then mine, politely returning them with a gracious bow, a signal to move on. The olive-green tent was close enough to touch. More Pledge Officers greeted us at a white velvet rope. "Please state your districts."

Florence and I looked at one another, then down at our ID badges clipped to our backpack straps. "Lancaster County, Alliance District 307," Mom answered. "Both of us."

"Right this way." Another curt, polite nod from the Pledge Officers. Our new friend Herb could've taken a lesson in manners or two from these guys. Mom and I took hesitant strides forward. I glanced behind us, searching the line for Mason. I spotted his gray suit jacket and the bandage on his neck, and his mocha eyes found mine. A whisper of a smile touched my lips, and I sent him an awkward wave, almost robotic. He returned the gesture with an encouraging nod and then the tent tarp fluttered, calling me back. The olive-green flaps lifted and rolled up at the sides, welcoming us inside.

A no-frills panel awaited us, a collection of plastic tables arranged in a semicircle, matched with garden benches and wood crates for seating. A mix of men and women lined the makeshift panel, in similar uniforms as the Pledge Officers, only with personal name tags stitched to their pockets. Unlike their counterparts and the tense Intake Officers we'd interacted with on the road here, the judges lounged casually on their homespun chairs, as if expecting neighbors for lunch. Coffee-tin place settings dressed each table, filled with sprigs of fern and an assortment of flowers, each tin distinctly different, resting on blue-and-white checkered cloths. The random decor added an oddly homey touch to the cold, damp space. Being in Western Washington was like being on a picnic, waiting for the bears to bring you pails of fresh honey from the beehives, and the birds to air-deliver you plump blackberries on a bed of twigs. Florence stalled before the semicircle. I scurried around to stand to her left.

"Peace and wellness to you, friends," one of the judges said, a lumberjack with serene, patient eyes. Serene because he'd probably been out collecting honey and twigs with the birds and bears. Picnics and chopping wood in the fresh air would make anyone calm.

The pair of Pledge Officers who'd escorted us into the tent presented us before disappearing back outside. "Florence and Joanna Kowalski," they announced. "Ready to present."

"Excellent," Mr. Lumberjack said, eyes sparkling as he smiled at us. Dimples peeked through his beard. I decided he was only fifty percent lumberjack, and the rest of him was teddy bear. "My name's Levi." I glanced at his name patch. Of course it was. "We're happy you're here, and we trust the journey's treated you well, despite the situation brewing out there."

"Yes," Mom mumbled, "it's quite the situation."

Levi shuffled through some papers. "Well, once you're admitted to our little slice of heaven, you'll have plenty of opportunities to learn all about the nuts and bolts of our community. In the meantime, however, I take it you've been briefed on what Burtonshire is all about, and that we'd like you to share your talents with us before you advance to the next step, yes?"

"Yes," I answered. "I do have one question first, though."

"Can it wait?"

"No."

"Okay, then." His shoulders shook with amused laughter. "Talk to me, friend."

"Is there a reason the terminal is empty? It was just our bus . . . and another group of recruits. Did you shut the ferries down? Or is this place deserted because of the," my fingers curled into air quotes, "situation?"

"*Ding, ding!*" He pointed at me like a game show host congratulating a contestant on the right answer. "Quite the loaded question, friend. We're running behind schedule today, but I'll do my best to fill you in. We've seen some interesting developments in Western Washington the past few days. It's been exceptionally quiet, and the ferry terminals have all shut down until further notice. That wasn't our call. People weren't traveling, workers were sent home. A lot of fear out there right now, friends. A lot of fear. Just so happens you were on one of the last two busloads. That line you see out there represents the last batch of recruits invited to join our community." His snow-white teeth flashed with another million-dollar smile. "Isn't that just super? Aren't you thrilled? It sure makes us happy. Right, friends?" He turned to the other judges, blinding them with his pearly whites. Harmonious cheers swept the semicircle.

"Doors are closed now, correct?" Florence shifted.

"You got it, Mama Bear. Burtonshire's Founders Council made it official just this morning. Many other colonies already closed their gates. We held out as long as we could, but it was time for us to do the same. You'll be on the last boat to the island. Beginning today, no one else is permitted on or off."

"No one?" Florence's eyes narrowed. "Indefinitely?"

"Everything's tentative, Mama Bear. Only the founders will make scheduled trips to the mainland, for necessary supplies or emergency medical care. If, and only if, they feel it's safe. As I've said, you'll learn more once you're admitted. Our community takes good care of one another. You'll be in excellent hands. Now . . ." He leaned forward, cracking his knuckles. "Can your other questions wait?"

I nodded.

"Super. In that case, it's showtime!" He clapped and stood, announced our names into a walkie-talkie, and in seconds, a group of guards hurried from a roped-off section at the back of the tent to the center of the ring. Wheels squeaked as one of the uniformed women rolled a little utility cart over, stationing it to Mom's right. A sheet draped the top, covering its contents. Another woman returned Mom's archery bag, and she happily swung it over her free arm. She squared her shoulders, balancing both the case and her backpack's weight. I peeked over at the cart.

"Joanna," Levi said, "we see you're a professional clothing designer. Are you willing and prepared to serve Burtonshire by providing wardrobe essentials for the community?"

"Yeah, I can do that. I have some sketches of my work if you'd like to see them."

"Absolutely!" Levi beamed, dimples sharpening. Warm grins floated from the other judges. They exchanged enthusiastic nods, leaning forward in anticipation. "No pressure, Jo," Levi said with a laugh, as if we'd known one another since elementary school. "Whenever you're ready, 'kay?"

His chipper energy made my skin itch. It really was time for that shower.

"Sure, okay." Removing my backpack, I bent down to unzip it and rifle through the contents. I walked toward Levi, handing him the sketchpads. Florence's stare burned the back of my neck as I stood there, waiting for feedback like a contestant on one of those reality TV talent shows. Levi assessed my designs, passing them to the judges. They each took their turn observing, responding with collective approval.

"Thoroughly impressive!" Levi extended a hand, returning my sketches. "No doubt your skills will be a tremendous gift to the community. Let's see your work in action, shall we?" He clapped again, signaling the guards at Mom's side to remove the sheet from the utility cart. I swung around to watch the demonstration. Like magician's assistants, they swiped the sheet away, uncovering two items, the first a sewing machine, with some fabric and a basket of supplies beside it, and on the lower shelf, a small, ancient Casio keyboard. I swallowed a laugh at the thought of Mom playing that thing.

"Jo," Levi's voice ruptured the mental image, "how about you present your offering first? Nothing fancy, of course. Just whatever you can whip up within the next five minutes."

"Five minutes?" I gulped.

Levi's exuberance made my face hurt. He was high on life, this one. And probably a stash of happy pills. "Sorry, friend. Due to the nature of the situation, we're really pressed for time. I'm sure you understand."

"Oh, I do, but . . . I'm not sure what I can realistically make for you in under five minutes. I have other skills. I sing, too. Mom and I perform together, actually. Right, Mom?"

"Performed," she said. "Past tense."

"Past tense?" Levi's head tilted. "You're a classically-trained pianist as well as a vocalist, are you not?"

"Yes." Florence replied begrudgingly. "But I'd like to present a different skill." Panic bubbled at her omission. I knew she hadn't played a note since the Turn, but now was not the time for resistance. I needed her to show up, needed the old Florence right now.

"Say it ain't so!" Levi feigned a disappointed frown. "Jo won't sew for us, and Flo won't perform? Oh, friends. What a bummer."

"What could I possibly sew for you in five minutes?" My

tone was clipped. My brain scrambled to cook up a way out of this. "We have other skills. So, what's the problem?"

"Joanna," Mom's cautious whisper reached for me, but my agitation flared. I was exhausted, hungry, dirty, and already done with Mr. Happy Camper and his cult-juice-drinking gang. I'd witnessed Mom go through hell and back, had said goodbye to everything familiar, lost all sense of self and direction and was now combating a monsoon of disorientation thanks to time zone changes, sleep deprivation, and the overwhelming change in surroundings. It was time to get on that boat and touch down on that island.

"Aw," Levi's tone bordered on condescending. "Well, Jo, I have to say, we were really counting on seeing your design skills at work, and your records here indicate your mother is a brilliant performer. It would be a real shame to deny us such incredible talents. You have so much to offer!"

The judges nodded in unison, faces pouty.

"Exactly," I snapped. "We're more than fabric and stage shows. There's more than one way for us to serve your community."

"Okay," Levi said, studying me carefully. "I'm listening. How so? In what other ways do you intend to contribute?"

"You already know our background, correct?"

"That's correct, but—"

"So, you've heard and seen—" I waved my sketchpad in the air, "what we can do. Honesty is an important value on your island, right?"

"Absolutely, my friend. It's the cornerstone of our colony's belief system."

"So, out of respect for your time and our dignity, why not just trust us? Believe what the records tell you. Take my sketches for face value. We'll help the community as best as we can. We won't cause any trouble. We'll live simply, quietly. No drama. All we want is a safe place to rest our heads. A little peace, just like everyone else. You're worse off without us—I can promise you that. We're passionate about what we do, and we work hard. What I *can't* do is perform in this circle like a trained monkey to try and convince you in less than five minutes how valuable I am." Crossing my arms, I clutched the sketchpad against my chest. "Since we're being honest."

Levi's hand brushed his beard. The judges cleared their throats, eyeing their wristwatches. "I appreciate that argument," Levi began, "I really do, Jo. And in your defense, you're right." He shrugged. "We need you. We care for one another on Burtonshire, we all have a job to do, and I get the impression you're a woman of your word. I don't doubt you and your mother will be vital assets to our community. But you seem to be missing the point, here, friend."

"Enlighten me."

"Your admission isn't simply about your abilities. It's about your willingness to share them. Your commitment to our united mission. We need to know your heart's in it, see?"

I held my breath and my tongue, watching the sparkle in his eyes dull. Doubt touched down like the gentle mist outside —not a full-on rain, but a slight, barely-there trickle. "I understand."

"*Ding ding!*" Levi winked, lighting up again. "Now you're pickin' up what I'm puttin' down, friend. Excellent. So, now you see my predicament. We want you to *want* this. For the sake of time, though, I think we'd be willing to let your presentation slide, right, all?" He cast a brief glance at the other judges, even though everyone in this tent knew his opinion was the only opinion. "Your sketches and records do speak for themselves, and if you solemnly pledge to supply our community with the clothing it needs, then we have a deal. However . . ." Rising to his feet, he turned a crooked gaze on my mom. "Florence's lack of enthusiasm to present a musical offering is more concerning. Tell me, Mama Bear. Why the aversion to show us your talents? You claim you no longer perform, but your records indicate otherwise."

I stepped in front of Mom, blocking her from Levi's intrusive stare. "I told you she has other skills. She said she'd like to present something else."

"I can see that." Levi's head cocked to one side. He glanced at the archery case. "Florence? Answer the question, please."

I moved again, blocking his view. "There are children on your island, right?"

"Excuse me?"

"Kids." I rolled a shoulder.

"Of course. What does that have to do with—"

"What about the disabled? The elderly?"

"What about them?" His eyes lowered into thin slits.

"Did you turn them away when they got stage fright in the admission ring? When they were mentally or physically incapable of performing at your command?"

Another crack of his knuckles. "Of course not. We've always taken these factors into consideration during the admission process."

I chanced another step in his direction, arms dropping to my sides. The sketchpad dangled from one hand, dangerously close to slipping, just like my courage. "Well, let's say your records are incomplete. Let's say my mom's incapable of performing right now, not unwilling. She's not feeling well, not feeling herself. She's not refusing to present an offering, she'd just like to show you a different skill. How about those factors for consideration?" I probed his twinkling, beady eyes, challenging him to offer up a shred of compassion buried beneath that transparent facade. He locked gazes with me, launching a staring contest. The first one to look away would lose.

"Physical or mental exhaustion, illness, injury—these are all valid considerations in the admission ring, Joanna. In your mother's case, however, I really must insist that she either demonstrate her musical talents or forfeit her place on the boat."

"She can play piano and sing. You already have it on record. She's had a tough trip. Please, cut her a break."

"Again, it's not merely about *if* she can play. I need to see that she *wants* to, need to hear it from her mouth, not yours. Music is the primary offering listed on her record, the offering she promised to contribute in exchange for admission. And if she'd like to be on the boat with you, I'll need her to pledge a commitment to provide music instruction, entertainment, mentorship, and more to the community once she arrives on the island. We all have assignments in Burtonshire, and this would be her gift to us. Since the birth of our colony, we've discovered that music education and entertainment is crucial to our quality of life, especially in our community. Island living doesn't suit everyone, you see. Makes some of us a lil' stir-crazy. Music lifts our spirits."

"You're not honest." I shook my head. "You're a bully."

"Jo." Mom's plea only sharpened my determination. "Forget it. It's fine. I'll sing, or play, or whatever they want."

Levi's jaw worked and he looked at his watch. He still wore a smile, but it no longer touched his eyes. "A bully?" He ignored Mom's surrender. I'd poked the bear and now he wanted me to put me in my rightful place. "No. More like a realist. I hold the key to the kingdom, and from where I'm standing?" The skin above his dimples tightened as his gaze raked over us. "Even rock stars are expendable. Either your mother presents the musical talent that earned her her ticket here and pledges to accept her assignment, or she won't be joining you on the boat. Are we clear, friend?"

My eyes drifted shut as I fought the urge not to lunge at him. "Crystal."

"Super."

Movement suddenly rustled in earshot. "Enough," Florence cut in, saddling up beside me. The sharp, fast sound of a zipper sliced to the left and then her bow rose, eliciting a simultaneous intake of breath around the semicircle. Levi staggered back, reaching for his walkie-talkie. Pledge Officers braced themselves, lifting their taser batons, shifting their stance. From observing her for years, I sensed the whirlwind of calculations that flashed in Florence's fed-up, determined aquamarine eyes: angles, range, draw weight, sight, target, release. The sound of splintered wood snapped throughout the tent. I flinched as a small explosion of ferns and flowers reverberated on the main table. Mom struck one flower coffee can, then another, the smooth turnaround from quiver to release so fast, my vision blurred. One pop after another, she nailed each place setting, wiping them out clear across the semicircle, blowing the other judges back and up, right off their seats. Lowering the bow, she turned to the utility cart, flicked on the old portable Casio, and her fingers flew over the keys. An abbreviated version of Chopin's Étude Op. 25, no. 12 filled the tent, each note exaggerated as she hammered the tune. When she was done, she swung back around and stood politely before the judges, gently clasping her hands in front of her.

A twitch at the corner of my lips threatened to crack my stony poker face, but I willed it away. I couldn't let them see me sweat. Not now. My lungs pulled in a silent, steady breath. "You should see her with a baseball bat," I said flatly, with a blasé shoulder roll.

"That was unnecessary," Levi said, winded. Fire spread in his eyes as his chest rose and fell. He took a measured step forward, gaze latched onto my mother. "But effective." He tugged lightly at his collar. "Wouldn't you say so, friends?" The judges wobbled back to their seats with uncertain laughter. "We like initiative around here. We like it a lot." With a furtive glance at the defensive line of Pledge Officers, Levi called off his watchdogs and walked carefully to his seat, stamping his stack of papers.

"Florence and Joanna Kowalski, do you hereby pledge your allegiance to the Isle of Burtonshire, to serve and protect its beloved community? Do you solemnly swear to never harm, deceive, or steal from the Founders Council or your fellow residents?"

My shaky hand found Mom's. I looked up at her, waiting.

"We do," she said, squeezing my fingers.

"Friends and witnesses," Levi surveyed everyone in the tent, "do you hereby acknowledge Florence and Joanna Kowalski as neighbors and partners? All in favor, let it be known." Murmuring softly, the Pledge Officers, Levi, and other judges bowed their heads and placed one arm across their chest, palms over their hearts. Two guards appeared behind Levi, gesturing for us to join them as they pulled back a section of the tent, offering a pathway for us to follow.

"Peace and wellness to you, friends," Levi said, stepping aside. "Welcome to the Isle of Burtonshire."

Checking first to make sure we had all our belongings, Mom and I walked forward, accepting the invitation. Gloomy light flooded us as we stepped outside the tent and walked down a ramp, where the other accepted recruits and a large, docked fishing vessel awaited. Taking our place in line, we both exhaled.

"Now what?" I leaned back against the ramp's rail, glancing around for Olivia or Mason. Any minute now, we'd all be setting sail for the final leg of the journey. Fatigue's gravity pulled at me.

"We leave it all behind. Start again."

"We can't leave everything, Mom. Not really."

"You never know what you're capable of until life forces your hand, darling."

An unfamiliar longing coasted through me like a spirit passing through an inhabited body, searching for a host. What did you do when all you had was a medley of heart-achingly happy memories from the past to decorate the present with, to place on the shelf and pick up again and again, as the future unrolled before you? Everything before Dad's lie was happy. Blind love was happy love. For all the bad we walked away from, the good still existed. It was what I knew, what I chose to keep. I looked at the fishing vessel, our ticket out of here, but saw only a cracked chasm, one that was breaking and splitting off into two separate realms. We couldn't stay still, and we couldn't go back. The boat wasn't an answer, but a decision to be made.

"Can we play pretend?" Mom asked wistfully, turning to face the mountains. "Make this our new stage? This can be our next ever after."

"A happily ever after, I hope."

"I hope so too."

The city was a masterful thief; it knew Florence well. Slowly, expertly, it siphoned her joy, deposited it into its criminal reserve, until one day, there was nothing left to steal. I knew this because I'd been there the whole time. I'd witnessed the demolition. As an integral part of our usually confounding, often infuriating symbiotic mother-daughter relationship, I not only had the pleasure of becoming a part of the collateral damage, but I also became inextricably linked to the thumbprint it left on her life. Not that I blamed my mother. I didn't. She didn't ask for any of it, which was why I accepted the blatant codependency that effortlessly boomeranged between us now, and why I wanted nothing more than to fill her up again.

"We can do whatever you want, Mom," I answered, admiring the fog-filled forests hovering in the distance. "Whatever will make you happy."

"Can you believe it? Our very own theater." She beamed as the line began to move, guards welcoming us aboard the vessel. She was already on the boat, waving goodbye to the mainland, serene and radiant. "Me, you, and island life, darling. That'll be enough for me."

The boat left the dock, carrying us from one kingdom to the next. A mechanical groan churned beneath the deck, the water gliding sleekly by. We watched the mainland slowly disappear, absorbed by the placid horizon. The echo of a shrill screech, visceral and inhuman, suddenly showered the distance, dispelling our tranquility and silencing everyone on board. The sound drowned us in a deep undertow, and my heart floundered, abandoning ship.

A sheer whisper leaked into the salty air, mine or my mother's, I didn't know. "I just want to go home. Please, God, just let us go home." The vessel cruised along. Mom stepped forward, gripping the deck rail. The ghoulish shrieks stretched across the waters. Dread flooded my veins, and I moved closer to her side, closer to my compass.

THANK YOU FOR READING!

If you enjoyed this book, please consider leaving a rating or review.

WANT MORE FROM R. M. CARPUS?

Sign up for her mailing list at **rmcarpus.com** for an exclusive FREE read and updates.

Want to continue the saga?

Check out THE DOPPELGANGER, an Isle of Burtonshire Novella. Available at most major book retailers.

Meet R. M.'s partners, D. M. Million and C. C. Thomsen, at **impossiblethingspublishing.com**. Together, they bring you new supernatural suspense anthologies each year.

You can download **Through the Woods Vol. 1** and **Under the Sea Vol. 1** for FREE today, available from most major ebook retailers.

ACKNOWLEDGMENTS

This project would not have been possible without Jesus Christ, my Heavenly Father, and the kind, inspiring people I am fortunate enough to call family and friends. You know who you are. Thank you for the joy you bring to my life and the countless ways you show me unconditional love. Special thanks to my indie girl gang, Domenica and Cathy, for taking the ITP journey with me. I'm so thankful for our bond and for your incredible support. You ladies are pure magic, mixed with a healthy dose of snark. May we always be united by our love for the written word, '90s nostalgia, and the emo-goth kid in us all. I cannot wait to see where you're headed next and what the future holds for you both in the publishing world. Your cheerleader for life, Rach. xo